61 THREADNEEDLE STREET

A Novel

L.E. Ricker Schofield

61 Threadneedle Street
A novel by L E Ricker Schofield

Illustrations, cover and design by Rachel Reddy

ISBN   13:978-069-212-4666
        10:069-2124-667

Printed in the United States of America
2019

This book is dedicated to the hope that Ben and Billy are amicably reunited in heaven.

ACKNOWLEDGMENTS

First, to my son-in-law, David Maurer, who somehow retrieved this manuscript from the technological graveyard where all my obsolete word processing discs were buried. He then spent considerable time deciphering them, line by line, to save me from having to retype my whole book.

To Mt. Holyoke College, whose reference librarians allowed me to spend hours in the stacks or the basement archives perusing the histories of peoples and places relative to my story.

Extremely helpful was the University of Pennsylvania dissertation by William Herbert Mariboe, <u>The Life of William Franklin 1730 (1) - 1813</u> "Pro Rege et Patria", copyright 1962.

To Tomas Axel, deceased, my English professor at the University of Massachusetts in 1986, who wholeheartedly approved of my starting point for *61 Threadneedle Street*.

A book by Willard Sterne Randall was also very informative.

To my one-time agent, Helga Maas Potter, who succeeded in getting me a reading from St. Martin's Press, NY.

To the nun at St Paul's Chapel, NYC, who let me and my friends into the sacristy so I could confirm that William Franklin's epitaph for his wife, Elizabeth Downes, still hung to the side of the altar where he had it installed. The nun was also surprised to learn that the Royal Governor of New Jersey's first wife was indeed buried beneath the altar.

These same friends and I also toured Proprietary House in Perth Amboy, the capital of East Jersey. On another trip to Levittown, NJ, we saw the sign which confirmed that William Franklin once owned the property, which was his Strawberry Hill Farm.

To my late husband, George, who took me to London, where I saw Threadneedle Street for myself. We also went to Philadelphia to see the Franklin graves, Christ Church, and all the historic sights of the city.

61 THREADNEEDLE STREET

BEN AND BILLY

London, England
November, 1758

Middle Temple alumni Sir William Blackstone was powerful at the podium, his voice resounding through the vaulted expanse of Westminster Hall. "You men of law," he said, addressing the graduating class of 1758, "are the guardians of the English constitution--delegated to watch, to check and to avert every dangerous innovation."

Spontaneously, candidate William Franklin responded silently to Sir William's trust, committing his life and pledging his loyalty to the mother country. His bosom swelled with filial pride as he made a lasting covenant: For King and Country. England forever.   So shall it ever be.

Billy expelled a long, inaudible sigh to release the emotion that welled from the very pit of his stomach.   For the first time in all his twenty-eight years, he felt like a man with a separate identity, a man with a destiny all his own.   The feeling, though strange and unfamiliar, was intoxicating, making him lightheaded and almost giddy.   And no wonder.   He was poised to step out of his ever more famous father's lengthy shadow and cast one of his own making.

From time to time sustained bursts of applause and scattered bravos interrupted the address long enough for Billy to scan the sea of fashionable white wigs before him in search of his father and their friends.   Ah, there they are, he mused, Mrs. Stevenson and Polly on either side of him, naturally!   If only Mama and Sally had come, today would be perfect.   Well, almost perfect.   He put Betsy's hurtfully heartless letter out of his mind for the time being.

Mrs. Margaret Stevenson was the widow in whose house the Franklin's lived, having rented four furnished rooms on the second floor of the modest residence at No. 7 Craven Street.

Although Billy praised her hospitality and Christian concern, he resented the endearing friendship that had blossomed over the past year between his father and their landlady, feeling as he did a strong sense of duty to guard his mother's interests in her absence.

Mary, nicknamed Polly, was Mrs. Stevenson's 18-year-old daughter, who had fallen hopelessly in love with the tall, dashing law student from America. Unfortunately, the young man had arrived in London engaged to someone else, a beautiful, wealthy aristocrat from Philadelphia named Betsy Graeme. As a result, Billy's feelings for Polly were purely platonic from the start, and much to her dismay, she became a mere absentee sister, a replacement for his 15-year-old sister, Sally, his closest confidante and friend.

Billy was surprised to see that his father's attention was fixed on him rather than on Blackstone and that he appeared to be basking in the sinfulness of pride. Resisting the impulse to acknowledge the rare compliment, Billy turned away to allow his Papa a brief moment to indulge. After all, why shouldn't Benjamin Franklin feel proud? His only living son, the son of a Philadelphia printer, was being called to the bar by the Middle

Temple, one of the four prestigious and renowned English Inns of Court. Besides, Billy knew full well how upset his father would be if someone caught him breaking one of his own tenets. These were the thirteen hard-and-fast rules the 17-year-old runaway from Boston had devised shortly after he first stepped ashore in Philadelphia and walked up Market Street with little more than lint in his pocket and determination in his heart. With a bent for self-improvement and goaded by a penchant to succeed, this ex-New England Courant apprentice meant to avoid the pitfalls of adolescence by adhering to his daily disciplinary regimen. The tenets included humility, temperance, silence, frugality, industry, cleanliness and chastity, and Benjamin would be the first to admit that at such a tender age, the last rule was extremely hard to control; however, Benjamin tried his best to walk the straight and narrow, to build up a good reputation and to amass a tidy nest egg for early retirement.

Billy, on the other hand, who had never known hardship, lacked the hunger of the elder Franklin and found his steady diet of stringent regulations about as palatable as a dose of salts. Frugality, for instance, was unnecessary for a boy who never had to pinch a penny to survive, and Resolution a bother.   No, the younger Franklin had no qualms or pangs of guilt about feeling proud on his graduation day, the day of the first major accomplishment of his life.

Warmed by the flurry of pre-commencement activity, Billy hadn't noticed how chilly it was in the Hall until now.   The cavernous room was unheated but for a profusion of candles and the abundance of human warmth, and he worried that his father might take sick as he had their first winter in London.   His concern was short-lived when he noticed that Mrs. Stevenson and Polly, who had nursed him back to health then, were tucking his black woolen great coat snugly around his shoulders.

As Blackstone finished his address, Billy felt a wave of exhilaration wash over him as he awaited the conferring of degrees and his name to be called.   "WILLIAM FRANKLIN", the speaker presently announced.   He summarily approached the podium flashing a broad, satisfiable smile.   It was official at last.   He was William Franklin, barrister.

At the conclusion of the benediction, the entire assemblage rose to honor his majesty.   As the graduates recessed down the aisle toward the vestibule, Billy could hear his father singing with gusto, "God Save the King".

He was also aware that he himself was attracting the attention of many alluring women and acknowledged them with a slight nod, a gently raised brow or the trace of a smile.   They responded by opening their ivory fans and fluttering them as he passed.   Socially, he was choosy and mingled with no one but the upper crust, and his popularity among these ladies was conspicuous.

Lacking the sophistication of the socialites, Polly waved. Billy responded with a soft laugh and a sigh, sharing with her his relief that his studies were over and his future all but assured.

Following the barristers, the crush of well-wishers poured into the anteroom, but having the advantage of height Billy was easy to spot.   To his surprise the first person to single him out was Blackstone himself.   Billy was well aware of the young man's outstanding legal reputation; nevertheless, it was common knowledge that he was a poor mixer and tended to shun such social settings, which made Billy feel especially honored by the gesture.

After he formally introduced himself, Sir William inquired,

"Tell me, Mr. Franklin, what are your future plans, private practice or a crown appointment?"

"To serve the crown, Sir."

"In the colonies?"

"Wherever I am sent."

"You shouldn't have a problem. With the Franklin name and unbeatable credentials, the world's your oyster, he replied, paraphrasing from Shakespeare's "Hamlet".

"Hopefully, a winning combination," Billy replied, thanking him for his encouraging words. Although he was accustomed to people crediting his good fortune to the power of Benjamin's increasing fame, he wondered momentarily whether it would ever be possible for him to achieve absolute independence.

"By the way," Sir William added as he turned to leave, "please tell your father that I would like to meet with him sometime before he sails back to America."

"Thank you, Sir. I know he'll be delighted." As Billy watched the 35-year-old genius take to the sidelines and thread his way through the throng to the exit, he wondered what his own status would be seven short years hence. Besides being a brilliant lawyer, he heard that Sir William was compiling a four-volume tome entitled "Commentaries of the Laws of England" which he planned to dedicate to Queen Charlotte Sophia.

"We're over this way, Billy," Polly called as she carved her way through the crowd to his side.   "I wanted to be the first to congratulate you," she said grasping his only free hand.   Of course, she wasn't the first if she had witnessed the many subtle expressions of praise and admiration he had encountered just minutes before.

"Thank you, my sweet," he replied, brushing her cheek with a perfunctory kiss.   "Just a minute.   Do I know you, young woman?" he teased, following close at her heels.   "The eyes are familiar...but"

Polly pulled him up short and whispered, "Didn't you know, William Franklin, Esq., in England, at eighteen, I'm already considered an old maid."

Billy chuckled inside, conscious of the fact that Polly had tried to make herself look suave by powdering her flaxen hair with starch and styling it with a chignon and loose-flowing curls at the nape of her neck, which created the effect of making her widely-set hazel eyes predominate--or were they green tonight?

"Ah, here you are, my Doctor of Jurisprudence."
Benjamin reached up to embrace his towering son as their small circle of closest friends gathered round to share the momentous occasion and to shower Billy with laudatory accolades.

"An enviable achievement," said Mr. Collinson, tapping his cane excitedly on the stone foyer.   "A real feather in your cap."

Peter Collinson and Benjamin had become dear friends through their correspondence over the years, and it was he who was influential in arranging a meeting between Benjamin and Lord Granville, the president of the Privy Council, when he first arrived in London as the agent for Pennsylvania.

"A milestone in your life," added Mr. Strahan, the English publisher who shipped law books to Billy to enable him to study initially under famed Philadelphia lawyer, Joseph Galloway, until the Franklins were scheduled to sail to London.   At Benjamin's request he also chose one of the Inns of Court for Billy to attend and saw to his early enrollment.

"A furlong, certainly, but never a mile," said Benjamin in his laconic fashion.   "A degree in itself does not guarantee success."

"Aptly put, Papa.   An axiom worthy of the *Almanac*."

They all laughed heartily, but then the mood changed as Benjamin's face took on a sad expression.   A tight smile made furrows form around his mouth and he said, "My only regret is that Deborah and Sally are not here to share our joy."

"And Aunt Jane," Billy added soberly.

"I've written Deborah many times and urged her to come to England," said Mr. Strahan, "but she insists she is too terrified to cross the Atlantic."

"In all honesty, after making the crossing myself, I can't say I blame her," said Billy.

"Come now.   I admit we had a harrowing experience, but it was extremely interesting."

"My father truly amazes me.   We were nearly shipwrecked on the rocks off Falmouth Harbor, and he calls it interesting.   I still shudder when I think of that night."

"We came on deck and a light as 'big as a cart-wheel' glared upon the treacherous coast," Benjamin added matter-of-factly.

"Believe me, I thought it was Judgment Day."

"Thank God for lighthouses!" Polly exclaimed.

"Remind me, my dear, to investigate this subject further.   I must encourage the construction of more lighthouses in America."

"A topic for a lesser day," said Billy, who was eager to begin celebrating.   "Polly, would you be a good sport and take my gown and physical wig home with you?" he asked, gently touching the shoulder of her cloak.

At his touch, she took a shallow breath (all her corset would allow) and held it until he removed his hand.   "Certainly," she replied, helping him off with it.   She clutched it to her breast, feeling the warmth of his body and the smell of his cologne.

Benjamin beamed as he watched the two, young people conversing, since he wanted nothing more than to promote a match between his son and Polly, the apple of his eye.   Why he was so taken with her from the start was perfectly understandable, because she shared his enthusiasm for science and philosophy.   During his recuperation they had spent hours discussing his experiments like father and son had always done.

Marriage or even a romance between them was totally out of the question as far as Billy was concerned.   It wasn't that he didn't appreciate her keen intellect or jovial spirit, it was the fact that she didn't stimulate him physically as his heartthrob, Betsy, had done.

Billy changed from his long-bobbed professional wig to a more fashionable white bag wig. Its human hair was greased, whitened with starch and brushed back smoothly from his forehead. A black bag held the queue and prevented the powder from marring his new brown velvet coat.

"We men are going to the tavern for a short celebration."

"You'll be at The Chapter, right," Polly replied innocently, more of a statement than a question.

"As a matter of fact, we will not," said Billy abruptly, unable to conceal his displeasure. Why must Papa confide everything to Polly, he thought, noticeably irked. "The Chapter caters to printers, The Hell to lawyers," he remarked, setting her straight. Why does she need to know the pubs we frequent to drink our beer? he asked himself.

"I'm sorry. I shouldn't have interfered," she whispered sheepishly. She bit her lower lip and strained to hold back the tears that were filling her eyes.

"Whichever you prefer, my son," Benjamin said, intervening like a parent in a sibling squabble. "Are you agreeable, Mr. Strahan and Mr. Collinson?"

"I'd say The Hell is fitting, said Peter, "as soon as we see the ladies to their carriage."

Before linking arms with Benjamin, Mrs. Stevenson told Billy how proud she was of his accomplishment, and Billy responded by planting a kiss on her cheek.

Outside, the oil lamps were lit illuminating the pedestrian walkways, but beyond the posts that separated them from the cobblestone streets was the murkiness of twilight. A pack of links carrying their blazing torches high converged on the throng leaving Westminster Hall bargaining for hire. "Four farthings, portal to portal," one hawked. "A half-penny," another competed.

"Before the ceremony I took the liberty of hiring our linkboys," said Billy, holding the door open, "trustworthy lads. They will be waiting by our carriages."

It had taken Billy fifteen months to get used to London's noisy mobs, her peddlers, beggars and pickpockets. His father was prone to brag that 'not an idle man, and consequently, not a poor man was to be found in America,' by contrast.   When Billy first arrived, he was compassionate, gullible and inexperienced, doling out money right and left.   He had great difficulty tolerating the persistent harassment everywhere he went.   Not until he saw a crippled man run and a tyke who came no farther than his coat cuff pick a pocket, did he understand the desperation of the city's poor.

"Look," Benjamin remarked as he helped Mrs. Stevenson into the coach, "a Gibbous moon."   It bulged like the stomach of a woman pregnant with child.   The moon, however blurred and barely visible through the filmy soot screen overhead, shed a dim light, like lamplight through a dirty chimney.

Six days a week the furnaces at the silk mills and the plate makers belched coal particles into the sky, but on Sundays, a Londoner's only day of rest, the fires were banked, clearing the air somewhat.

"Take the ladies straight to 7 Craven Street, Strand," Billy ordered the linkboy, attending strictly to the business at hand.

"Don't tarry too long," warned Mrs. Stevenson, "or you'll ruin my rarebit."

"You know the way to a man's heart," Billy called, as the carriage wheeled noisily away.   He bit the bait, because he knew his father could not be lured by the prospects of a good meal, no matter how enticing the apple puffs smelled that morning.   His Papa had lived too long on the borrowed maxim, 'Eat to live, not live to eat'.

The Hell was bedlam when the four men arrived, but Richard Jackson, a lawyer of the Inner Temple, with whom Billy had spent the latter part of the past summer, beckoned them to join him.

"How do you feel being William Franklin, Esq.?" he asked, clasping Billy's outstretched hand.

"As anxious as a thoroughbred at the gate."

The metaphor Billy chose to describe his present feelings stemmed, in the first place, from his love of horses and the sport of racing.   Secondly, it reflected his ambition to succeed in his own right, on his own merit, to run his own race.   Up until now he had followed in his father's footsteps, walking into a job as Benjamin vacated it, like the absentee position he now held as Comptroller of the Post Office for the Northern Colonies.   The symbolic remark

also had an occult meaning, meant for father and son only.   By

equating himself to a 'thoroughbred', Billy was saying that his

newly acquired status as a J.D. would perhaps override the stigma

of illegitimacy, a brand too deep to remove completely but give

him a degree of respectability.   Although he dutifully considered

Deborah his mother, the true identity of his genealogical mother

was never divulged to him.   The fact that he was a bastard was

grist for vicious political opponents and had been a bone of

contention with Dr. Graeme, Betsy's highly influential father.

"Of course, I'm alluding to my desire of being appointed to

a good post as quickly as possible," he replied, raising his glass.

"Good things in good time," said Mr. Collinson, offering

the toast.

"Here!   Here!" they shouted, raising their mugs.

"To the future Mrs. Franklin, Miss Betsy Graeme of

Philadelphia," Richard added with a flourish.   "I'm certain that

she must be impatiently awaiting your return."

Ben and Billy exchanged sidelong glances and lowered

their drinking cups but said nothing.   Inappropriately timed, a

group of raucous revelers at the other end of the pub challenged
another to a drinking contest.

"I'm sorry," said Richard, getting the message.   "I thought
that 'absence made the heart grow fonder', he mumbled
apologetically, borrowing the ancient maxim from the Roman poet,
Propertius.

The others sat swirling their beer slowly, not knowing quite
what to say, waiting for an explanation.

Billy fingered the handmade silk watch chain, a
remembrance Betsy had sent to him in New York while he waited
to embark for London and wondered whether they should have
carried out their plan to secretly marry before his departure.   "Her
letter arrived while I was away at Portsmouth," he began.   "She
was outraged!   Said I was a neglectful suitor because I had not
written to her faithfully with every packet.   Her love must have
been very fragile, in need of constant reassurance.   I never
realized..."   His voice trailed off momentarily.   "She accused me
of having a change of heart.   If I had, I would have told her so.
That was our agreement!"

"You are reasoning with your heart, my son," said

Benjamin, "and only dealing with one aspect of her outrage. Your supposed neglect of her is a superficial excuse, a private problem.   The underlying cause of her fury is of a public nature, namely, your recently published article exposing the contemptible acts committed by the Proprietors against the Pennsylvania Assembly.   My guess is that Dr. Graeme had something to do with the writing of that letter.   In all likelihood my son's exposé created quite a stir in the Penn camp and at Graeme Park.   It's all my fault.   I was too ill to write it myself."

"She succumbed to her father's pressures after all," added Billy, shaking his head.   "I misjudged her maturity or lack thereof."

"A father can be an overwhelming influence," Benjamin concurred.

"And that's not all," Billy exclaimed, pounding his fist on the table like a gavel.   She called my father malicious!   And to think that I told her over and over again that I loved her almost as much as you, Papa.   Well, I swear to you all that I will never write to Ms. Graeme again.   Ever."

"It's probably just a lover's quarrel," Richard said, trying to make light of it.   "Put yourself in her place.   She's was lonely

and probably terribly afraid of losing you."

"Well, Mr. Jackson, Miss Graeme has done exactly that!"

"We are acting like a bunch of Cimmerians," said Mr.

Strahan, pointedly goading them into higher spirits.

"To bachelorhood!" Billy toasted, clicking his mug all

around.

"To my son and his future," Benjamin said, standing.

"To Billy and his future," they echoed.

Billy stood, his gold cuff buttons flashing in the firelight

"To Papa," he said, sharing the limelight.   "For your love, your

friendship, your generosity over this past year and your countless

indulgences throughout my life.   I am forever in your debt."

"Wealth is not his that has it, but his that enjoys it,"

Benjamin quoted facetiously from *Poor Richard*.

"For those of you not privy to my prodigal habits, I am

being ribbed for living beyond my means."

"Drink up, gentlemen," Benjamin replied, laughing.   "It's

time to go home to supper."

A blustery southwest wind barred the door, forcing the men

to put on their beaver tricorns to anchor down their wigs before
stepping outside.   Open hearth fires burned in every London
house that November night, sending ribbons of smoke to envelop
the moon.

HISTORY REPEATS ITSELF

Chapter II

July 4, 1759

"Whoa!" Peter reined the bay mares to an abrupt stop on his master's order.   He was one of two slaves the Franklins had brought with them from America.   The other was King, who had recently run away, like Billy's pony had done when he was a boy of eleven.   Brokenhearted, he had placed an ad in his father's *Gazette* saying that if anyone found and returned her, they could ride her whenever they wished.   From this sad experience, Billy learned the meaning of the phrase, 'Finders keepers, losers weepers', as well as a hard lesson about human nature.   It seems the thief took the latter half of that bargain literally, because the unshod bay mare, branded IW on her shoulder and buttock, was never returned.   His luck wasn't much better with his runaway slave.   King, he learned, had found greener pastures by being taken in by a pious lady in Suffolk, who converted him to Christianity and saw to his education and general improvement. Although Billy knew of his whereabouts, he had no compulsion to retrieve the mischievous rascal.   In fact, the thought of eventually selling him to the lady had crossed his mind, but he decided to let the matter ride, since he was no longer obligated to pay for his keep.

Besides, on this clear, drizzle-free, early summer day, Billy was not preoccupied with horses or servants.   A far more urgent and perplexing problem had arisen to demand his attention.   He learned that he was going to be a father!

Getting out of the carriage, he strode off across London Bridge to think.   Peter followed at a respectable distance, edging the coach into the stream of traffic with the agility of a sculler navigating a tiny vessel on the busy Thames.   Normally at mid-morning Billy would be working, employed as he was as his father's secretary for the time being, but with the *Historical Review* published, he had little else to do but sit back and wait for the fur to fly when he divulged his predicament to his father.

Hesitating, he feigned interest in the demolition of the old private dwellings and business establishments cluttering the bridge and then, leaning over the railing, watched the glut of red and green boats jockeying for position on the congested river below. Billy had ridden bareback through the entire winter and spring seasons, beguiling maiden and lady alike with his charm and good looks as he circled their constant round of parties.   He was a gay blade who had suddenly been unbridled by his breakup with his fiancée in America.   One hard-and-fast lesson he learned by throwing caution to the wind was that freedom goes hand and hand with responsibility.

How can I support a child?   Obviously, I can't.   But I must, or I'll go to jail.   His mind flipped from one agonizing consequence to another.   Will this scandal jeopardize my appointment?   It can't.   It mustn't.   I won't breathe a word of it to anyone except Papa.   Papa.   How will he take this news? Will it destroy our relationship?   That I couldn't bear.   He massaged the bridge of his long, slender nose to ease the throbbing pain in his head.   For sure he'll bring up Polly.   I know he blames me for her leaving home broken-hearted to live with her aunt in Wanstead, but I will not allow Papa to choose a wife for me.   I do not love Polly and do not intend to marry her, just as I do not intend to marry the mother of this unborn child of mine.

Feeling squeamish and washed-out from torment and lack of sleep, he straightened up stiffly and threw back his head to let the warm, gentle breeze that filled the sails and powered the ships clear his troubled mind and knead his sin-filled soul.   In no time at all the haggard look waned.   He had made his peace and would leave his destiny to providence.   Presently, he flagged Peter and instructed him to take the long route home past St. James Park.

On the way, they passed the windowless tenements, evocative and enduring reminders of the unpopular glass tax. They stood like monuments of defiance, where families lived like Cimmerians with no ventilation and no daylight.   In order to keep from dwelling on his own dilemma, Billy fictitiously elevated himself to a position of authority and imagined how he would rule, given a similar situation.

As a royal governor, let us say, I would have to remain neutral, walk the middle ground between subject and King.   Papa says that 'the waves do not rise but when the winds blow'.

Misjudging the people's tolerance could be a danger, but would

they resort to violence over such a trivial grievance as a glass tax?

I hardly think so.   Non-use is harmless civil disobedience, but

revolt is out-and-out treason!   In any event, this tax has generated

revenue for sundry purposes, including the ongoing war with

France and the Indians of America, so I don't believe it will be

rescinded anytime soon.   The poor devils!

"It was so out!"   The shrill, young voice rising above the

normal clamor of Fleet Street interrupted Billy's train of thought,

and he peered from the carriage to see two boys bickering over a

game of marbles.   He summoned Peter to stop in front of Temple

Bar, a popular meeting place for actors, authors and poets.

"Was not!" the defender protested.   He stuffed the

disputed aggie into his pocket with his grubby little hand and

waddled off into the mob as fast as his bowed legs would carry

him.

"Was too, you cheatin' cripple," the other one yelled,

shaking his fist.

The boy with rickets was no doubt tired of using the

hackneyed phrase, 'Sticks and stones may break my bones, but names will never harm me', because he did not return to retaliate.

Billy's chest muscles tightened as he glared at the name-caller with eyes as cold as agate.   Sitting in judgment with him like a mute jury were the shriveled heads of rebel partisans still pegged to the facade of Temple Bar since the Jacobite uprising after being publicly hanged and beheaded on Kensington Common.

"Giddyap."   Peter tapped the reins lightly and the horses stepped out.

Like the deformed lad in the street, Billy had grown callous to name-calling at an early age, too.   Bastard was not a pretty label either, but a mark of shame and disgrace.   In many instances, such subjection would deaden a boy's spirit and instill in him a permanent feeling of inferiority, but thanks to his father, who treated his son with the utmost respect and instilled in him a high degree of self-righteousness, Billy became thick-skinned and somewhat of an elitist.   "An empty bag cannot stand upright," Benjamin was prone to say; in fact, he took pride in his son and did not hesitate to introduce him to the most influential, the most prestigious people he knew.

"Ugh!"   Billy nearly gagged.   The stench, he saw with

dismay, came from the corpse of a horse left to rot in the middle of

the road where it had evidently dropped.   He reached for his cane,

removed the end and sniffed the vinegar-soaked cloth it contained,

which was the proven preventative of the day against

contamination.   Dead cats and dogs were commonplace in the

kennels, the open sewers that carried away the wastes of London's

filthy streets.   But a horse!   A horse was as sacred to Billy as the

cow to the Indians or the apple to Aphrodite.   He closed his eyes

to the unsightly horror and ordered Peter to head for home.

Thinking again of the ordeal he faced, Billy couldn't help

but wonder whether his father harbored any misgivings about the

identical error he had made thirty years ago.   If he did, he wore no

guilt on his sleeve.   He stroked his clean-shaven chin and tried to

second-guess his reaction when he told him that sometime in

February he would be the grandfather of a bastard baby.

THE PRODIGAL SON

Chapter III

The wooden stairs creaked spitefully announcing Billy's arrival.   "Is that you, son?" Benjamin asked, not looking up from his writing.

"Yes, Papa," Billy replied, taking off his coat and hanging it on a peg by the door.   Benjamin was seated at the gateleg table facing the window.   Billy plopped down on the edge of the settee behind him, nervously wringing his hands.

"I'm just finishing up a letter to your mother, telling her of our proposed trip to Scotland."

Billy winced.   What if he had botched that up too?   The University of St. Andrews had recently bestowed an honorary Doctor of Law degree on his father, a great personal triumph for a mostly self-taught man, and having him receive it in person was to be the highlight of their trip.   The other reasons paled in comparison, namely, introducing Billy to England's most notable masters and sightseeing.   "Please add that her dutiful son sends his love and affection."   Billy's voice was rough and ragged, causing Benjamin to look up.

"Is something the matter?" he asked, removing his small, round-rimmed glasses, laying them on the table and placing his feather pen back in the inkwell.   Showing concern, he pushed back the Chippendale armchair, stood to stretch his neck and back and turned to face his son.   "Mrs. Stevenson said you left without a bite of breakfast."

"I'm afraid I find myself involved in a very regrettable situation," he began with extreme hesitation.   For someone so articulate, Billy was having a deuce of a time verbalizing.   His shoulders slumped, and his eyes avoided his father's by roaming about the airy sitting room.

"Do you wish to discuss it?   No problem is unsolvable," Benjamin prodded as he eased himself into the Hepplewhite chair opposite his obviously disturbed son.   He leaned back and

patiently waited for a response, his right thumb supporting his chin
as it customarily did when he pondered an observation.

Unable to make his confession face to face, not wanting to
see the disappointment he feared would be reflected there, Billy
got up and crossed the room to stare out unseeingly upon Craven
Street.   Although his Crown appointment and accompanying
Benjamin on his upcoming trip to Scotland might be in jeopardy
because of his irresponsible behavior, what mattered most and
foremost was the preservation of the wonderfully close relationship
he shared with his father.   Scenes from last summer's trip to
Ecton fancifully replaced the window panes: finding grandfather
Franklin's estate, roaming through the converted stone
schoolhouse that was once the old homestead, watching excitedly
as Peter brushed the moss from the gravestones in the churchyard
and uncovered inscriptions legible enough to copy and send back
home.

Mustering courage, he began. "I find myself involved in a
totally untenable predicament."

"Go on," Benjamin replied, not changing his position.

"I've gotten a woman into trouble, Papa," he stated evenly.

"The baby will come sometime in February."   He stood as still as a palace guard.

Benjamin's arm fell from his chin like a strut dislodged by a severe blow and lay flaccid in his lap.   "Well, what do you know!" he exclaimed, seemingly talking to himself.   "History repeats itself."   He rose at once and went to his son's side.

"I'm sorry, Papa," Billy said, embracing him.

"Look," Benjamin said commiserating, "'the passion of youth is not easily governed'.   After, all, who am I to talk!   Does anyone else know about this?" he asked, sounding the alarm.

"Not a soul."

"Our saving grace is that we are expert at keeping a secret."

"But, Papa, I am in no position to raise a child!"

"Don't worry.   It will be properly cared for.   I shall see to that."

Billy's shoulders slumped as the heavy weight he had been carrying for weeks was lifted from them.   "How can I ever thank you, Papa," Billy questioned, no longer avoiding his father's eyes.

"You've heard me say this before, but I'll say it again. 'None but the well-bred man knows how to confess a fault or acknowledge himself in an error'."   For some time the two men stood arm in arm and watched as an unwelcome shower passed through, spoiling London's rare sunny, summer day.   Linked by more than bonds of blood, they shared a mutual admiration, one that transcends age and raises an impregnable, natural barrier to affront.

Billy stood tall and squared his shoulders, relieved that he had been exonerated and freed from this highly inconvenient and untimely burden.

August 8, 1759

Up to this point, suppression of the deed appeared to be successful, and for the Franklins, absorption in plans for their upcoming trip supplanted the prickly affair in their minds.   The lengthy itinerary included stops at the Staffordshire potteryworks and the salt mine areas of Liverpool and Lancaster, places they had missed the previous summer.

"Are you certain you've brought along enough clothes?" Benjamin asked Billy facetiously as Peter loaded the trunks atop the coach on departure day.

"Now let me ask you a question, my dear Papa," Billy bantered once he was satisfied that his over-size trunk was securely stored atop the post chaise.   "Would it be fitting for the son of DR. BENJAMIN FRANKLIN. to be presented to the illustrious Lord and Lady Kames or the learned scholar, Adam Smith, or the Rev. Carlyle looking like a pauper?   I should say not!"

"My first mistake was telling you that I'd rather have it said that 'He lived usefully than He died rich'."

They both had a good laugh as they climbed aboard. Benjamin thrived on raillery such as this, and their playful exchanges continued as they left the Black Swan en route to Birmingham, a city of about twenty-three thousand.

Billy's lack of thrift and frugality, inculcated over the years by a doting father, had become a way of life.   His taste for clothes was Parisian -- the best wools, the most elegant brocades, the finest cambric.   Bills he could not meet came from 'Christopher' the tailor, 'Forfar' the hatter and 'Regnier' the clothier.   As a result of these extravagances, his indebtedness to Benjamin rose with every buying spree, but Benjamin kept a running tally, and with every new debit entered, his hold over his son tightened.

"Your company gives me untold pleasure, Billy," he exclaimed, patting his arm affectionately.   In a rare show of emotion, a lone tear surfaced, and Billy surmised by the blank expression that his father was reliving the painfully traumatic day when his other son, four-year-old Francis Folger, who was too weakened by the flux to be inoculated, sadly died in the smallpox epidemic of '36.

In his own mind's eye, Billy saw the child-size marker his parents had placed in Christ Church burial ground bearing his brother's name.   He went there often to visit it when he was home. Francis was remembered by everyone as 'the Delight of all that knew him'.

Although the process of inoculation was crude in 1736 (the deadly virus obtained from the pustules of the infected with a needle and thread and transmitted through an incision to the healthy), it spared many people.   Billy was among them.   He was six at the time.

As they proceeded down Holbrook Street, church bells began to peal evoking additional, grisly reminders of the baleful epidemic.   Billy would never forget them ringing in Philadelphia after every sixth death, and some days they rang more than once. So many people died that the bodies had to be buried upright in a potter's field.

Benjamin had nodded off before they crossed Oxford Street, although Billy wondered how. The wide, metal wheels clattered and clanked on the uneven cobblestones with every turn, grinding the cinders strewn over the street into ashes as a millstone grinds wheat into flour. The brick ovens located at the edge of town mixed soot from the kilns with clay to make good, strong building bricks, which was a positive result. The negative effect of the process, however, produced sickening, foul-smelling air that eventually roused the elder Franklin.

Billy buried the unpleasant recollections he had exhumed about his little brother and returned them to the crypt of his memory, because he and his Papa were on their way to Birmingham and points north, setting out on a new and exciting adventure. Benjamin's love was part and parcel of his life, and he thanked God that he had not been disowned because of his loose and reprehensible behavior.

They passed the time reminiscing about the whirlwind they

trailed in Maryland in '45 as well as the foolhardiness of the kite

experiment in '52.

"That was a harebrained thing to do!   We're lucky we're

here to talk about that one," Billy reminded his recklessly daring

father.   "Or should I say I'm lucky!" he added stroking his chin

and giving Benjamin the eyes.   "So long as the end justified the

means, which I believe it did," Benjamin replied, patting the back

of his son's hand.

"Right!" Billy responded playfully.   "Anything for the

advancement of science!"   He was well aware that whatever

tickled his father's curiosity piqued his own as well, mainly the

foibles and phenomenon of nature.

Any observer could see that they were happy and content in

each other's company.

"Look, Papa," Billy cried, pointing to a field of low-

growing plants.   "Aren't they strawberries?"

I do believe they are," Benjamin replied, stretching his neck

to see.   He tapped the roof with his cane and Peter stopped.

Getting out to investigate, they found little fruit left to sample this

late in the season, but to husbandry-loving men like the Franklins, tasting was secondary. They were already aware of the berry's delectable quality but what interested them more was the soil in which it grew. Billy rubbed the damp earth between thumb and forefinger much as a clothier examines the quality of a fine piece of silk.

"I'm definitely going to cultivate these on my farm," Billy announced, popping a juicy, red berry in his mouth.

"Well, then, 'since diligence is the Mother of good luck', we'd better be off and make some contacts so you can get a job, buy that farm, and plant those strawberries," Benjamin joshed good-naturedly.

As Ben and Billy traveled further north into the upland moors, their eyes feasted on hills smothered in pinkish purple heather and valleys whose tessellated floors of spiny, yellow-flowering gorse resembled an unending mural of geometric diversity. Father and son oo'd and ahh'd like youngsters seeing their first fireworks display.

"'Britain, land of the Angles'," Benjamin quipped, testing his brand of subtle humor on his son.

"With a capital A," Billy quickly answered, not to be

outwitted.

"Just testing your gullibility. Keeping you sharp. You know, son, I was just thinking of the time we had a discussion about my concern for your generation, its aimlessness, lack of purpose and loss of direction. I was sincerely troubled because I feared I'd raised a 'country gentleman' whose life was totally consumed with frivolous pursuits, weekly balls, plays at Plumsted's warehouse, horse racing, fishing, hunting, things I'd never had time to do myself. To pay off one debt after another, I had to keep my nose to the grindstone, be industrious, hardworking, build a respectable reputation, because dependability was important for an upstart businessman."

"And I still recall your words of wisdom on that occasion," Billy replied, knitting his brow in concentration. "'You know, my son, a person can be born with a highly capable brain, but like the good earth, if it is not well tilled and sowed with profitable seed, it produces only ranker weeds'," he riantly quoted verbatim.

"Ah, yes. You were cut from a different cloth."

"Will you ever forget the time I ran away to fight the French?"

"You were only knee high to a grasshopper!"

"I was fifteen.   I often wonder where I'd be now if you hadn't come in time to fetch me off that ship.   By the way, there's something I always meant to ask you.   You brought me back, yet you didn't tie me down.   In fact, you encouraged me to join the military, as I recall.   Why?"

"Adventure was in your blood.   I knew that.   Besides, there was a sore throat epidemic in Philadelphia that summer, remember?"

Not wanting to dwell on epidemics, Billy mused about his army career.   I was an eighteen-year-old with army time under my belt and an expedition to the Ohio Indian territory to my credit. You became prosperous while I was away while I became arrogant."

Benjamin chuckled softly.   "What the devil did you say anyhow?"

"I told you that I thought you 'had enough money for both of us'."

"And what was my reply?"

"You replied gruffly that 'you intended to spend what little you had yourself and that I could see by your goings on that you were as good as your word'." They both laughed until they cried. Grimacing, Billy bobbed his head in retrospect. "You must admit that I came close to becoming a country gentleman, so close." Billy needed a private moment to indulge in a blissful fantasy in pantomime, so he closed his eyes and pretended to be resting. He pictured himself as the master of the expansive Graeme estate in Bucks County with Betsy at his side. In his letter to her on May 16, 1757, shortly before the packet left New York and carried him away to England, he disclosed this ultimate ambition. Benjamin's mention of Plumsteds and the use of the words 'country gentleman' had hit a soft spot. He'd met Betsy at the warehouse, and along with his passionate desire to marry her had also evolved the dream of one day being a member of Pennsylvania's aristocracy.

"We're here," his father said softly, nudging him.

Billy bolted upright, not wanting to miss a thing. Luton Hoo, the stately mansion of Lord Bute, a man whose closeness to young Prince George was no secret, loomed in the distance. It was surrounded by lush pastures with creations of topiary art lining the driveway in perfect symmetry.

"Welcome to my home," Lord Bute said as the Franklins alighted from their carriage. "Any friend of Caleb Whitefoord is a friend of mine," he assured them. As soon as they were seated comfortably inside, he took from the pocket of his pink riding habit several letters of introduction, which he handed to Benjamin.

CROSSCURRENTS

Chapter IV

"The Firth of Forth," Billy enunciated without the slightest slip, the tongue-twister rolling smoothly off his articulate tongue. "How majestic it is in the moonlight," he whispered, breathless from the splendor of the sea and landscapes beyond: massive Edinburgh Castle, its outer wall of rock plunging precipitously into the cavernous ravine below and historic Holyrood Abbey, the former residence of Scottish royalty, the most celebrated being the infamous Mary, Queen of Scots, who was beheaded by her cousin, Elizabeth I for plotting to kill her.

"From here," said Benjamin, completely mesmerized, "it appears that an arm of the North Sea is reaching inland to empty the mouth of the River Forth, with the city of Edinburgh cradled in the crook of its elbow.   Then in the blink of an eye, the sight vanished as stealthy, filmy clouds slithered by to drape the helpless

moon in a gauzy coverlet to extinguish its luminescence and

blacken the night.

Billy soon found the people as overwhelming as their

scenery.   It seemed that all the prominent members of society in

Edinburgh and its environs were in a state of readiness for the

Franklin visit.   After just a little more than a week, he was in such

high spirits and bursting with so many tales of things he'd done and

dignitaries he'd met that he sat down to relate them to his sister,

who was not quite as privileged as he.

'September 10, 1759

Dearest Sally,

Someday you, too, must see Scotland.   Papa and I are

greatly impressed with its physical beauties as well as its

hospitable and friendly people.   After a journey of over three

weeks and four hundred miles, we arrived in Edinburgh on

September 2nd and almost immediately were made honorary

guildbrothers of the city.   We have been staying in Prestonfield since the 8th at the home of Sir Alexander Dick, who is the

president of the College of Physicians.   He is begging us to stay a

week, but you know what Papa says about house guests -- 'Fish

and visitors smell in three days'.   If he decides to decline the

invitation, I pray God he does not express our regrets in that

fashion.   There is a bowling green on the grounds, and they have

taught me how to play.   There are six alleys 20'x120' long, each

having a shallow trough running its entire length.   The object is to

roll a lopsided, wooden ball down the alley and see who comes

closest to the jack (a small ball which is placed at the opposite end

before play begins).   To our host's surprise, I seem to have gotten

the knack of it rather quickly, because I have been winning most of

the wagers.   I bought you a muff and a tippet (the same shade of

blue as your eyes) but will not be sending them until we get back

to London, which should be sometime next month.

Your ever affectionate brother,

Billy'

Benjamin decided to stay the week at Prestonfield after all,

and Billy noted wryly when they left that there wasn't the slightest

taint of discord in the air.   On the contrary, compared to the ceremonious reception they received upon arrival, their farewell

was emotional and difficult, like the parting of lifelong friends.

They returned to Mrs. Cowan's flat in Edinburgh, and the

partying continued.   It seemed that while the Franklins were out

of town, all the most notable minds of Edinburgh had conferred to

arrange a schedule of nonconflicting parties for their two guests of

honor on their return to the city.

Benjamin rapped on his son's door.   "Hurry!   We'll be

late.   And don't forget the *Historical Review*.

"Coming," Billy called, smoothing the ruffles on his shirt

for the umpteenth time.   Dismissing Peter, he tucked the leather-

bound publication under his arm and hurtled down the four flights

of stairs, catching up with his father before he reached Milne

Court.

"Dr. Robertson's residence," Benjamin directed the

postman as they boarded.

"Aye, Sir.   I know it well.   That is the grand Elizabethan

house just inside the west gate."

The powerful horses strained audibly as they scaled the

formidable incline of the Canongate.   At the top of the hill they turned right onto the Cowgate, and from there on in, the going was easier down the main street.   The two celebrity passengers relaxed and leaned out to admire the flush of the late afternoon sky, the infinite band of radiance fusing every color of the rainbow into a fleeting work of art.

Nearing their destination Benjamin gave Billy some last-minute coaching.   "Adam Ferguson, who is a channel to Lord Bute, is also expected to be here tonight.   See that you talk to him."

"Because Lord Bute is a link to the heir apparent."

"How quickly you learn protocol, my son."

"I've had a mentor par excellence."   Glancing sideward, Billy noted that Benjamin had enjoyed the compliment.   God, how I love my father, he thought.   I'd follow him straight into hell, if need be!   He's not only my father but also my best friend!

"More wine, gentlemen?" Dr. Robertson asked.

"Thank you, but no thank you," replied Benjamin laughing. "If I drink another drop or eat another morsel, I shall have to lie down and place my stomach beside me."   He pushed back his chair and proceeded to light his pipe.

"Then we shall all relax by the fire and enjoy some more conversation."

Billy, whose dislike of tobacco was a handy excuse to leave the table, joined Adam Ferguson to chat by the hearth. Relying on his stint in the military as a common bond, he struck up a conversation about the war with France. "It appears that General Wolfe will have a showdown with Montcalm in Quebec any day now."

"Perhaps the battle is already over. News travels so slowly across the Atlantic. What do you think? Does Wolfe have a chance?"

"Only if he is well supplied with men and materials, concentrates his forces on one target and attacks from strength."

"I agree," said the former fighting chaplain of the Black Watch Regiment. "Victory will never be achieved with a half-hearted assault."

By this time, war talk monopolized the entire conversation.

"'If France is forced to let go of the tail, isn't she apt to turn around and bite the dog?'" Benjamin propounded in his usual enigmatic way.

Unamused, Rev. Carlyle questioned in disbelief.   "Are you suggesting, Dr. Franklin, that England will be invaded?"

"I pointed out several vulnerable spots to my son as we traveled northward."

The group erupted like a volcano, spewing forth an assortment of denials and arguments.

Suddenly, Billy stepped forward to take the floor.   "I feel," he said, taking a deep breath and stretching his torso to attain his full stature, "that after the French are defeated in North America and the West Indies, the remainder of the war will be confined to the Continent."

"You surprise me, William," Benjamin retaliated, "when you relegate the acquisition of the Caribbean Islands on a par with the conquest of the French possessions in North America. Overall, they are of little importance."

"But trade is all-important.   Sugar and molasses are valuable commodities and could profit the empire greatly," Billy contended.

A spent log crashed between the andirons, sending red-hot embers aloft.   The onlookers stood like waxed figures, apparently stunned by the unexpected confrontation between father and son.

Letting the matter drop, the sage receded to a seat by the window to sulk in silence while Billy, remarkably unscathed by the exchange, returned his attention to his charmed and admiring audience.

Needless to say, the ride home was uncomfortably quiet. In a way, Billy was glad, because he had a great many things to mull over in his mind. Of late he'd been aware of something fermenting inside of him, but he'd never vented it until this evening. Speaking his mind and having his opinion count had been an extremely satisfying experience, a real shot in the arm for his budding self-confidence. Although he realized that his show of independence had no doubt been a shocker to Benjamin, he felt that their ties were strong enough to take the jolt. Like it or not, the old dyed-in-the wool Whig, an ally of the artisan, had raised a Tory son, who hobnobbed with aristocrats and Anglicans with the ease and alacrity of a true blue blood.

On the way back to the flat, Billy was so caught up with lingering regrets over their falling-out on the one hand and wondering whether he had made points with Adam Ferguson on the other, that he was oblivious to the stench created by people flinging the contents of their chamber pots out of the windows and into the streets before the dung collector made his nightly rounds.

Benjamin, still nursing his grudge, stirred but otherwise remained sullen and withdrawn.

Putting the tiff between them to rest for a minute, Billy concentrated on the prospects for his immediate future. Since both fame and fortune were coveted equally, he decided to devise a strategy that would guarantee him not only station and personal redemption but monetary rewards as well. Self-reliance hinged on two things. First and foremost, he needed a post, a position of eminence, power and distinction. Secondly, he needed a wife, someone with a handsome dowry and exceptional qualities: intelligence, grace, sophistication and charm. Dwelling on the latter item first, he pondered his possibilities. Polly was not in contention. Billy never gave her a second thought, which the matchmaker claimed had broken her heart. Then, for some reason, the amber-complexioned Barbadian beauty to whom he had been introduced at Lady Percy's party before leaving London appeared in his mind's eye. He envisioned her in a

Gainsborough-like painting, a landscaped portraiture, feeding the ducks in St. James Park and dressed in a gown of pale yellow brocade accented with a filmy chiffon scarf flounced about the neck and secured in the V of her décolletage.   Her name, he recalled, was Elizabeth Downes.   Strange, he pondered, that I should single her out at the very moment I am contemplating choosing a suitable bride.   H'm, he thought.   She is a definite maybe, perhaps even a genuine possibility.

Benjamin, who appeared to be catnapping, apparently felt a chill and shivered.

"Are you cold, Papa?" Billy asked, ending his reverie.

Benjamin nodded, his wounded pride salved by his son's solicitude.

Billy unfolded the tartan robe that lay on the seat beside him and tucked it about his father lovingly.   "Don't you dare get sick on me now," he joshed, trying to make amends.   "It isn't everyday that one receives a Doctor of Law degree!"

"Ah, yes," he replied with renewed vitality.   "Then we'll each have a title."

"We'll start our own dynasty," Billy added, egging him on.

"How does that sound?"

"Like music to my ears!"

"The FRANKLIN dynasty.   It has the ring of majesty, grandeur, sovereignty, don't you think?"   Billy caught the expression of joy in his father's face as he alighted from the carriage and stood momentarily in the torch's brightness and felt confident that their relationship was back on an even keel and that, except for this minor, isolated incident, their compasses were pointed in the same direction.

Before turning in, Benjamin confided, "Do you want to know the God's honest truth, Billy?" he asked, stroking his chin. "I think you could charm the horns off the very devil!"

"Like father, like son," Billy admitted with a redemptive grin.   "Goodnight, Papa."

"Goodnight, son."

PAY THE PIPER

Chapter V

"Richard!" Billy called, cupping his hands around his mouth.   The expanding ice bellowed a reply, and soon after, his friend appeared from under one of the arches of Westminster Bridge, his wooden skates skittering over the bumpy surface like knuckles across a washboard.

"Will," he hollered, "how many arches would you guess there are?   Fourteen!" he shouted, answering his own question.

"Humph!" Billy snorted as he brushed the snow aside and plopped down on the dock to attach his skates.   "Discover the cause of typhoid.   Then I'd be impressed," he retorted indifferently.   Mutely he cursed himself for agreeing to go to the frost fair with 'omniscient Jackson' in the first place.   How in God's name could he feign interest in the boring details of steel and stone or find amusement in a hasty pudding-eating contest when at this very minute his child was about to be born?   But for the sake of expediency, he would simply have to fake it.   At least it would kill a couple of hours.

Richard skidded to an abrupt stop inches from a corner pile and sat down to rest.   "I read somewhere that it cost £389,500 to build, and it's..."

"Are you sure you weren't a docent in a former life?" Billy ribbed, deciding to play along.   "Okay, length?

"1,223 feet."

"Construction time?"

"Eleven years."

"Opened in?"

"1750."

"That's incredible.   Now let's go."

"The sad thing about this new structure is that it made the old horse ferry obsolete."

"I agree," Billy added nostalgically.   "The old ways are often more romantic and colorful."

"But slower and much less dependable.   Can't stop

progress, you know."

Billy chuckled to himself and wondered whether Richard
ever dated the same girl more than once.

"Is Miss Downes coming to the fair?" Richard asked out of
the blue.

"Elizabeth is visiting relatives in Laberton until Friday."

Richard zipped around sharply to face Billy, skating in a
zigzagging, backward motion.   "Aha.   So that's why you
accepted my invitation so readily today," he said, needling him.
"You had nothing better to do."

"I shall remain silent for fear of incriminating myself,"
Billy replied, taunting him back.

"You're not getting off the hook that easily, Mr. Franklin.
Did I detect a degree of gladness in your voice when you said
Elizabeth was out of town?   Am I to assume that there is
disharmony in Camelot?"

"Nothing of the sort," Billy stated boastfully.   He spun
around to skate backwards alongside Richard to prevent further
scrutiny.   Admittedly he was glad the woman he had chosen to
marry was away.   There was less chance of the sordid affair

reaching her ears.   If she learned of it, perhaps she would jilt him, and all his carefully-laid plans would be shattered.   He wanted desperately to confide in Richard, who had become like a brother to him, having worked together on the *Historical Review*, but he dared not.   Sympathetic to America's problems, politically astute, socially prominent and financially well-heeled, Richard was one of many people Billy did not want to alienate.   In fact, there was no doubt in his mind that before long, Richard would have a seat in Parliament.   In an attempt to mollify and divert his friend's all too perceptive line of questioning, Billy offered, "I'm taking her to Covent Gardens on the 22nd to see 'Samson'.   Why don't you invite someone and come along?" he asked casually, his warm breath visible in the frosty February air.

"That's this Friday.   Pretty short notice.   Why not," he blurted out after another moment's hesitation.   "I wanted to hear the Stanley organ concert anyway."

"'Samson' is playing.   I'm sure of it," Billy reiterated.

"Didn't you know? There's a concert before the play."

"What time?" Billy asked, mocking him.

"Six-thirty.   Come on!   Let's race!   The loser buys the

cider and gingerbread."

Hugging the north bank, they raced neck and neck toward St. Paul's, its masterly dome rising hundreds of feet above the city. The old church was destroyed in the Great Fire of '66; the present landmark, designed by Christopher Wren, did not open until 1710. Having reached their first destination, they cut cross-lots and headed for the tent-shaped shacks clustered against the opposite bank. Billy was dead set on winning now that a wager was at stake, since he suddenly remembered that he didn't have one solitary copper farthing in his pocket. He had used his last one to pay the messenger that morning and had sent all the silver shillings remaining from his monthly allotment to the midwife. No one would ever suspect money in a package the size and shape of a book. At least he hoped it was ingenious.

A small crowd gathered on the fringe of the fair to wager on the two-man race in progress, which rivaled the traditional hasty pudding-eating, grinning, whistling or yawning contests any day.

The lead seesawed back and forth, and Billy feared he had lost when, three-quarters of the way across, Richard shot past him, head and torso bent, arms flailing.   Then all of a sudden Richard

plowed into an unsuspected mound, an obstacle they later learned

was made by two youngsters who used it to support a target board

for their snowball pitching duel.

Amid a mixture of hoots, cheers and jeers, Billy rushed to

help Richard to his feet.   Unhurt but limp from laughter, he said

weakly, "I concede."

With skates in hand, they moseyed about drinking cider and

eating gingerbread Richard bought from the roving hawker, Tiddy

Doll, a colorful character clad in a long white apron, who carted

his cakes in a basket and whose presence was as familiar at a

Tyburn hanging as here or on a corner of the Strand.

"Ah, here's something I must get you."

"Twenty-four farthings for one line of print?   That's

preposterous.   Don't be foolish."

"A few copper coins is hardly an extravagance.   Consider

it a memento of your sojourn in England, a remembrance from

me."

"As you wish."

They got on the tail end of the line and passed the time

joking, talking and eating glossy red apples that Richard purchased
from a vendor who passed by with his wheelbarrow.   "You never
said much about the ceremony at St. Andrew's.   Was it a grand
affair?"

"Forty some people attended, including university students
and faculty.   It was a banner day for Papa, though, a distinction
he's coveted for a long time."

"Were you at least mentioned for your part in the kite
experiment?"

Billy stopped chewing as a person does when he chomps on
an eggshell.

"Don't say it.   You're right.   It's none of my business."

"Next," said the printer.   "Name, please."

"William Franklin," Richard answered, placing the six
coins in his outstretched palm.   "My God," he persisted, refusing
to let the matter drop without making his point, "you could have
been killed!"

"It never occurred to me to be afraid," Billy added, stroking
his clean-shaven chin.   "As the saying goes, 'If you're born to get
drown, you'll never get hung!'"   Judging from Richard's roar of

delight, Billy felt confident that his crafty manipulation and simulated cheerfulness had done the trick.   True to his nature, his private grievances were not open to public view.

Finishing the certificate, the printer handed it to Richard. "Daredevil William the Fatalist," he said with a flourish, "I present you with this testimonial in recognition of your outstanding feat of courage and adventure."

Billy took it and read aloud: "WILLIAM FRANKLIN WALKED ON THE THAMES FEBRUARY 20, 1760."

Benjamin's sniffles had worsened into à full-blown cold by the time Billy got home, and he was burning up with fever.   Mrs. Stevenson had given him a dose of quinine and had sent Peter to fetch Dr. Fothergill.   She fussed about nervously picking up the scads of newspapers littering the room, and Billy, feeling like a fifth wheel, offered to get the ipecacuanha from Nanny, the cook, in case the good doctor prescribed an emetic for him.

He padded softly down the stairs and found her stirring a steaming kettle of soup, thinking that her stubby, shapeless form always reminded him of a sack of potatoes.   Not wanting to appear expectant, he did not ask if there were any further messages for him or his father but instead used his eyes to survey the kitchen in search of one.

"How is Dr. Franklin?" she cried.

"He's sleeping," Billy said wearily.

"Is there something you want me to do, Master Franklin?"

"Yes. Please take the ipecacuanha up to Mrs. Stevenson and sit with Papa until the doctor arrives."

When she was gone, Billy made himself a cup of tea and went into the parlor to wait for a knock at the door. For as long as he could remember, his father's well-being was always his overriding concern, but uppermost in his thoughts tonight were his own personal, nagging problem and divided loyalties, the feeling of being torn between parental duty and paternal responsibility. Resisting the urge to panic, however, he relied rather on the promise his father had made him, that when the time came, he could depend on his know-how and his monetary help.

His entire private and public future hung in the balance, and there was nothing he could do but leave the unfolding events to providence. Certain that it was going to be a long night, he closed his eyes and fell fast asleep.

Rousing him gently, Nanny whispered, "Master William, your father is asking to see you."

"Has the doctor arrived yet?"

"He has come and gone."

Billy went up immediately to his side and sent Mrs. Stevenson down to supper.   He hated her constant doting and disapproved of the Stevensons becoming like a so-called second family, but he kept his growing resentment to himself.

"Have you heard anything further?" Benjamin asked without opening his eyes.

"Not a word, Papa."   He took the cupping glass from the table and began to suction blood to the surface, a procedure commonly used to alleviate congestion.

"A false alarm, no doubt."   He put his hand over his son's to indicate that he'd had enough cupping.   "Your allotment is there in the chest," he whispered, opening his watery eyes and looking squarely into Billy's.

The younger Franklin expressed his thankfulness with a passing smile and then asked, "What time did Mr. Strahan finally arrive?"

"After three.   The King's printing took precedence over the Franklins' finances."

Billy laughed softly, his hopes buoyed by his Papa's brief spurt of humor.   "Did he bring the large sum you asked him to deliver?"

"No, he didn't.   I told him about the baby."

Billy tilted his head to one side like a person does when he hasn't heard what is said and wants it repeated.   His face paled and his eyes probed his father's for an explanation.

Reading his son's mind, Benjamin propped himself up unsteadily on one elbow and whispered, "You know the law.   The government here does not deal kindly with a man who fathers an illegitimate child and does not arrange for its support."

"I'm well aware of that," Billy countered softly, restraining his anger and dismay.   "And you know the infant mortality rate. Fifty percent of the babies in England, if not still born, die before the age of two.   If this happens to my child, God forbid, then telling Mr. Strahan has served no useful purpose."

"Straney will be acting in my stead.   I trust him with our

secret and you must also," Benjamin concluded.   Considering the matter closed, he slumped back down on his pillow.

"I do not intend to go to jail.   I intend to…"

"Intentions.   Poppycock.   Useless as circumstantial evidence.   Talk.   Pounds pay for a wet nurse, not talk.   The same is true for care, lodging and schooling.

"And the mother's settlement?" Billy broke in sheepishly as he checked his father's brow with the back of his hand.

"The coordination of last-minute details is so crucial. "Oh, dear me, why did I have to get ill this week of all weeks?" Benjamin cried, blaming himself and bewailing the fact that his son felt betrayed.

"Nonsense," Billy quarreled.   The fault is all mine."

"Regardless, we agreed that it would be prudent for you to remain as anonymous as possible, the one exception being, of course, the midwife, who is legally bound under oath to know your identity."

Ending the sordid exchange of disturbing details, Billy checked his father's head again for fever and changed the subject. "I'm sure Dr. Fothergill told you to rest, drink lots of water and try to get down some of Nanny's wonderful home-made soup.

Sighing, Benjamin lay back on his pillows, his vitality sapped, his fever recurring. "Time, tides and babies wait for no man," he managed with a disarming wink.

"He seems to be taking his good old sweet time."

"Headstrong like his father."

"And his grandfather."

Benjamin reached for Billy's hand. "Don't worry, son. Our secret is safe with William Strahan. He will handle the matter expediently

"I hope so."

"I know so. For years I have trusted Straney with my money. Now we shall entrust him with our flesh and blood.

Billy adjusted the covers and blew out the candle, but before leaving the room, he tiptoed to the chest and removed his money. In that instant, the fire on the hearth flared, flashing a larger-than-life image up the wall and halfway across the ceiling, a magnification of both man and deed.

Dawn came on the 22nd and still no word. Billy spent a

sleepless night, reading most of it, or trying to, and pacing the rest.

Adam Smith's latest writing, '*Theory and Moral Sentiments*', a gift

to father and son when they visited Edinburgh, lay face down on

the rumpled bed.   It was a provocative work equating moral

attitudes with sympathy, a philosophy that ran counter to Billy's

belief in legal obligation and sense of duty and honor.

Considering the current state of affairs, perhaps the subject was too

relevant, too touchy.   But William Franklin was not a closed-

minded individual, so that wasn't it at all.

The truth was that his mind was elsewhere--a back room, a

hideaway in an isolated corner of London, imagining as best a man

could the agony of labor, a pain soon forgotten, he was told, after

the joy of delivery.

Billy felt sickish, partly because of lack of sleep but mostly

because time was slipping by, and in a few hours Elizabeth would

return.   Then his mind began to play tricks on him.   The form in

the bed giving birth was hers, writhing, sweating, screaming.   He

squeezed his eyes shut to blot out the transformation, to end the

fantasy.   He had to go out.   He felt trapped,

Dressing quickly yet quietly, he checked on his Papa and

stole, like a thief in the night, out of the house unnoticed.   He felt

an overwhelming urge to ride bareback in the crisp, morning air to

clear his head.   Despite the early hour, Peter was up and bridled

his horse.   Riding bareback was his own private cure-all, a

panacea for all ills.

From Craven Street, he reined left onto the Strand, deserted

now but after eight would be crowded and noisy.   After passing

the King's Mews, he rode up Cattle and Hog Streets and so on out

of the city.   Like an analgesic, the wind and the animal's rhythmic

gait combined to sweep away the cobwebs of pessimism and self-

doubt spun by his one immutable, thoughtless act.

A naturalist at heart, Billy relished the out-of-doors,

especially the farmlands.   Here amidst dormant fields and barren

apple orchards he found renewal.   Already rejuvenated, he slowed

the rented steed to a walk and headed back, patting his shoulder

gently.   An occasional oak, remnants of a one-time abundant

forest, housed new litters of squirrels, their leafy nests deftly

deposited in the trees' naked, bobbing boughs.   Billy stopped to

marvel at their ingenuity and to ponder the miraculous nature of

the deciduous cycle.   He wondered how David Hume, the noted philosopher he had met at Dr. Robertson's party, could remain a skeptic after experiencing half a century of springtimes.

The aroma of coffee brewing and biscuits baking greeted Billy as he entered the modest clapboard house on Craven Street. Since there was no escaping Nanny's watchful eye, he poked his head into the kitchen to report on his whereabouts.

"Land of Goshen, Master Franklin.   You're going to get yourself killed riding alone with all those murderous and thieving highwaymen and footpads on the loose."

"First," he replied absently, seeing a sealed note on the edge of the table, "they'd have to catch me.   Is that message for me or my father?" he inquired with tempered eagerness, his voice sounding strangely guttural.

"Saints preserve us.   I nearly forgot, bein' so worried about Dr. Franklin and all.   The messenger just said, 'Give this to Master Franklin right away'," she added, handing him the note. "Nobody in his right mind would wake a body out of a sound sleep—only if it was a matter of life of death, I suppose."

"No matter, Nanny, and to relieve your mind about Papa, he had a peaceful night.   I'm going up now to see if he's awake and ready for some breakfast."

"I hope to God he'll be up and about soon."

"I agree," he replied, hastily making his exit before she noticed how his hands were shaking. Unable to stand the suspense a second longer, he broke the seal as he scaled the stairs and read: "The child is a healthy boy." He cupped his hand over his mouth to prevent an outburst of pent-up emotion then tiptoed into Benjamin's room to tell him the news. "Papa," he whispered, shaking him gently, "you are a grandfather. You have a healthy grandson." Too congested to speak, Benjamin raised both arms to embrace his son, his tears of joy and relief expression enough. Totally wasted by even this scanty amount of physical exertion, he lapsed back into a sound, peaceful sleep.

Billy was so elated that he wished he was the town crier and could shout his good news to every passerby on the street, but since he was honor-bound to keep the baby's existence under his hat, he stifled his emotions and concentrated solely on coming up with a fitting name for the boy. William Temple Franklin, he mused, alias William Temple for the time being.

COURTING BETSY NO. 2

Chapter VI

After a rousing and exhausting gavotte, Betsy and Billy

escaped from the crowd jamming the three main ballrooms and

joined the stragglers in the Northumberland House gallery, a

stately room where the Percy ancestral lineage was lavishly

displayed, beginning at the time of William I.   With such

distinguished genealogical peers, one would never suspect that the

duchess' chain of succession contained a link tarnished by

illegitimacy, the spoiler being the bastard son of Charles II.   This

incidental aside, first-timers, overwhelmed by the room's opulent

grandeur and awed by the lifelike portraits surrounding them,

roamed about mesmerized as Billy had also done nearly two years

earlier when he was a neophyte in high society.

Tonight, however, Billy was aware of only one figure, the

dark-haired beauty nestled at his side.   Knowing of a more

secluded spot in the gallery where they could have a little privacy

and hold a conversation without interruption, he took her there,

beneath the full-length painting of their hostess.

"Wasn't it marvelous of Lady Percy to give us tickets for

the coronation?" Betsy exclaimed, looking up at it.

"They're scarce as hens' teeth!   I've been told that seats in

the Abbey are reserved for the King's favored people."

"Just be sure you get back from Holland in time, my

sweet," she cautioned with a kiss.   She slipped out of his embrace

and headed in the direction of the powder room.

"Neither hell nor high water could keep me away," he

replied under his breath to his benefactress on the wall.

By now he and Betsy were regulars at Lady Percy's routs,

adornments, and like the paintings, admired for their charm and

elegance.   If the truth was known, however, Billy had carefully

and intentionally invaded the Tory social circle, a stronghold, he

calculated, whose hierarchy would inevitably win the power

struggle when King George II died.

If his prediction was right, George II's grandson, George

William Frederick would take the throne, oust the incumbents and install followers of his own choosing.   If this design succeeded, William Pitt would resign and Lord Bute would become prime minister.   Lord and Lady Percy, being both Tory and High Church, would automatically shift into favor and inherit the courtly clout of the deposed Whigs.

Pitiably, the Northumberland House gambit was not Benjamin's cup of tea, a circumstance which was certain to generate discord between father and son.   Satisfied with the direction of the political winds and his positioning in them, Billy turned his full attention to wooing and winning Miss Elizabeth Downes, an affiliation that also displeased his father.   Benjamin's dream of one day having Polly as a daughter-in-law died hard.

With the resumption of the music, the gallery had cleared when Betsy returned.

"Isn't this lovely?" she said, slipping into his outstretched arms.   "Bach's "Minuet in G."   It's one of my favorites."

He whirled her about the floor, their eyes feasting on one another as they danced the dance of lovers.   "Must you go to Bath for the entire summer?" he whispered, drawing her closer.   "I don't see how I'll stand it, Elizabeth. And why Bath of all places?" he probed with a hint of suspicion.

"Why William Franklin! I do believe you have a jealous streak!" she teased, holding him at arm's length.

"From what I hear, it's a breeding ground for matchmakers."

"Fathers send their daughters there just to meet mates who will improve the stock," she chided him playfully.

A pained look crossed his face at the thought of losing her to some seductive libertine, and he suddenly realized that the driving force behind his wooing was not economic greed or social standing but love and desire. It surprised him to discover that he was capable of loving another woman the way he loved his first Betsy back home. To prove to himself that his broken heart had mended, he said, "Betsy, I want to ask you something, but I am in no position to do so at this time, when my future is still uncertain. God willing, that day is not too far off."

"So this is where you two lovebirds are hiding." Lady Percy appeared holding the hand of a very young boy, her whalebone-hooped skirt swaying to and fro as she walked.

Fashion conscious to a fault, her dress was certain to be a replica of a French creation received on the latest fashion doll, an exquisite mauve and periwinkle flower-studded brocade with wide paniers extending beyond each hip.

"Our own private ballroom," Billy replied, kissing her hand for the second time that evening.   "Did you mind?"

"Heavens no, my dears.   Regulars like you are at liberty to come and go as you please."   "I didn't want you to miss Johannes' performance, Elizabeth.   I know how you love music. Johannes," she said, "I would like you to meet my friends, Miss Elizabeth Downes and Mr. William Franklin.   He's from America."

"Where are you from, young man?" Billy asked, getting down on his haunches to face the boy.

"I am Johannes Mozart from Salzburg, Austria."

"Johannes is here to play the harpsichord for us."

"How remarkable for one so young," Betsy said aghast.

"Wait," remarked Lady Percy, bubbling.   "Tell them WHAT you're going to play."

"A piece I composed myself."

"How old are you anyway?" Betsy asked, astounded.

"Five."

"That's incredible!" Billy exclaimed as he took Betsy's arm and followed them to the main ballroom.

Watching the amazing child genius in utter astonishment, Billy suffered a major pang of anxiety, comparing his own meager accomplishments with those of this small boy, who was only a pint of cider and still wet behind the ears.

Later that night, alone in his bed at Craven Street, he gave himself a lengthy pep talk. "You'd better get on your horse, William Franklin!" he exclaimed as he drifted off to sleep.

All spring Billy wanted to propose. The words were on the tip of his tongue more than once, but his hands were tied. He still had not been offered a post. He was a poor prospect for a wealthy, West Indian heiress, who could have her pick of the lot whenever she chose. Having nothing better to offer, he showered her with attention and affection, filling her evenings with permissible pastimes: cribbage, backgammon, dancing and theater. David Garrick, their favorite actor and a close friend of Richard

Jackson, gave a command performance of "King Lear" at Drury

Lane on May 28.   Ardent and loyal fans, they returned on June 3

to see him play "Hamlet".

All too soon, with the heat of summer, came vacation time

and the forced, worrisome separation.   For their last rendezvous,

Billy decided that St. James Park, her favored promenade, would

provide the best opportunity for a private talk.   Arm in arm, they

meandered along the narrow, gravel path to a secluded spot behind

a honeysuckle-covered wall that cordoned them off from the rest of

humanity.   They sat together on a bench so close that not even a

ray of sunlight could shine through between them.

Taking his hand she raised it to her lips.   "I'll be with my

family," she said, trying to reassure him, "and you with yours."

Getting no response, she put his hand back in his lap and leaned

forward to pet a fallow-colored fawn that had wandered by looking

for a crust of bread.

"Don't you see, Betsy?" Billy blurted out.   "We're merely

pawns, figurines on a chessboard, letting everyone else manipulate

our lives!   Was it your wish to go to Bath or my idea to go to

Holland?   That's what I've been sitting here contemplating."

"Patience, William, patience," Betsy cried, throwing herself in his arms.

"You sound like Papa," he said, kissing a tear from her cheek. "He says, 'He that can have patience can have what he will'."

"In more ways than one," she offered submissively, slipping back into his embrace, the meaningful connotation intended not being entirely lost on her amorous suitor.

But at that moment, another adage came to Billy's mind: 'He who hesitates is lost'. Tilting her chin, he gazed into her large, brown eyes and asked, "Miss Downes, will you marry me?"

"Today if I could, Mr. Franklin," she replied with not the slightest hesitation. Locked in a loving embrace, they sealed their betrothal with a long, fervid kiss.

Moments later he held her at arm's length and said in a tone reminiscent of a man whose hunger for love has only now been amply filled, "I'm afraid, my sweet, that I cannot officially ask for your hand in marriage until my appointment comes through and my professional future is more definitive and secure."

"I understand completely, my darling," she assured him.

"I have a feeling that something positive will happen soon after the coronation.   I ask you, why did we get seats in the Abbey when even your father did not?"

"I rest my case," he concluded, not wanting to spoil the moment.

Nevertheless, now that he and Betsy were secretly engaged, Billy needed to balance his juggling act deftly to avoid any pitfalls. The wisest path to follow, he decided, was a 'safest in the middle philosophy', biding his time by appeasing his disapproving Papa while he pleased his newly-intended wife.   The tightrope he walked consisted of the family purse strings, which were kept rigidly taut by his loving but domineering father, and the thing he feared most was that Benjamin might be provoked into returning to America prematurely, thereby cutting off his lifeline before he was ready to survive alone.

To offset his frequent trips to Bath, therefore, he threw himself wholeheartedly into making preparations for their trip to Holland.   Billy counted on his father's insatiable zest for travel to get his mind off the proverbial triangle.   As much as he adored him, he would not have him meddle in his love life like he had his naïve little sister Sally's.   Through his chronic matchmaking, he had paired her with young Billy Strahan long before she had even reached puberty.

Believing as he did that his union with Betsy Downes was ordained by God, Billy vowed to overcome any obstacle hurled in his way until it was consummated, even breaking his father's heart, if that's what it took.

THE PROPER CONNECTIONS

Chapter VII

"It's a holy war, I tell you!" Richard shouted to Ben and Billy above the howling wind as the three braced themselves against the mainmast of the midget-sized sloop and held fast to the rigging as another salty wave doused them.

"Between Neptune and Poseidon, I suppose you mean," Billy sputtered, reading Richard's predictable mind.

"You guessed it.   The Romans against the Greeks in a battle for supremacy of the sea."

"And here we are plunk in the middle of it in a damn, old overcrowded washtub!" Billy crabbed.

"Ohhhhh!" Richard gasped, gaping at the wall of water breaking over the deck.

"That's not the mighty roar of Neptune that you hear, my

learned companions," Benjamin interjected matter-of-factly before the next dousing, "but merely a seasonal display of nature on the rampage."

"If this is nature in the raw, Sir, then it's not for a feint-hearted fellow such as I," Richard confessed.

"Nor I," echoed Billy, hanging on for dear life.

The tiny vessel pitched and rolled, trapped in the briny, opalescent deep, its helpless captain and his battered boat drifting further and further off course away from London.

"Man overboard!   Port side!" a seaman hailed from his perch in the crow's-nest.

"Throw out the line!" the captain ordered the bosun.

Off to the south, southwest, a threatening drum roll commenced, followed by a jagged blade of lightning that slashed the slaty-colored sky before being snuffed out by the turbulent sea.

"All passengers below deck!" he snapped at the three holdouts, relinquishing the wheel to the coxswain.   "Get below, I said, before the whole lot of you ends up as shark bait!"

But single-mindedly, before anyone could stop them, the Franklins kicked off their shoes and jumped overboard to aid in the rescue.

"You foolhardy, asinine jackasses!" the captain bellowed.

"Never mind your bellyaching, you old salt," Richard snarled, scooping up their shoes with one hand while he gripped the railing with the other.   "Toss those men a line before they drown!"

Ben and Billy, both powerful swimmers, plowed toward the bobbing, thrashing form with hawser in hand.   In no time at all they reached him, slipped a noose securely about his middle and signaled the captain to heave ho.

"Please don't put me back on the boat," the seasick lad pleaded.

"Trust me, son.   I know exactly how you feel.   Come on now.   Don't fight me.   As soon as your feet hit dry land, you will feel fine."   Breathing hard, Billy boosted him aboard and then assisted his father.

Richard made the sign of the cross with his only free hand and two pair of sneakers

"Good God," Benjamin exclaimed while he was wrapping himself up in a warm blanket supplied by a member of the crew.

"He's no more than a slip of a boy.   How old do you think he is,

Billy?"

"No more than fifteen, I'd guess," Billy panted, swallowing

a very large mouthful of crow.   He glanced at his father who was

nodding his head and chuckling, no doubt recalling a similar

incident as many years ago.

Now that everyone was safely aboard, the authority of the

captain was brought to bear.   As the hatch opened, Billy took one

last breath of fresh air before going below after the others.   The

boy was still retching and mumbling over and over again that he

wanted to go home as he staggered back to the galley with his slop

bucket.

During the next hours, no one escaped the misery of

seasickness, not even the veteran sailor, Benjamin, who always

boasted that it was simply mind over matter.

With nothing more to lose, Billy tried mental diversion as

an antidote.   Thinking about the runaway brought thoughts of his

own son, already sixteen months old, who was being comforted

and coddled by someone other than a member of his own

immediate family.   Although his visits to the London

boardinghouse had been few and far between, he had infixed the memory of each indelibly in his mind.   His first recollection was the pudgy face of a passive, tightly-swaddled infant; the second, a round-bottomed towhead, giggling and struggling to keep his balance while the household's pet dog licked his face and thirdly, the surprised yet proud look of a toddler walking unsteadily from place to place on his own.

Tormented by unrelenting nausea, crammed indignantly like lading on a slave ship, Billy rode out the storm withdrawing into himself to take his mind off his misery.   Feeling duty bound to share his travels with Sally, he mentally composed a letter, detailing for her the scope of events he had experienced on his month-long Holland holiday.   Mustering up a feeble smile he concluded:

'...I can assure you that on board (our sloop), there (is) no such thing as 'Inside Contents Unknown'.   For my part, whatever I might have been formerly, I think I must now be one of the best natur'd men living, as old Neptune...(is taking the) opportunity of depriving me of every bit of (gall) I had in my body..'

I must remember to jot that down in my journal, he thought

pretentiously, forgetting that the whole idea of a Neptune/Poseidon

conflict was Richard's from the start.   Betsy will be amused at the

mythological cause-and-effect reasoning behind my soul's

thorough purging.

Suddenly the hatch opened and a square of sunlight flooded

the dank quarters.   "In the nick of time," Richard moaned.   "I

was beginning to wish I was dead."

One by one, they dragged themselves up the wooden stairs

out of the reeking cubbyhole and onto the fresh-smelling, rain-

swabbed deck to try to regain their sea legs.

"Do you still believe it's mind over matter, Dr. Franklin?"

Richard asked, pitching his new hat into the channel.

"'He that speaks much, is much mistaken'," Benjamin

quipped, quoting from *Poor Richard*.

"I can't top that," Billy said, following suit and pitching his

tricorn out over the rough, billowy surge.

"Ahoy, Captain," the lookout shouted.   "Land to

starboard!"

A great cheer went up at the sight of it.

"The bad news," said Benjamin, squinting as he scrutinized

the distant shoreline, "is that we shall not be landing in London."

"But we must!" Billy fumed, his face clouding with dismay.   Tuning everything out around him, he felt sick again at the thought of missing the coronation and not fulfilling the promise he made to Betsy that he would be back in time to attend. "Where are we anyway, Papa?" he asked, having missed the captain's announcement.

"A cape about sixty miles north of London called The Naze."

"Why the hell are they dropping anchor?"

"For heaven's sake, William.   Where've you been? Didn't you hear the captain?   The old tub's sprung a leak."

Billy threw up his hands in silent submission and made his way to the bow of the boat for solitude.   He had a pressing problem to ponder, a real stickler, one that concerned his Papa. Should he or should he not tell Benjamin that he was to march in the King's procession and that he and Betsy had tickets to sit in the Abbey during the coronation ceremony?   Let's be honest.   The renowned Doctor was not accustomed to being upstaged by his offspring.   After much deliberation, however, Billy decided to hold off.   There was no need to hurt his father's feelings

unnecessarily, because as things stood, it appeared that he was

going to miss the chance of a lifetime himself.

Much to Billy's surprise, the leak had been a blessing in

disguise.   Forced to work his pumps full tilt, the captain was

compelled to make a run for shore, enabling the threesome to get

to London in plenty of time for the coronation.   Even more

thrilling for Billy was having Betsy on his arm as they attended the

royal festivities.

And to his total surprise, as it turned out, although Billy

found that telling his Papa of his good fortune was an abominably

painful task, he was relieved by his jubilant reaction.   "Now you

can see why it was so important to cultivate the proper

connections," he had said, taking the bulk of the credit.   "Our

brief stop at Luton Hoo did you no harm."

Despite all the plaudits, however, during the following

months, when no job offer materialized, Billy noticed a gradual

change in his father's disposition.   He was like a fish out of water.

In the back of his mind, Billy feared that Benjamin's restlessness

would cause him to book passage and set sail for America.   He wondered whether being slighted at the time of the coronation had anything to do with it.   Billy leaned back in his desk chair and folded his brawny arms across his chest, fretting that for someone who is forever in the limelight, a slight of that magnitude must have smarted.

Having solved nothing by speculating on whether his father's dejection was brought on by homesickness or wounded pride, Billy focused his thoughts on a more immediate consideration, an affordable present for his son's second birthday.

"I just saw Dr. Franklin get out of a carriage, and I think he's headed here," Richard announced, peering around the corner of the cubicle, a compartment he supplied gratis in exchange for access to the records of the Pennsylvania Assembly in Billy's possession.   Billy spent more and more of his time of late amid his copious files, preferring his peaceful little sanctuary to the tension-charged atmosphere of the Craven Street apartment where he and his father were constantly at each other's throats over Betsy.

"What's Papa doing out on a day like this?" Billy cried, rushing to the window.   Snow had been falling steadily since early morning whitening the soiled city and snarling transportation.

"He wouldn't venture out in such weather for love nor money. Unless..."   A sketchy smile creased his face.

"Your assignment!" Richard exclaimed wide-eyed.   "What else could it be?"

"Papa's been talking about going home.   He accomplished what he came to do."

"And a success story it is, securing taxing power over the Penns' lands."

"Yes," Billy said absently.   "Or it could be mother.   She needs him, especially since my grandmother died."

"Such a horrible tragedy!"

"What can I say.   The poor soul was old, 86, lost her balance and fell into the fire."

"God!   What a way to die!"

"My mother's a strong-willed woman," Billy said aloud. For an instant, though, his mind raced back to their relationship after he moved out of the house, how wretchedly she treated him. They didn't even speak to one another when he stopped by to see his father on business.   Was I really 'the greatest Villain upon Earth' as she claimed to one of Papa's workers, did she hate me for living when her four-year-old son had died, or was she jealous of

the closeness and high regard Papa and I have for one another?

Billy had to leave it there when Benjamin arrived.   "What

in the world brings you out in such vile weather, Papa?" he asked

hastily, brushing him off and ushering him toward the fire.

Billy's hopes soared when he noticed that Benjamin was looking

and acting like his old self.

"Don't get the wrong impression, Billy," he said, planting

his hand firmly on his son's shoulder.   "It's not news of your

appointment I've come to deliver, I'm sorry to say."

The letdown left Billy feeling empty and deflated, like the

air had been knocked out of him.   What then?" he asked, with a

trace of impatience.

Benjamin eyed Billy over the tops of his steamy glasses.

"On April 30th, Oxford, the most famous and prestigious university

in the world, is granting you an honorary Master of Arts degree

and me a Civil Law degree.   What do you think of that, Mr.

Jackson?" he boasted, his voice quivering with excitement and his

face reflecting the bold expression of a victor.

"Whooeee!" Richard whooped, tossing the papers he had

been holding up at the ceiling.   "You lucky stiff, William Franklin!   "Congratulations, Sir," he said to Benjamin, pumping his hand.

"Papa, I'm so happy for you," Billy cried, hugging him. "For me, too," he added, recovering from the initial shock.   "You have no idea how long Papa's waited for this, Richard.   Year after year after year they blackballed him.   Right, Papa?"

"That turncoat, Rev. William Smith, blackballed me is more like it."

"The provost of the Philadelphia Academy," Billy explained, filling Richard in.

"The institution I inspired him to create.   Once he got control, he ousted me as chairman and replaced me with a Penn adherent.   Well, the battle's over and I've won at last.   Now Rev. Smith and I will both be Oxford honorees."

"Victory is sweet, Dr. Franklin."

"But vengeance is sweeter," he replied with a wink.

Slowly Billy began to comprehend the impact the distinction could have on his social as well as his political future. He suddenly felt more optimistic than he had in months regarding his billet, and, hopefully, this distinguished honor would help to assure the Downes family of his worthiness and promise. Maybe, just maybe *this is the catalysis I've been waiting for.* "My motto is that 'it doesn't hurt to be titularly endowed when you're monetarily deficient'," Billy quipped, drawing laughs all around, especially from Benjamin.

"Let's go celebrate," said Richard, grabbing his coat. "Where'll we go, the Star and Garter or the Dog Tavern?"

"I have a better idea," said Billy. "Since it's so nasty outside, suppose we stop by Caleb Whitefoord's Wine Shop. "I'll buy a bottle of Madeira, and we'll toast our triumphs at Craven Street."

"A masterful plan," Richard jibed, "but I'm buying."

Like three, jolly musketeers, they boarded the carriage and headed for Caleb's place.

NOVA CAESAREA

Chapter VIII

With picnic basket in hand, Billy crossed the Pulteney Bridge and walked briskly along the bank of the turbid river Avon until he reached the appointed spot.   He spread a cloth for lunch and sat on the grass to wait, feasting his eyes on the ancient wonder not far off that was only recently discovered, the domical ruins of the Roman baths and the old priory, built over seventeen hundred years ago.   After what seemed an eternity, he saw Betsy hurrying toward him.   Jumping up, he ran to meet her.

"Sorry I'm so late," she apologized, catching her breath, "but Mr. Gainsborough had to finish my portrait, since I won't be back to Bath again this summer."   She gave him a loving smooch on the cheek.

"You won't be back ever again without me," Billy said,

drawing her close and kissing her like he'd never done before. "I'm a very lucky man," he said hoarsely, tracing the outline of her delicate facial features with the sentient touch of a sightless man. "I adore you."

"And I you," she murmured, rapt with joy.   Suddenly she pushed him back and shrieked, "Are you trying to tell me something, William Franklin?"

"It's come through!" he whispered, giddy with pent-up emotion.   My appointment's finally come through!"

"What is it?   Where is it?   Please, Billy," she begged, "don't keep me in suspense!   Tell me or I'll die!"

Abruptly, he became very serious, acting as secretive as one of Fielding's Bow Street policemen.   Lowering the pitch of his voice and glancing in all directions to make sure nobody was around, he said, "the royal governor of Nova Caesarea."

"New Jersey?"   From the inflection in her voice, Billy knew that the news was somewhat of a letdown.   He knew she was praying for Barbados.

"You'll love living between New York and Philadelphia," he added quickly, capitalizing on her love of city life.   "And you'll be near my family.   You and Sally will get along

splendidly."

"Of course we will, governor," she replied, recovering

somewhat from the shock.   "You needn't worry about me, my

darling.   I'm tougher than you think.   As long as I have you by

my side, I can adapt to anything."

Bending down, he nuzzled his head in the crook of her neck

and whispered, "Within a month or so, my precious, we shall

finally be one."

Betsy trembled from the sensation.   "In that case," she

said, wriggling free, "I suggest that we get down to business and

plan our wedding."

"After we eat," he said, getting the bottle of wine from the

basket and opening it.

"The innkeeper's wife packed enough food for Gargantua,"

Betsy exclaimed as she spread the wide selection on the white

linen cloth.

After toasting everything from their happiness to their

future home to George III's reign, Betsy added hesitantly, "Why

did I get the feeling that you are afraid someone will overhear talk of your appointment?   You're not in danger, are you?" she cried,

the scary thought apparently startling her.

"Not physical peril, my sweet, but until I kiss the King's

hand, any number of political intrigues could occur.   Let me start

at the beginning.   In January Papa and I learned from our contacts

in Whitehall that Governor Hardy of New Jersey had disobeyed the

King's instructions regarding the appointment of two judges."

"Faux pas," said Betsy, judging rightly the seriousness of

the offense.

"A blunder of major proportions.   Lord Bute, a staunch

advocate for tighter control over the administration of the colonies,

was furious over Hardy's imprudence and provocation and decided

to recall him.

"To set an example."

"Exactly.   Hardy's demise will clip the wings, so to speak,

of the neighboring governors, forcing them to heel.   The whole

idea is to limit a provincial assembly's autonomy."

"But wouldn't the lieutenant governor step in?"

Billy smiled, appreciating her unusual perception.   "Tom

Pownall is in contention, and Lord Bute is obligated to grant him

the right of first refusal.   Papa and I think he will decline the
offer."

"Then I don't understand.   Who else is a threat?"

"You will soon learn as a member of the Franklin family
that although we have a host of allies, we also have some very
powerful, bitter enemies, who would like nothing better than to see
Papa and me both divested of every public trust.   For example, if
the Penns got wind of the fact that I was next in line for the job,
they would fight it tooth and nail."

"What could they possibly say?"

Billy shifted uneasily and then stood up.   Betsy didn't stir.
He snapped a small sprig from the willow and walked to the
water's edge, stripping the catkins from it and releasing the downy
seeds from their cell-like pods.   Lacking buoyancy and unified
strength, the ineffectual, airy tufts, one by one, succumbed to the
prevailing current and vanished.

She went to him and took his hand.

"What can they say?" he repeated, stroking her slender, un-
callused hand.   "Villainous, vengeful, ugly, debasing things,
humiliating disclosures meant to destroy my reputation and

disgrace me in the eyes of my constituency.   Papa and I have felt

the sting of their venomous attacks before and survived.   But this

may be different," he worried, his voice dropping.

"What does anyone know that's so damaging?"

"One thing in particular," he sighed.   "It's only fair that

you hear this from me before we publish our banns, and there's no

kind or tactful way to say it."

"What for heaven's sake?"

"That I'm the illegitimate son of Benjamin Franklin."

"Good grief!" she exclaimed, doubling over with laughter."

Stunned and embarrassed by her seeming repulsion.   Billy

dove impulsively into the river and began to sprint across.

"Come back, Billy," she cried, wading in after him.   "I

already know *that*, and it doesn't matter."

Stopping and treading water, he questioned cynically,

"How did you find out?"

"My brother, the priest, insists on being my self-appointed

guardian.   I thought you were going to tell me you were *divorced*

or something."

"Divorced?" he boomed, charging the air with unbridled

laughter.   Racing to shore, he felt billowy, much like a criminal does, he surmised, when given a stay of persecution from the Charing Cross pillory.   Picking her up, he said gently, "I've got to get you home before you have an asthma attack.   I want my bride to feel fit on her wedding day."

"I love you, William Franklin," she whispered in his ear.

London

The drenching rain of the previous night that ended the month-long drought had soaked thirstily into the parched earth, leaving no puddles for Ben and Billy's steeds to splatter as they loped at a leisurely gait a mile or so outside of Westminster.   The air was dry and fresh, unlike the sultry dog days of early August. They rode in silence, drinking in the scenic tranquility and relishing their last day together.   In the pastures cows grazed, while in the fields farmers, who were early risers, too, toiled at their back-breaking labor, plucking from the endless rows of cabbages and carrots the insidious weeds that threatened to choke and stunt the normal growth of their precious, yearly crops.

Shifting in his saddle, Benjamin scanned the panorama,

fixing the sight firmly in his mind.   "It may be years before I view

it again.   Maybe never, if I cannot persuade Mrs. Franklin to

return with me."

"Betsy's very disappointed that you won't be here for our

wedding.   So am I."

"I'm sorry, Billy, but I can't risk losing my assembly seat.

It may jeopardize my whole political future.   Sailing this late, I

still may not reach Philadelphia before the October l4th election.

Five years is a long time to retain a power base in absentia."

"Hogwash!" Billy exclaimed.   "This rumor, that your

support is eroding, smells fishy to me.   It only surfaced after our

'friend', Rev. Smith, visited London.   I say that when you get

back to Philadelphia, you'll be welcomed with open arms."

"You may very well be right, my son.   It might be nothing

but a vindictive plot cooked up and transmitted through the

grapevine by the archenemy you named, but true or false, I don't

want to push my luck.   Aside from that, I confess that for many

months now, I have felt 'like a thing out of its place, and useless

because it is out of its place'.   I am ready to go home," he

admitted, sounding tired and melancholy.

"I understand, Papa," Billy said.   "And so will Betsy."

"I'll go to see her later today to explain." Benjamin replied. Suddenly he pulled his horse up short and listened.

Billy reached for his pistol and checked their bearings. "We've strayed into Finchlea Heath, I'm afraid, and the thundering hoofbeats you hear are not those of a welcoming party.   We'd better turn to and ride."

"We'll give those contemptible marauders a run for their money."   Benjamin whipped out his gun, cocked it, and like entries in the Egham races, they took off.

"Stay with her, Papa, and keep low," Billy shouted, bringing up the rear.   "This is no time to take a spill!"

In hot pursuit, the thieving band gained ground.

"Duck, Papa!" Billy yelled, seeing a low-hanging branch in his path.   But it was too late.   Benjamin passed under it, leaving his new gray wig dangling on a snag, grotesque but comical.

Within the hour Ben and Billy were lounging on the levee at the bottom of Craven Street, laughingly commiserating over the loss of Benjamin's expensive hairpiece and of their bizarre deliverance from the marauding bandits.

Looking at the rising sun, Benjamin said he hated to go inside but must begin the tedious task of packing up his belongings.   "Before I do," he added, becoming subdued and serious, "there are a couple of matters we need to discuss.   People are going to wonder why you didn't accompany me home. Maintaining silence about your appointment and marriage will be very difficult for me, especially since we agreed that I cannot even risk telling your mother, sister or Aunt Jane.   What am I to tell them?   With bad weather coming it could be months before a packet arrives in Philadelphia with a copy of *The London Chronicle*, which will carry the public announcement of the two events.

"The truth is always good.   Say I merely decided to stay in London a bit longer."

"That should be harmless enough to keep the Penns from 'smelling a rat."

"If they do, my goose is cooked!   Remember, until you read it with your own eyes, mum's the word."

The adage I wrote for the '47 edition of the *Almanac* comes to mind: 'A Slip of the Foot you may soon recover, but a Slip of the Tongue you may never get over.'   "So far so good."

"Perfect advice, Papa.   Now let me offer *you* some.   If we manage to pull this off," he responded, pointing a finger at his father to reinforce his sincerity, "it should give you sufficient satisfaction to bury the hatchet and put an end to this personal vendetta forever.   For your own good, I might add."

"Don't underestimate the rancor of your adversaries. When this news hits the press, that William Franklin has been named the next royal governor of New Jersey, they'll be fit to be tied.   He te-heed softly, reveling in the success of their well-plotted, political intrigue.   What tickles me most is that their ranting and raving will be like 'closing the barn door after the horse has been stolen'."

"I'm sure they won't take this lying down.   They'll get in their licks somehow."

"We may not be home before springtime.   Maybe by then the dust will have settled."

Benjamin looked skeptical.   "Another thing, how much have you told Betsy?"

"She knows about my parentage."

"Did you tell her about Temple, too?"

"No."

"Good.   No need to yet.   It's a well-guarded secret."

"Once I am invested and married, I plan to take your advice and write a Will that will protect my wife and son, but I shan't tell Betsy about Temple until I feel the time is right, conceivably that could be several years from now."

"Both wise ideas.   Don't worry.   The boy is in good, loving hands".

"The thought of leaving the little fellow here all alone kills me, though."

"I sympathize with you.   After all, I am his grandfather."

"I know," he said, hanging his head.   "Is there anything else we need to cover?"

"When I get to Portsmouth, I shall write Polly.   The poor child is so distraught."

"It wasn't in the cards, Papa."

"I make no bones about it.   I hoped against hope that you would eventually come around, but love goes where it is sent.   I abide by your decision and will take it upon myself to write to the dear girl to say our goodbyes as tenderly as humanly possible."

"You have a way with Polly, Papa. You'll know what to say."

"She's like a daughter to me. I shall miss her terribly. And now I must finish my packing before I go to bid my good friends farewell," he said, getting to his feet with Billy's help. "There is one thing more I wish to say. I want you to know that you have made these last five years very happy for me and have given me many wonderful memories that I will never forget and will always cherish. Marry your Miss Downes if you must. I give you both my blessing and my approval."

Billy hugged him tight, unable to speak, experiencing that old familiar feeling of camaraderie with another secret shared, another bond accrued. Unabashed, tears streamed down the faces of both men.

AN 18th CENTURY WEDDING

Chapter IX

September 4, 1762

Reminding Billy of their lengthy courtship, the center aisle

of St. George's Church on Hanover Square stretched like an

unending path, distancing him from the woman he loved.   Billy

adjusted his new blue satin vest, then stood erect as the prelude

began.   Richard double-checked his pocket for the ring before he

settled down next to his friend.   Billy took these last few minutes

of freedom for introspection, reliving the intoxicating moment

when he received his commission, the meaningful words still

ringing in his ears: '...Know you that We, Reposing Especial

Trust and Confidence in the Prudence, Courage and Loyalty of you

the said William Franklin...have thought fit to Constitute and

Appoint you...to be our Captain General and Governor in Chief in and over our Province of Nova Caesarea or New Jersey'.   It's

official, Papa, wherever you are.   We did it!

As the prelude ended his bridesman stirred, jolting Billy

from his preoccupation.   Chills traveled up and down his spine as

the stately 'Jeremiah Clark Trumpet Voluntary', the wedding

march of royalty, commenced, its powerful strains reverberating

through the hallowed tabernacle.

Although Billy had anticipated this long-awaited moment

for an eternity it seemed, his breath caught in his throat when

Betsy appeared in the arched entranceway on the arm of her escort.

She was a fluff of embroidered white silk and silver lace, with a

lace point cap crowning her un-powdered brunette hair, which was

coiffed away from her face and hung in large curls at the nape of

her neck.   Adorning her stomacher was a solitary diamond

brooch, a family heirloom, that glittered and sparkled in the filtered

yet dazzling light from the late morning sun.   This was

conservative in comparison to the diamond-covered stomacher

embossing Princess Charlotte's white and silver tissue gown when

she married George III.   But then again, the princess' wedding

dress also doubled for her coronation gown, killing two birds with

one stone.   Billy remembered it well.   The train was so long that
it took ten attendants to carry it.   He looked approvingly at the
modest length of Betsy's as she floated gracefully toward him on
the pompous waves of sound past many rows of empty pews.

"The garter's white," Richard wisecracked out of the side of
his mouth, trying to get the bridegroom's goat.

"Blue," Billy retorted in like manner, defending his love's
honor.   Blue was the color normally worn to symbolize the
blessed Virgin Mary.

Suddenly a light dawned and Billy realized that Richard
was pulling his leg.   Mary (Polly) Stevenson was unkindly known
in London's social circle as "Virgin Mary."

On Parson Downes' cue, Billy joined his bride at the alter
rail and waited for the spine-tingling processional to end.   At long
last, her brother began: "Dearly beloved, we are gathered together
here in the sight of God..."

In snatches, he heard the Solemnization read from the
century-old Book of Common Prayer.   In between, he recorded
mental images of the elegant setting to relate to Sally: the
magnificent east window made of 16th century Flemish glass "...is

not by any to be enterprised, nor taken in hand, unadvisedly, lightly, or wantonly, to satisfy men's carnal lusts and appetites, like brute beasts that have no understanding; but reverently, discreetly, advisedly, soberly, and in the fear of God."

James Thornhill's exquisite masterpiece, an altar painting of 'The Last Supper'.

"First, It was ordained for the procreation of children... Secondly, It was ordained for a remedy against sin, and to avoid fornication; that such persons as have not the gift of continency might marry, and keep themselves undefiled members of Christ's body. Thirdly, It was ordained for the mutual society, help, and comfort, that the one ought to have of the other, both in prosperity and adversity..."

The choir boys, angelic-looking cherubs, dressed in red vestments and white cottas...

"I require and charge you both, as ye will answer at the dreadful day of judgement when the secrets of all hearts shall be disclosed, that if either of you know any impediment, why ye may not be lawfully joined together in Matrimony, ye do now confess it..."

There was a moment of silence.   Since Billy, in all good conscience, did not consider Temple an *impediment*," he went on to make his vows with the self-assurance and intensity of a bona fide bachelor.

As the obligatory exhortation continued, Betsy tilted her head to exchange confidences with Billy, her wide, innocent eyes motionless and penetrating, her dark complexion the velvety texture of a morning-glory.

"Wilt thou have this man to thy wedded husband...?   Wilt thou obey him, serve him, love, honour, and keep him in sickness and in health; and forsaking all other, keep thee only unto him so long as ye both shall live?"

"I will."

There they were.   The words he'd been waiting so long to hear.   He felt slaphappy, punch-drunk at the thought of having her all to himself from this day forward forevermore.

Shortly before noon they knelt together to receive the Holy Eucharist while the young choristers, their voices clear and euphonious, sang the communion hymn: 'Therefore we, before him bending; This great Sacrament revere; Types and shadows have their ending, For the newer rite is here; Faith, our outward

sense befriending, Makes our inward vision clear'."

As luck would have it, London got its daily sprinkling

precisely at noon, dampening the cobblestones of the square but

not the spirits of the governor nor his radiant first lady and their

small entourage as they emerged from the church onto the

columned portico in a flurry of animated excitement.

"Rain on your wedding day is a good omen," Richard

shouted above the tolling of the bells.

"Thank you for the lovely service," Betsy cried, hugging

her brother.

I wanted to elope to Gretna Green, but for some strange

reason, she wouldn't hear of it."

"Pay him no mind, Jonathan," said Betsy's sister.   "He's

always kidding."   As pregnant as she was, she was finding it

difficult to perform her final duty as a bridesmaid, that of gathering

up Betsy's train and folding it neatly over her arm, so Billy gave

her a hand.

"A sense of humor's a rare quality," replied the parson.

"And to find someone who appreciates it and does not take offense is rarer still," Billy answered, complimenting his new brother-in-law.   "I understand that you're not coming to St. James Street while the ladies change or to the Mall to walk but will meet us later at the Mitre."

"Yes.   I'll see you there.   A perfect choice.   Henry Cole will prepare you a wedding feast fit for his Excellency, the Governor!"

"I'm afraid you cannot address me 'His Excellency' yet, because my audience with the King has been postponed until next Wednesday."

"Your carriage awaits," said Richard with a sweeping bow.

Pelted by a shower of rice, the traditional symbol of fertility, the couple dashed to the seclusion of Betsy's fine coach.

While he waited for his wife to change from her negligee to a silver and white sacque dress, Billy curbed his impatience by jotting the following note to William Strahan: 'Dear Sir: Your friend...is this moment arrived at the land of matrimony and, (to continue the seaman's phrase), hopes to get safe into harbour this night.   I know you and Mrs. Strahan will sympathize with Mrs. Franklin (for so I am now happy to call her) and me in the 'unbounded joy this long wished-for event occasions...'

After composing a brief announcement about his appointment and marriage for Straney to publish, he sealed the letter and blew out the candle.

TIT FOR TAT

Chapter X

February 12, 1763

Having made the rounds of their friends and Betsy's relatives, Billy booked passage on the Philadelphia Packet, which departed from Portsmouth in mid-November as part of a convoy under the H.M.S. Nightingale.   Overnight, their lives changed from a fairytale to a nightmare.   Winter crossings were known to be notoriously dangerous, and this one proved no different. Battered by high winds and heavy seas, the convoy limped back to Plymouth for repairs, giving the seasick passengers a good month to recuperate and time to make out Wills and buy hefty insurance policies.   Billy did both.

The second attempt, although scary and eventful as well, was more successful, and by February 6, they were a mile off the

New Jersey coast, only to be greeted by yet another winter storm. Finally on February 12, Captain Budden was able to moor the Packet at Lewes, Delaware, a hundred miles or more south of his original destination. With ice choking the river, Philadelphia was totally inaccessible.

Debarking in a blinding snow storm, the newlyweds nevertheless thanked God for delivering them to dry land. Their elation was short-lived, however, when they discovered that even the most elemental conveyance was as scarce as a wooden nickel.

After depositing his wife at the local inn for safe keeping, Billy and his new servant, John, set out with stubborn determination to scour the town in search of suitable transportation. Luckily, procurement was his forte. In the '55 Indian uprising, as a captain under General Braddock, he'd been a whiz at scaring up anything from Conestoga wagons to horses and fodder to feed them.

In a couple of hours, they returned in an open sleigh, pulled by two of the most pitifully bony old nags Betsy had ever seen. "From all appearances," she mused, trying to keep a straight face, "it seems that status carries little weight here in America."

Billy threw back his head and roared, surer than ever that he'd married the right woman. Much to his surprise she had remained cheerful, uncomplaining and resilient, taking each leg of the long, arduous journey in stride.

"Didn't I warn you that a crossing takes everything out of you?" he joshed. "Well, in addition to losing a few pounds, it also seems that I have unfortunately lost my touch in the bargain."

"Let me be the judge of that." She squeezed his hand as he helped her into the rickety sleigh. He followed and nestled close to her, covering them with a mantle of furry bear skin.

Outside of their cozy love nest, snow blew and the wind raged, drowning out the tinkling of sleigh bells and making eerie sounds as it thrashed through the naked, shivering trees. It pruned the deadwood and toppled shallow-rooted scrubs and sturdier perennials severely weakened by dry rot and time.

February 19, 1763

"Governor Franklin, Governor Franklin, the cavalry's coming!" John's mouth was so stiff from the cold that he had trouble forming the words. "See their red coats?"

Two heads poked out from under their warm, furry coverlet.   "Either my eyes are deceiving me," said Billy squinting, "or I would swear I see a detachment of Grenadiers from my old unit approaching."

"Is that an illusion or do I see a closed carriage up ahead?" Betsy cried, half standing.

Billy was up now, too, looking for a familiar landmark, a beacon.   Then he saw it, the spire of Christ Church, the steeple he had worked so tirelessly to have erected before his sojourn to England.   "We're home, Mrs. Franklin," he sighed.   "Papa must have gotten my message, because if I'm not mistaken, what you see is not a mirage, my love, but our welcoming home party, and you can bet all the tea in England that Papa's arranged it.

Momentarily, Benjamin and Sally were alongside with the Guards breaking rank and surrounding the sleigh, shouting their congratulations and greetings.   Jumping down, Billy threw his arms around his father, then his sister before he helped Betsy alight.   Not bashful at all, Betsy hugged Sally as if they were long-lost friends.   Benjamin kissed Betsy on the cheek, glorying in their safe crossing but immediately escorted her to his closed carriage.   After much hand shaking and back slapping with his

Grenadier friends, Billy thanked them heartily as they closed ranks

and marched home.

Billy joined his wife in the carriage while Sally

accompanied her father back to the Market Street house on her

dapple-gray mare.

"What a wonderful reception," Betsy exclaimed, all smiles,

"and now I know why you love your sister so much.   She is

simply delightful."

"She's always been there for me.   We're very close."

"On the other hand, I wonder what the Penns will have to

say about our grand entrance into their city," Betsy mused.

"I assume news of my good fortune has preceded me,

giving our foes ample time to rake me over the coals both publicly

and privately.   Hopefully, for your sake, my darling, they have

already vented their anger

"How you underestimate me, my sweet."

"True.   You've come through this ordeal with flying

colors so far," he replied, kissing the tip of her exquisitely-shaped

nose.   "I'm very proud of you."

Within minutes, the jolly foursome entered through the general store that Deborah ran, climbed the stairs to the second floor and burst into the warm, comfortable, unpretentious Franklin home, one of several rentals the Franklins had occupied over the years in the same vicinity.

"I can't stand the suspense any longer, Papa.   How did the election go?"

"I won handily.   You were right.   That confounded rumor was a lot of humbug."

"Congratulations!"

"You mean the wave literally smashed the porthole and gushed into your cabin?   I would have been terrified!" Sally exclaimed, eying Betsy with an incredulous stare.

"Hush, Sally," said Benjamin quietly.   "Kindly change the subject before your mother hears you.   There's no need to alarm her needlessly, since our children are here safe and sound to tell us about it."

"Frankly, Betsy said to Sally with a wry grin, grasping her about the shoulders in a sisterly fashion, "all I worried about was saving my trousseau."

"Welcome to Philadelphia, Mrs. Franklin.   Governor Franklin, it's good to have you home," Peter said as he helped them all out of their heavy, snowy cloaks.

"A veteran seafarer like you can readily imagine how delighted we are to be ashore, Peter."

"Yes, Sir!" he exclaimed with a broad, knowing smile. "Mrs. Franklin's waiting in the parlor."

The gleeful cavorting abruptly stopped.   Billy took a deep breath, trying to calm his butterflies.   With arms intertwined, the couple followed Benjamin and Sally to join Deborah, who was embroidering by the toasty fire.   She stayed seated but removed her newly-acquired spectacles and put away her sewing as they entered.

At first glance, Billy was struck by the startling resemblance between her and Sally, the short frame, stout figure and round, full face, likenesses that were not perceivable in the gangly adolescent of thirteen he had hugged good-bye almost six years before.

Billy approached his mother cautiously, much as one might a snapping turtle, leery of the sharp, quick tongue that had stung him so mercilessly throughout his youth. Although he expected a lukewarm reception himself, he prayed that she would be cordial to Betsy. Unlike Benjamin, Deborah had worshiped Betsy Graeme, and at this moment, Billy had no way of knowing how his mother felt about their breakup. "Mother," he began gingerly, stooping to give her a peck on the forehead, "I want you to meet my wife, Betsy. Betsy, this is my mother."

"I'm very pleased to meet you, Mrs. Franklin," Betsy replied sweetly, clasping Deborah's outstretched hand.

"Why, your hands are like a cake of ice. Billy," she snapped, acknowledging his presence for the first time, "pull up a chair by the fire for this poor dear and get her a shawl from the sideboard there in the dining room."

While he was doing her bidding, Billy overheard Deborah's next remark, which cut him to the quick.

"You must forgive Billy. He always was one to stand on ceremony, a regular show-off with his highfalutin manners."

"Is that your famous apple pie I smell?" Billy asked as he wrapped his wife in wooly softness and redirected his mother's attention to the feast that was spread on the dining room table. A mouth-watering blend of herbs and spices filled his nostrils, making him ravenous.

Apparently having a bellyful of her mother's nitpicking, Sally jumped in to rescue her brother.   "Papa," she said, "here we are standing around like bumps on a log while Betsy and Billy are probably in dire need of a glass of your best Madeira to warm them."

"Here, here," said Benjamin, applauding the idea.

After toasting their nuptials, Billy's appointment, the two safe passages, their health and, finally, King George III, the composite little group splintered briefly before going in to dinner.

Sally, who seemed completely enthralled by Betsy's cosmopolitan attitudes and stylish dress, never left her side.

No wonder, Billy thought, as he watched them from across the room where he and his father had retreated to gloat over the success of their concerted efforts and to compare notes on the various reactions on both sides of the Atlantic.   The girl is nineteen years old and has never been further east than the Passayak Falls.

Later that evening the two men sat alone before the smoldering fire as though hypnotized, basking in the afterglow, peacefully at ease and perfectly satisfied.   The smoke from Benjamin's pipe rose lazily on the coolish currents as the heat from the flickering embers waned, gradually reducing the last of the logs on the hearth to charred and dusty ashes.

"We plucked this plum right out from under their snobbish noses, Billy.   I hear Adams called it 'backstairs intrigue' while others labeled it 'shrewd politicking' and a 'burlesque on all Government'."

"Humph!" Billy grumbled with disdain apparent in his voice.   "When the deck's stacked against you, it's fair play to have an ace up your sleeve.   John Penn referred to it as a 'shameful affair,' I understand, and believes the people of New Jersey will protest against this 'indignity' that has been thrust upon them.   Do you?"

"I think he's in for a big surprise."

"From all indications, then, the opposition was unsuspecting and totally shocked."

"It hit them like a 'Thunder clap'."

Wednesday, February 23

The prolonged winter storm persisted, which left the men no alternative but to go to Billy's inaugural ceremonies without the women. Despite the bad going, the intrepid travelers reached Bristol in time to dine, and after thawing out a bit, pressed wisely on, not wanting to tempt fate by making the risky crossing to Trenton after dusk. Fortunately, the ice was rock solid and formed a natural causeway as sturdy and functional as London Bridge herself.

The following night they lodged in New Brunswick, situated on the shore of the Raritan River ten miles or so southwest of Perth Amboy, the East Jersey capital. It was an unprosperous town of about 130 families, more renowned for its beautiful women than the aesthetic appearance of its buildings.

Benjamin was asleep as soon as his head hit the pillow, the synergetic effect of porter, pipe and fatigue. Billy's future hung in the balance the following day, and he lay awake thinking, wondering whether Penn's prediction would prevail: Hearsay has it that Penn believes the people in my province will 'remonstrate' against such an 'indignity' being thrust upon them, he fretted.   So

I am a 'base-born brat'.   What of it?   In Jeremiah, the question is

asked, 'Can the Ethiopian change his skin, or the leopard his

spots'?   Then neither can I reverse the circumstance of my birth.

More false prophets, like Rev. Smith, I suspect.   Sour grapes.

He turned over and went to sleep.

February 25, 1763

   "I, William Franklin, do solemnly swear that I shall

'execute all things in due manner ...(under my) Command

...according to such Reasonable Laws and Statutes as now are in

force or hereafter shall be made..."

   '...We do hereby declare Ordain and Appoint that you the

said William Franklin shall and may hold, Execute and Enjoy the

Office and place of our Captain General and Governor in Chief in

and over our province of Nova Caesarea or New Jersey together

with all ...the Powers and Authorities hereby Granted unto you for

and during our Will and Pleasure.'

   Upon hearing the very words that had brought his world

crashing down around him, Josiah Hardy, the ousted governor, never blinked an eye but stood like an impassive Stoic, the shock

and insufferable humiliation he most certainly was enduring

visibly unapparent.

At the conclusion of the induction ceremony in the Council

chambers, the Middlesex Troop, the cavalry unit that had ushered

the Franklins into the city earlier in the morning, waited to escort

them and the accompanying dignitaries to the courthouse, where

Billy's commission was to be publicly posted.   A throng of well-

wishers, defying the elements, lined the route to hail their new

chief with cheering, applause and shouts of approbation.

"This is an enthusiastic vote of confidence, my son."

Benjamin's voice was husky, his eyes misty with emotion.

"I think it's safe to say that I have East Jersey in my pocket,

but West Jersey is still an unknown."

"If the acclamation you receive in Burlington is half this,

you won't have a thing to worry about."

Looking happy and self-assured, Billy shrugged off his

bulky fur cape for his father to hold, climbed the courthouse steps

and waved to the crowd, savoring the warmth of the limelight and

glorying in the delectable sweetness of revenge, hoping the

message of his joyful reception carried all the way to the Penn

mansion.

BURNED BRIDGES

Chapter XI

Trevose
March, 1763

Billy slipped out of the warm, canopied bed as quietly as humanly possible, fumbled for a fresh nightshirt in the dark and, after changing, carefully groped his way across the unfamiliar room to a chair by the east window.   For more than an hour, he sat there and watched the mellow shades of morning, luminous harbingers of a bright, new day, change the complexion of the heavens from opaque dullness to hues of nightless splendor.

Not far away, Betsy slept again peacefully, curled up like a kitten with a full tummy whose appetite has been amply and pleasingly gratified.

Too soon, the crest of the sun emerged above the horizon

and climbed with unfaltering precision from bristly limb to bristly limb of a distant pine, a stark silhouette against a backdrop of blue and fulgent yellow.   Before he had time to shield her from its full-blown glare, the pushy intruder burst into the room and rousted her from sleep.   "It can't be daybreak already," she moaned, yawning drowsily.

"Good morning, sleepyhead.   Too much bed; not enough sleep I'm afraid," he whispered devilishly in her ear as he covered her up.

"The bed's cold.   Come warm it for me."   She nibbled his earlobe and ran her lips slowly down the length of his neck and buried them fiendishly in the crook of it, an enticement that never failed to initiate an immediate reflex.

In this heightened state of bliss, Billy cared little about the shameless sun's blatant spying and worried even less about whether the walls of Trevose, the Galloway's Bucks County mansion, had ears.

They soon discovered that they did; otherwise, their hosts were extremely perceptive, because an appreciable time later, someone knocked at the door.

"Who is it?" Billy asked, leaping to his feet and plopping his wig on his head askew.

"A servant, Sir, with your breakfast."

Betsy slid down under the quilt to smother her laughter and to hide her flushed face, the classic look of a blushing bride caught in the act.

Trevose was a honeymooner's paradise and the Galloways exemplary hosts, who accorded Betsy and Billy all the privacy and privilege of royalty.   Lingering over breakfast, picking at the remaining morsels of cornbread and apple cobbler, he studied the lovely woman he had married as she sat opposite him leisurely sipping tea from cream-colored queen's ware, the latest creation by Wedgewood.   It did his heart good to see her so relaxed and at ease.   After a few weeks under Deborah's thumb, she had become tense and uncomfortable, undoubtedly sensing the undercurrent. Although his mother had held her tongue in Betsy's presence, in private, she had lashed out at her son for shattering Betsy Graeme's life, going so far as to accuse him of infidelity.   Billy was floored to learn that she was 'eligible' yet and found it even harder to believe that she was still carrying a torch for him.   Brushing the accusations aside as the ravings of a bleeding heart, Billy

dismissed them from his mind.

"What a magnificent view," said Betsy.

"Isn't it, though," Billy agreed with a hint of envy.

The sprawling estate extended from the mountaintop manor

to the shores of the Delaware below.   In between, were acres of

hardy apple trees, pruned to perfection, a sharp contrast to the

adjoining forest, whose jumbled mass of twisted shapes and sizes

weirdly appeared to him as an imaginary army of unclad stick

figures, crippled and sickly-looking.   It jarred him to think that

his mind would play such crazy tricks on him.   "Betsy," he said,

refocusing his attention, "look over there."   He pointed toward the

wharf.

"At what?   All I see is a boat tied up at the pier."

"That's a shipload of Galloway iron ore bound for England

ready to set sail as soon as the ice breaks up.   Forget that for now.

Look directly across the river.   That's the site of your new home,

Burlington, the capital of West Jersey.   Billy had decided to tell

her on the spur of the moment, feeling she was in a proper frame of

mind to face the disappointment.   Her heart was set on living in

Perth Amboy, a short ferryboat ride to Staten Island and New York City, the elite centers of culture and entertainment.

Saying nothing, she hung her head and bit her lip.

"The house at Amboy was built by the Proprietors not the province, so I don't think it would be wise for us to live there," Billy explained. "I've rented us a lovely brick place facing the water," he added hastily, trying to soften the blow. "It's only temporary. In due time the Assembly will build us a suitable residence. In fact, I shall make that my first order of business."

"My home will always be in England," she replied in a whisper, her voice shaky, her lower lip trembling.

"Oh, my darling," he cried, realizing for the first time how homesick she was. He went to her, knelt down and put his head in her lap. "If it were in my power, I would 'put Great Britain under sail, bring it over to this country and anchor it near us'."

She bent over and tenderly kissed the top of his head.

Burlington
Weeks Later
        "Billy! Sally!" Betsy called excitedly, running halfway up the stairs, "Papa's here! What a wonderful surprise," she cried,

hugging him hungrily.   "The last we heard was that you were in

Virginia inspecting the post offices."

"I was," he replied, returning her warm-hearted embrace,

"but I decided to make a slight detour on my way to New York, the

next stop on my circuit, and try to persuade two very lovely ladies

to join me for a couple of days."

"Did you hear that, Sally?" she exclaimed as her sister-in-

law flitted down the stairs.   "New York!   Billy!   Papa wants me

and Sally to go to New York."   She was bubbling over and her

eyes were wide with excitement.

Arriving on Sally's heels, Billy replied nonchalantly,

playing the devil's advocate, "I'll have to think about it."

"Let your conscience be your guide," said Benjamin, the

conspirator, "but keep in mind that saying no would not only be

cruel and inconsiderate to the ladies but a tremendous letdown for

your dear, lonely Papa."

"Contrarily, if I said yes, then the shoe would be on the

other foot, and I would be lonely," Billy argued, playing his role to

the hilt.

"How selfish of me," Betsy cried, dropping Benjamin's arm

and running to her poor, forlorn husband.

"Stop it right there." Sally exclaimed, stamping her foot so hard that the windowpanes rattled.   "I'm wise to you jesters, and it's time I called your bluff.   The truth is you're both being hatefully cruel, deplorably inhumane and..."   She went on to recite the whole litany of abuses, giving them a well-deserved taste of their own medicine.

Somehow the pranksters continued to maintain their deadpan expressions, but underneath, like Benjamin's oil and water experiment, Billy, at least, was convulsing up a storm.

"If that's the way you want it," said Sally, impishly contorting her hands and fully intending to tickle her brother into submission.   "Fess up or else..."

"No!   Not that!" he exploded, raising both arms in unconditional surrender.

"I ought to be furious with you, William Franklin, but I'm too happy to be cross.   Turning to her father-in-law, she said, "You must be parched.   Is it always this hot here in June?"

"Hotter sometimes," he replied, mopping his brow.

"Oh my," Betsy cried with a fleeting frown.   "Matty," she

said to a young servant who was standing a respectable distance off, "please bring Dr. Franklin a cold drink."

"Yes um."

"Yes, what?" she asked sweetly.

"Yes, Mrs. Franklin."

Betsy smiled and nodded her approval.

"Please don't bother, Matty," Benjamin said to the girl in his usual benignant way.   Addressing Betsy, he said, "I stopped at the Blue Anchor, so I'm well watered."

"The refresher our Papa needs is a long, relaxing swim in the pristine waters of the Delaware.   Am I right?   I could use one myself.   It's hotter than blazes upstairs."

"What have I interrupted, anything important?"

"I was writing to Straney, asking him to publish my first speech before the Assembly in *The London Chronicle*, but it can wait."

"I'll go tell cook to set an extra place for dinner," said the hostess.   "Sally, would you please get John to put Papa's things in the other guest room.

"Whoa!" said Benjamin, stopping them all in their tracks.

"Who said I was staying?"

"We did," the women stated in chorus.

Billy stepped aside and waited patiently for the coddling and coercing to subside, certain that he held the kicker.   "It's a pity you won't be here for the big bash tomorrow night," he said dryly.

"Down at the point," said Sally.

"In your son's honor," Betsy added.

"You're twisting my arm."

"All the notable gentlemen and their ladies have been invited," Billy offered, alluring him with a pinch of spice.

"Well," said Benjamin, clearing his throat, "I know when I'm licked.   You outnumber me, but just so you know," he forewarned the victors, "Sunday morning I shall be up and on my way bright and early, so you two" he admonished, pointing a finger at them, "better be packed and ready."

This was to be a festive night, an inaugural celebration, in effect, an open house hosted by unhostile constituents for a popular governor, the state's twelfth.   The mood and tempo of the evening were set early on when, as the Franklins were preparing to leave the house, a troubadour, a virtuoso violinist, met them at the door playing a lively tune. He escorted them down the grassy slope, past an honor guard of pyramidal hemlocks and so on into the clearing where scores of revelers were gathered.

Sally and Benjamin got right into the spirit of things by clapping to the beat, but Billy maintained his reserve, suppressing a strong urge to join in and give vent to the ballooning exhilaration welling inside. He felt light-footed enough to float among the clouds and disappear over the horizon with the sun, the great ball of fire that was making its final curtain call of the day. Yet, as his mind soared in unbounded fantasy, his feet stayed firmly planted on the ground. At long last, he was casting a lengthy shadow of his own.

"An impressive turnout," Benjamin commented to Billy before he was engulfed by the swarm of cheering compatriots affirming their support with mugs and noggins raised.

Billy accepted the one offered him by the venerable judge and followed the fiddler to the platform to present a toast. Like a conductor who silences an entire orchestra with one stroke of his wand, Billy, holding his tankard high, stilled the crowd. The corners of his mouth, usually downcast, were upturned in a winsome smile as he paused to savor the moment.

With the encroachment of dusk, open Betty lamps illuminated the tables revealing mounds of cheeses and dried fruits, dozens of pumpkin pies, pickled beets and carrots, breads and crocks of apple butter, a sight as artistically pleasing to the eye as the parterre Lemon Garden in Philadelphia.

Then, taking a deep breath of warm summer air, redolent of roast pork and piquant venison, he began, projecting his voice for all to hear.   "To all of you for this heart-warming reception and," he closed, paraphrasing a saying by Confucius that he intended to be the hallmark of his administration, "to ACTION which speaks louder than WORDS."

"Hear! Hear!" they hailed.

As the musicians struck up a quadrille, the drinks were quickly set aside, and the gentlemen scampered about to find their ladies to form their squares.

Joseph Galloway signaled the Franklin party from the side-lines.

"Joseph, Grace," Billy said, greeting them, "wonderful of

you to come."

"A fine tribute, my friend."

"Wasn't this province supposed to be up in arms over your appointment?" Grace mocked with tongue in cheek.

"As Papa always says, 'Diligence is the mother of good luck'," Billy bantered back.   "Speaking of Papa, where is he anyway, Sally?"

"He bowed out.   Said he's bothered by a touch of gout," Sally replied as she and her partner took their place.

"Son of a gun.   He's probably off chewing the fat somewhere.   Now our set's one couple short."

"Let him be, darling," said Betsy.   "He's in his glory.   I'm sure another couple will join us."

"May we, Governor Franklin?" a man asked, stepping out of the shadows.   My name is Peter Jenkins, and this is Miss Elizabeth Graeme.

The dreaded moment had arrived.   Billy knew they would have to meet eventually, sometime, somewhere, but did it have to be here?   Tonight?   "Please do," Billy's dazed mind heard his wife say.   Sally stared wide-eyed at the Galloways.   The

Galloways stared back.

Then for a split second, Billy saw in his mind's eye 'a certain little Corner of a certain little Room, with all its long Train of soft attendant Ideas', the very words he had written to his beloved 'Charmer' six long years ago as he waited impatiently for Captain Ludwyck's ship to sail out of New York harbor.   While it was that passionate memory that sustained him during those first painfully lonely days and weeks of separation, it was also the hurtful memory that haunted him after he received her provocative letter, castigating him for, what seemed to him, trifling abuses.

Her eyes never left his face as he took her frail hand in his and put it to his lips with genteel civility.   My God, he thought, shocked at how peaked, drawn and spiritless she was, how did I so wrongfully misconstrue her feelings.   Betsy Graeme is still carrying a torch for me!   Mama was right.

Emerging from his stupor, he introduced Mr. Jenkins all around and then turned to Betsy Graeme.   "I believe you know everyone except my wife.   Miss Graeme, Mrs. Franklin.   Out of respect for the governor's lady, she made a slight curtsy.

Stunned by the surprise of his old flame's unexpected

appearance, Billy struggled to maintain his composure throughout the dance. He sensed the color fading from his face and feared his ghostly pallor would send an improper signal, one he did not intend to convey. By the same token, his heart was aching with pity and sympathy for the woman he once loved, for he could not fail to notice the look of anxiety and desperation in her telltale eyes, wrought, he imagined, by unrequited love. Briefly assessing his own current feelings after their unexpected encounter, the one-time supposed jilted suitor remembered being angry, disappointed and, yes, heartbroken for a time, but he had necessarily moved on, believing that the relationship was over.

Feigning a terrible thirst, Billy steered his wife in the direction of the refreshment tables before the final bars were played. Out of the blue he announced, "I've decided to accompany you, Sally and Papa to New York. Do you mind?"

"Mind!" she exclaimed, setting down her drink and squeezing his hand. "I think it's a wonderful idea."

"I think so, too. I think so, too," he repeated softly, looking over her head to the far side of the clearing.

ALL'S WELL THAT ENDS WELL

Chapter XII

Burlington
March, 1764

"I'm furious," Charles Thomson raved, picking up a glob of snow and hurling it angrily at a giant elm diagonally across Wood Street. "I can't believe your Rev. Campbell didn't mention the horrific massacre, not even once. Twenty Conestoga Indians murdered, butchered like animals and not a word said. Aha! It's probably because the slayers were Christians, Scotch-Irish Presbyterian frontiersmen," he qualified, noting Billy's disapproving frown.

Billy was glad he'd sent the ladies home in the sleigh after vespers. They didn't need to hear the grisly story again. "For God's sake, Charles, calm down. That happened back in

December."

"Two days after Christmas, let me remind you!"

"At the time The Reverend did condemn the Paxton Boys, prayed fervently for the victims and..."

"It wouldn't have killed him to say a special prayer of thanksgiving now that the threat is over," Charles broke in, exploding like a packed cannon.

"If you'd let somebody finish a sentence, you'd know that we did just that last week.   As long as you're placing blame, why don't you put it where it belongs.   Don't forget.   These frontiersmen were organized as rangers under the auspices of military authority granted by your provincial government to protect themselves against Indian raids.   All well and good.   But letting them take the law into their own hands when they made known that their avowed aim was to rid Pennsylvania of *all* Indians, friend and foe alike, was deplorable."

The ringleader of the Indian raiders was a defiant, 44-year-old Ottawa chief named Pontiac, who, after France's defeat by the British, had forged an alliance, a federation linking tribes from the Great Lakes to the Gulf of Mexico, in a vain attempt to subdue the fortifications guarding the frontier and to inhibit migration and settlement of the newly-acquired lands west of the Alleghenies, the legacy of a protracted and costly war. New Jersey, alone, had a war debt of £300,000.

"The attack was totally unjustifiable, I grant you," Billy added, agreeing wholeheartedly with his friend, "but what credence do you give to the plight of the Scotch-Irish settlers? For the most part your governor has ignored their cries for greater protection against Indian raids and harassment. Outrage festers just so long before it erupts into violence."

"If it's attention they wanted, it's attention they got. At any rate, the gory incident brought him to his knees. He did call for the murderers to be arrested, but when his orders were ignored, he called on your father, known as the epitome of candor and conciliation, to bail him out of the jam."

"Can you imagine John Penn asking a Franklin for help?"

"The governor was in a bind, and he panicked. With an angry mob of Paxton sympathizers on the warpath marching straight for Philadelphia to wipe out the remainder of the Conestogas, this course of action was his only salvation."

"Thank God Papa had the presence of mind to convince Penn to authorize a riot act, which sanctioned the defense of the city.   He was savvy enough to have military backup in place before he and three other peacekeepers rode to Germantown to confront the protesters face to face.   Although his most formidable weapon was his uncanny and intimidating gift of reasoning, he was sensible enough to take his gun along with him, too."

"You must be very proud of your father.   He saved the day."

"I am.   By dispersing that angry mob, he prevented further bloodshed."

"He showed them where the bear shit in the buckwheat," Charles blasted, abruptly apologizing to the governor for his vulgarity.

Billy erupted with laughter.   "How could you resist?   It was so fitting."

"Seriously," said Charles, "what bearing do you feel this crisis has had on proprietary government?"

"Frankly, I believe it's been dealt a deathblow."

"Benjamin would make a superb royal governor."

"He gets my vote, but changes of that magnitude do not materialize overnight; they develop at a snail's pace.   Even though Penn's recent failure bodes well for Papa and his followers, the proprietors and their supporters will fight a fierce tug of war to maintain their hold."

"Ousting them would be an uphill battle all the way."

"In English politics, an ally at Whitehall is here today and gone tomorrow.   Aside from that, what troubles me currently is that Papa stuck his neck out to champion a very unpopular cause and, as a result, may wind up losing his assembly seat in October."

"But he discharged a highly explosive situation.   The people ought to be grateful."

"That's the thanks he'll get.   You wait and see.   By God, it sticks in my craw!"

They walked the rest of the way in silence, each man absorbed in his own thoughts.   Billy erased the sickening image of the massacre from his mind and, instead, recalled the thrilling night in '48 when, as Weiser's aide, he sat around the Delaware's campfire shoulder to shoulder with Indian chieftains and English delegates alike and smoked the calumet, a memorable experience for a seventeen-year-old lad.

That recollection prompted visions of the vast Ohio territory and rekindled his lust for acquisition: rolling hills, fertile valleys, streams teeming with fish and forests abounding with timber and wildlife, furs, furs and more furs, which added up to riches beyond his wildest dreams.   He made a mental note to contact Croghan about possible investment opportunities.

Then, like a latent virus, his favorite hymn popped into his capricious mind, irritating him because he was enjoying his reverie.   They would have to sing that today, he grumbled to himself.   Helpless, he hummed along inaudibly:

A thousand ages in thy sight,

are like an evening gone;

short as the watch that ends the night,

before the rising sun.

The stanza, ending on a homophone, brought flashes of Temple's scanty repertoire flooding to the forefront supplanting the tune.   How time flies, he thought.   My son is four years old already.   With his handsome salary of £1200 coupled with the new loan he had inveigled from Benjamin before year's end to augment his perpetual indebtedness, he was free of stress, both parental and financial.

"After a weekend of your unrivaled hospitality, my wife will be spoiled indeed," said Charles as they reached the front door.   "She has talked of nothing but the yellow silk damask drapes and the thickness of the satin bedcovers, not to mention the exquisite tankards made by the Crown's own silversmith."

Billy cracked a smile.   "Betsy and I do enjoy the finer things of life, I'm afraid."

Off to the right of the walk, an upside down gray squirrel, his privacy intruded upon as he scavenged beneath the leftover snow for acorns he'd buried there last fall, righted himself, sat up on his hind legs for a second as though sculpted from stone and then, wearing the expression of the cat that ate the canary, scurried up the nearby oak and back to his cradle of young.

Burlington
June 4, 1765

"Five aye's, nineteen nays.   The nay's have it.   The

governor's salary shall not be reduced, but his request for a rent increase is denied," the speaker pronounced, thumping the gavel. "At this juncture, I suggest we recess and remove to the governor's home where some light refreshment awaits us in celebration of our sovereign's twenty-seventh birthday. This assembly is adjourned until two o'clock this afternoon."

The seasoned lawmakers sauntered outside into the dazzle of the summer sun still ruminating the pros and cons of this and that measure, bitching about the ruinous revenue tax imposed on them by Parliament the year before, and heatedly airing their views on Prime Minister Grenville's latest money-making scheme, the all-encompassing, unpalatable stamp tax, a piece of unjust legislation, they grumbled, which only added insult to injury.

They strode briskly along the river and up the walk, nodding to the militiamen manning the small brass cannons on either side of the front stoop, whose firings were to climax the testimonial.

Side-stepping any censure at least temporarily, Billy excused himself to go on ahead to check on his wife who, he explained, had a bad asthma attack during the night, which, regrettably, would mean that she would be unable to hostess their little celebration.

Inside the four walls of the Franklin's rented house, there was much ado, servants bustling back and forth trying to please, and the master, completely out of his element, unpleased that they were falling short. I must put it on my agenda to send for an English maid tomorrow, he decided.

Exasperated, Billy scaled the stairs three at a time and headed down the hallway to the crimson bedroom. His eyes focused on the carpet, a valuable Brussels-weave runner, one of an array of collectibles he'd recently purchased from the ex-governor of New York, but his thoughts were only concerned with his wife's well-being.

"Hush!"

Billy looked up to see Nona peering around the door with her finger across her lips. He cushioned his footsteps and tiptoed into the room.

"She's restin' easier, poor lamb," she said in an undertone. Nona's eyes were puffy and the whites bloodshot from lack of sleep. "I know'd when I heard that screech owl last night that we was in for a streak of bad luck." She brushed away the tears that spilled down her cheeks with a corner of her apron.

Billy noticed that the pockets were wrong side out, her way of fending off evil spirits. One day he had found her shoes upside down on the front porch and learned that she did this whenever she was approached by the cross-eyed man in town.

"I'll sit with Mrs. Franklin while you fix yourself a cup of tea. Get along, now," he urged, patting her on the shoulder.

"What about your guests, Master Billy?"

"They'll wait."

Nona smiled feebly and did as she was told.

The stuffy room was pitch-black once the patches of light that barged in with Billy's entrance and her maid's exit were snuffed out. The air was stale and noxious in the aftermath of the previous night's nightmare, Betsy's worst asthma attack ever. The only sounds came from a clock ticking methodically on the mantel and his wife's short-winded wheezing. As his eyes gradually adjusted to the darkness, the room's furnishings slowly came into focus. Going to the nearest drape-covered window, he drew back the curtain and inched up the sash considerably, inhaled deeply and then returned to the sickbed.   Little by little the minty, herbal

smell of hyssop water and horehound, the offensive stink of gum

ammonia, and the overpowering odor of balsam of sulphur

weakened.

Billy knelt, feeling a need to touch his wife.   In her

infirmity she looked pathetically frail, and it frightened him.

With feathery strokes, he smoothed her matted hair, suppressing a

lump in his throat as he pictured how fit she had been only the day

before, dressed to a tee, her long tresses coiffured into stylish

poufs, the idol of all the church ladies.

Awaking, Betsy said in a raspy voice, "Forgive me, darling,

for adding to your worries."

"You, my precious, are not to trouble that pretty little head

with money matters, the King's or ours.   Your job is to get well.

Remember, the Galloways are meeting us at the races in

Philadelphia on Saturday, and mother is expecting us for dinner on

Sunday."

"I'll be fresh as a daisy by then.   I promise."

Billy got to his feet and poured some Rhenish wine into a

goblet on the night stand.   Nona returned carrying a tray of odds and ends.   Worry was written on her wrinkled brow, and she

shook her head as she listened to her mistress's labored breathing.

"You'd better go now, Master Billy.   The gentlemen are waiting.

I won't leave her side for a minute."

"Thank you.   Please see that she sips this wine, and water,

lots of water.   Hopefully, they will relieve the tightness."

"A castor oil chest rub's what she needs."

Betsy groaned.

"Our girl's getting better already," he kidded affably.   He

checked Nona's tray for any unorthodox remedies and finding

nothing more than a mortar of eggshell powder and a bowl of thin

gruel, kissed Betsy on the top of the head and left the sickroom.

As he descended the staircase, Billy could tell by the

hubbub that the legislators had a few toasts under their belts

already.   Seeing him, they gathered 'round, commiserating with

him over his wife's malady.

"Is she improved?" asked Chief Justice Smyth, whose

appointment by the Crown the previous autumn had nullified

Billy's preemptive promotion of Associate Justice Charles Read to

the post and thereby forced the governor to eat his first slice of humble pie.   Billy realized he was taking a chance by forcing the Crown's hand, but faced with a prime vacancy when Robert Morris dropped dead of a heart attack on a dance floor, he courageously usurped his authority.   He was not at all surprised, however, when his first autonomous act was nipped in the bud.

"She is somewhat improved, thank you," Billy replied with a dim smile that betrayed his guarded apprehension.

"I say we forgo the cannon firings," someone suggested.

"I say we go ahead as planned," Billy countered.   "I know my wife; she's anything but a wet blanket.   It would disturb her even more to think she'd put a damper on her King's birthday celebration."

"To her health then," another proposed.

"To her health," they echoed, draining their glasses in one fell swoop.

"Now kind sirs, eat up," said the speaker.   "We have a long row to hoe before this day is ended."

Not averse to mixing business with pleasure, the assemblymen milled about munching, admiring portraits of the King and Queen in full regalia (a recent gift to the Franklins from his majesty) and lobbying for support of a pet piece of legislation.

"Tell us, governor," Bob Ogden said, cornering him.
"Your father's been in London since last December.   Isn't that
so?"

"I know exactly what you're going to say," said Billy,
holding up both hands.   "Couldn't he use his influence to stop the
passage of the Stamp Act?   Believe me, he and Richard Jackson
left no stone unturned.   Wait.   Let me read you what he wrote."
Going to his writing desk, he returned with a letter: 'We might as
well have hindered the sun's setting.   That we could not do.   But
since 'tis down ...and it may be long before it rises again, let us
make as good a night of it as we can.   We may still light candles.
Frugality and Industry will go a great way toward indemnifying us.
Idleness and pride tax with a heavier hand than Kings and
Parliament.   If we can get rid of the former we may easily bear
the latter'."

Billy folded the letter with deliberation and waited for their
reactions.   To his surprise, they did not condemn his father but,
instead, offered excuses for his tacit submissiveness, implicit
tolerance and unaccustomed naivete.

"A skunk smells less vile at a distance," a subdued voice murmured.

"Undoubtedly, he has not yet heard of the firebrand, Patrick Henry of Virginia, whose progressive resolutions declaring legislative independence are circulating throughout the colonies," another commented.

"Henry brazenly said, 'If this be Treason, make the most of it'."   The room buzzed with conjecture.   "How can Dr. Franklin be expected to feel the pulse of the people from across the sea?"

"News travels so slowly."

Billy took their remarks in stride but wondered whether he had misjudged the gravity of the situation himself.   Deep down he sensed the Stamp tax could become a major stumbling block to the peace and harmony he thus far enjoyed with his assembly, but, he thought, since they haven't even placed it on the docket this session, far be it from me to fan the flames of resentment by belaboring the thorny issue.   Orators like Patrick Henry make men's blood boil.   My approach is, the less said, the better.

"In any event," said the governor, placating them, "November is a long way off, and as my father says, 'a lot can happen between the cup and the lip'.   "In the meantime," he said,

raising his glass as a pivotal ploy, a transition as succinct and

smooth as the cleverest author's, "more pressing matters demand

our immediate attention.   To the province," he toasted, conning

his company and steering the ship of state into calmer waters, "its

people and its progress."

"To our governor," someone proposed, countering.

"To our governor!"

Billy nodded to acknowledge the compliment, relinquished

his glass and led the procession outside for the finale.   Smoke

from the cannons marred the cloudless sky with puffs of gray, like

debris tossed carelessly into virgin territory, vanishing slowly as

the lawmakers neared the meetinghouse.

Hearing a rumpus behind him, Billy turned and saw Nona

running toward him faster than he ever imagined she could,

screeching at the top of her lungs.

"My God, my wife!" Billy exclaimed and without further

elaboration, made tracks for home.

Nona collapsed in a heap on the grass, crying out

hysterically as he charged by, "She's as blue as blue can be, Master

Franklin.   I think maybe she's dead!"

DOUBLE OR NOTHING

Chapter XIII

Philadelphia

Arriving late at the Center Square course, Betsy and Billy waited on the outskirts of the crowd for the hullabaloo to subside before taking the seats Grace and Joseph Galloway had saved for them.

"We were afraid you'd gone to Sassafras Street, thinking they were racing there today," Joseph said, kissing Betsy hello.

"Welcome home, my friend," Billy said embracing him. "Just tell me in a nutshell.   How is Papa?"

"He's well and happy as a lark."

"Good," Billy replied, thanking him for the firsthand account.   "I see we missed the first race."

"We should have, too," Grace quipped, "because we both

lost."

"It's all my fault, Grace," Betsy was saying.   "My husband's been pampering me to death lately, letting me sleep till all hours."

"You do look rather sickly, my dear.   Is there something you haven't told us?"

"For Lord's sake, Grace," Joseph scolded, giving her the old evil eye, "aren't you being a little presumptuous?"

"Tsk! Tsk!" she retaliated.   "I'm a friend, not a busybody."

"Oh heavens no.   If I were," Betsy said wistfully but laughing for the first time in many days, "I wouldn't be green around the gills.   I'd be radiant."

"More than likely, a little of both," Grace joked, speaking from experience.   Talking about children evoked both pleasure and pain for Grace Galloway, since three of her four babies died in infancy.   Any stranger would have missed the passing look of anguish, but the fleeting, pained expression did not escape a lifelong friend like Billy Franklin.   "So tell me, Betsy," she said, pressing for an explanation, "what on earth's been ailing you anyhow?"

"It was just another of my chronic asthma attacks," she replied matter-of-factly, minimizing the seriousness of her latest bout.

"So help me God," Billy pronounced, his voice cracking as he made the sign of the cross over his heart, "I nearly lost her. I'm not exaggerating.   She was blue."

Unable to go on, he sat back to collect himself while Betsy filled them in on the ghastly details.   She leaned against him, knowing the anguish he was still suffering and went on to tell them about the miraculous thing that had happened.   "Dr. Lawrence told me afterwards that Billy probably saved my life."

"How?" they asked in unison.

"By accident, actually.   He hugged me so tight that he forced the trapped air out of my lungs, which allowed me to begin breathing normally again."

"Phew!" Grace exclaimed.   "That was a close call!"

"What a fright," said Joseph.

"You're telling me," Billy agreed, mopping his brow.

"Now," said Betsy with a petulant toss of the head, "enough of this gloomy talk.   I for one came here to wager and forget my troubles, so let's get down to business before we miss the next race." She scanned the list of entries and picked the No. 2 horse, Tallyho.

Grace and Joseph bickered back and forth, squabbling over which horse was the winner, hers or his.

After making their separate decisions, Billy placed all bets and returned to watch and clock his steed. The bugle sounded.

After two false starts, they were off. Through their binoculars, the spectators followed the contest patiently as the riders jockeyed for position, but as soon as they made the final turn and dashed for the finish line, pandemonium broke out. In the final analysis, a dark horse won, Joseph's placed and Betsy's took show.

Disappointed and exhausted from expending so much energy cheering him on, Betsy sat down to fan herself.

Billy checked his stopwatch and let out a war whoop.

"I'm glad one of us picked the winner," said Grace, tearing up her ticket.

"It's not that. In fact, I didn't even bet that race, because I wanted to time Tallyho."

Betsy and Grace looked at each other with raised eyebrows from under their parasols.

"Look at that time, Joseph."

"Mighty impressive for his first race."

"Why you old, incorrigible so-and-sos," Betsy pouted. "Now you tell me."

Billy couldn't stand seeing his wife unhappy. As a consequence, he was an overindulgent husband, and her every wish was his command. As a result, he was forever broke and up to his ears in debt striving to keep her in the opulent style to which she was accustomed. "How would you like to own Tallyho, my darling?" he asked in muffled tones.

"He is a beautiful horse, black as a raven."

"Then that settles it. I shall stay for the auction this afternoon and try to buy him for you."

The ladies tucked their bouffant skirts into the open carriage and prepared to leave for Trevose.

"Are you terribly disappointed that I'm not staying for the auction, darling," Betsy asked her husband privately. I'm betwixt and between.   The auction sounds so exciting, yet I can hardly

wait to see Elizabeth."

"Certainly not.   You get to see the child so seldom."

"I simply adore her."

"Elizabeth loves you, too.   She's been keyed up all week

knowing you were coming.   Hasn't she, Joseph?"

"Quite a handful, that little one.   You won't have a

minute's peace, Betsy.   I guarantee it."

"Forewarned, forearmed," Betsy blithely replied.   With

that, she reached down and, with all the conventional propriety of a

governor's lady, gave her husband a dispassionate peck on the

cheek.

The two men strode briskly behind the reviewing stand and

wended their way to the paddock.   The path took them along a

lane lined with flowering redbud trees and past a hedge of rusty

lilacs, whose blooms, although a week beyond their peak,

continued to perfume the air with their addictive fragrance.

"Are you serious about bidding on that colt?"

"Is there any particular reason why I shouldn't?"

"I'd be butting in if I said."

"I wouldn't be buying a pig in a poke, if that's what you mean.   He's a pedigreed horse."

"That's my point.   In tail-male, that's breeding lingo, Tallyho's the son of Herod, an ancestor of the great Arabian, Byerly Turk.   Because he is topnotch stock, dollars to donuts he'll bring a pretty penny."

"Money's no object, Joseph, when your dream is to have the finest stable in the province, and, besides, I promised Betsy."

One by one, the six offerings were led from the ring by their grooms and taken to the auction block in the adjacent grove of maples.   Uninterested in the rest of the lot, Billy stayed on the sidelines and waited for the pick of the lot.   In the background, the auctioneer's lightning-fast, singsong gibberish droned on: 70-70-70-80.   Do I hear 80?   80!   80-80-80-90.   Who'll give me 90?   90! Every so often, the mumbo jumbo was punctuated with "Sold to the gentleman in the nth row."

Joseph scratched his head.   "But aren't you putting the cart before the horse so to speak?   To the best of my knowledge, you don't have a stable."

Billy shook his head and grinned from ear to ear,

wondering how he could be so stupid.   "You must think I'm off my rocker."

"Impetuous to say the least."

"A lot of positive things have transpired in your absence, but, damn it, I feel like a traitor spilling the beans this way.   Betsy and I planned to tell you together."

"Don't feel bad.   At this very minute, Grace is probably wheedling the news out of your sweet, unsuspecting wife."

"I'll take your word for it, but just in case you're wrong, please do me a favor and act surprised tonight.   After all, we don't want to start a civil war."

"You lie and I'll swear to it," Joseph joshed.

"That's the spirit.   Well, believe it or not, within the next year, Whitehall is building us a governor's residence."

"It's about time.   Congratulations!"

"Merci´.   We're delighted."

"Granted, but if you will forgive my thickheadedness," Joseph mused, scratching his head, "I still fail to follow your logic when it comes to the thoroughbred.   A formal residence is a far cry from a celebrated horse farm."

"Hold your fire until you hear me out.   In my spare time, I've been scouting around for some prime tracts of land to buy up, five to ten acres at most.   I intend to start small, acquire my holdings piecemeal."

"Rome wasn't built in a day."

"Nothing ventured, nothing gained."

"One word of caution, if I may.   Never forget the primary rule of thumb: 'The successful man knows how far out on the limb to venture'."

"I'm well padded," Billy bragged, slapping Joseph on the shoulder as they went to take seats on the benches directly in front of the platform.   His cockiness stemmed from the resilient position he enjoyed, forever springing back from the brink of bankruptcy by dipping into his wife's rapidly diminishing dowry, a tidy sum she inherited at an early age upon her father's death, or by leveraging himself higher and higher with one loan after another from his well-off father.   All things considered, he had never experienced a hard fall financially.

Seeing Tallyho being led to the auction block, Billy listened attentively as the auctioneer established the thoroughbred's credentials.   Based on the colt's impressive lineal extraction, Sam Casey opened the bidding at £300, a figure aimed at weeding out timorous souls.   His tactic worked as the faint-hearted, overwhelmed by the immoderate amount, fled.   Billy bided his time.   In the interim, he examined Tallyho from head to hoof, marveling at his sleek, black coat, iridescent in the patchy sunlight.

Openly he was full of optimism, but, deep down, he had serious reservations.   Buying you will definitely set me back a peg or two, he figured, retreating briefly into his inner conscience, but in the long run, it'll pay off.   I'd feel a lot more at ease about this transaction, nevertheless, if I'd been successful in wresting control of my salary from the assembly before I left Burlington. It's a brilliant idea, if only I can get the Privy Council's approval.

The freeholders living on the Delaware islands, having decided to cast their lot with New Jersey instead of Pennsylvania, brought found money into the province's coffers.   Billy proposed that the quitrents be used to fund his salary and end his dependency on the whimsical lawmakers.   Although Billy's mind was busy pondering the advantages of tying his purse strings to a less erratic source, his ear was in tune to the bidding.

"£600," he shouted, figuring the time was ripe to move in for the kill.   His heart raced at the prospect of owning such a magnificent animal.

"£700," a woman at the rear challenged, her voice crackly and distorted by emotion.

Whistles pierced the charged air.   Joseph wriggled from side to side as though he'd picked up a splinter in his buttock.

"I have £700.   Who'll give me eight?" Sam dared, boldly upping the ante in £100 increments.

Billy raised his hand.

"I have £800.   Who'll give me £1000?" he pushed, skillfully nudging them higher and higher to strip them dry.

"£1200," came the outrageous bid from the brazen spoiler in the rear.   The voice, controlled now but curt and calculating, was a familiar one to Billy.   He didn't need to turn around.   He knew who his opponent was.   Betsy Graeme had found a way to shatter his illusion, a way to get even.

"Twelve hundred once, twice..."   Sam looked questioningly at Billy.   Getting no response, he concluded, "three times ...sold!   To the lady in the gilded carriage."

"It seems that my former intended is still holding a grudge," he said to Joseph, scarcely moving his lips.

"Carrying a torch is more like it.   I understand that she is so close to a collapse that her parents are sending her to England for a spell under the tutelage of your Rev. Campbell."   Billy's heart sank.

"Governor Franklin," Betsy called, addressing him formally.

"Excuse me a moment," he said to Joseph and walked over to her rig.   He was prepared to say the gentlemanly thing, that he was sorry for the pain he had caused, but he never got the chance.

"Was the price too rich for your blood, William Franklin?" she snapped, struggling to hold back the tears.

Billy absorbed the shock of her blow without flinching and watched her coach lunge away.

"That was cruel," said Joseph, coming to his friend's side but focusing his eyes on the ground.

"It's all right if it makes her feel better.   It was all a terribly painful misunderstanding."   Billy's voice had a faraway sound.   "As Papa says, 'If you do what you should not, you must hear what you would not.'   Maybe she's due her ounce of revenge."

THE POWER OF THE PRESS

Chapter XIV

Indian Summer, 1765

Outside, the moon and stars faded as the sky over Philadelphia lightened.   Clusters of clouds appeared, taking shape slowly, like the furnishings in the darkened front bedroom where Billy lay wide-awake, tense and alert, waiting for the roll of a drum, the mustering call of the mob.   What a paradox this is, he thought, shaking his head in disbelief.   Papa's been over there for almost a year lobbying against the Stamp Act while over here, Sam Smith's inciting a bunch of misguided, radical malcontents to maybe even go so far as to burn down his new house, a house he's never seen, telling them that the Act was all Papa's doing from the start.   Since I can't stop them single-handed, I must do the next best thing, take mother and Sally to Burlington until order is restored.   If I know mother, this will be easier said than done.

Not that I blame her.   After living in rented housing and cramped

quarters for thirty-five years, she's not about to abandon her home

without a fight.

Have I come on a fool's errand?   Maybe so., but it's my

duty to protect my family from possible harm while Papa's away.

What's that?   He raised up on one elbow and strained his ears.

Anybody who's ever slept in a strange house knows the feeling.

Under ordinary circumstances, noises are unfamiliar but

nonthreatening.   But these were not ordinary times.   The creak

of a beam becomes an ominous intruder; a field mouse in the attic,

a swift-footed scout; a barking dog, a bloodthirsty bloodhound.

To his relief, the only drumming he heard came from the ratatattat

of a downy woodpecker staking its claim to a distant pine, the only

alarm from a spirited house wren scolding an overly aggressive

blue jay.   I give my mother credit, though.   She has spunk.

She's full of piss and vinegar all right.   Why, last night I was

hardly in the door when she jumped down my throat and

demanded to know what fool would bite the hand that feeds him.

Before I could get a word in edgewise, she sniped that should they disturb her one iota, she was prepared to lick the whole kit and caboodle.

If it wasn't so damn serious, it might be comical.   Uncle John's flintlock Kentucky rifle is probably longer than she is tall, and the magazine she boasts about consists of a couple of horns of powder and a bureau for a barricade.

Tired of fighting the unbeatable duo of insomnia and vexation, Billy punched the feather pillow he had kneaded all night and, satisfied that it wasn't a slab of granite, got up, lit a lamp, relieved himself and shaved.   He blew out the flame, then moved a cushioned chair by the window to station himself like a sentry directly above the street, packing the loaded flintlock across his knees.   Since all seemed quiet and peaceful, with the threat of arson diminishing as daylight neared, Billy dared to turn his thoughts to his own burdensome problems in New Jersey.

Besides his mother's safety, a host of political dilemmas weighed heavily on his shoulders: a postwar depression with its resultant hard times and bankruptcies and law suits that could not be settled because of the unanimous resolve of New Jersey's lawyers to shut down the civil courts by defying the Stamp Act and refusing to buy the required, objectionable stamps.   And that

wasn't the half of it.   Billy's stamp distributor had resigned,

fearing for his life and property, and figuring out where to store the

confounded stamps was becoming a real kettle of fish.   For the

moment, they were safely stowed aboard the H.M.S. Sardoine, a

British frigate anchored in New York harbor, but Captain Hawker

had notified the governor that when cold weather set in, the ship

would go into dry dock, and he would have to take delivery of the

controversial cargo.

On top of this, House Speaker Bob Ogden had summoned

an unauthorized, ad hoc assembly meeting in Amboy at which a

former decision not to send delegates to the Stamp Act Congress in

New York on October 7th had been rescinded.   Should I have

nipped rebellion in the bud and dissolved the House, Billy asked

himself as he got up and opened the top drawer of the serpentine

dresser to take out his clean set of clothes.   It was my

constitutional right, of course.   Nonetheless, I believe I acted

wisely by steering a steady course, keeping a cool head and

avoiding a confrontation.

Look what almost happened in New York when Colden

responded to the threat with anger and arrogance.   My God, we were on the brink of civil war!   No, in order to maintain peace in the province; and to save my own hide, I'll follow the path of forbearance and humility.   "As I've always said, 'it is best...for a man to lower himself a little, rather than let others lower him'."

"Billy, are you alone?" Sally asked meekly, rapping gently.

Amused, Billy went to the door and opened it on a crack. "Don't worry, Sis," he whispered.   "I haven't gone berserk yet. Just thinking aloud.   I'll be finished dressing in a minute.   Is mother still sleeping?"

"Yes.   Thanks to you we all got some rest, but you probably got little.   I'll go rouse Sammy and get her to make us a special breakfast."

"And we'll converse in French.   Mine's a bit rusty, but it'll be fun," he said, thinking that any diversion might do her a world of good.

Her eyes brightened, and an anxious smile crossed her face.

Within minutes, he joined his sister in the dining room where he found her sitting at the table in a flood of lamplight reading the *Pennsylvania Gazette*.

"Bonjour, mademoiselle" he greeted, keeping his end of the bargain.

"Bonjour, monsieur" she replied with an impressive French accent.

"Must be something juicy for you to be so absorbed," he said, gaping over her shoulder.

"You are going to flip your wig when I read you this, big brother."   She motioned for him to sit.

Playing along, he sat obediently and folded his hands in his lap.   "In French, remember," he badgered, poking fun at her. With Sally, he could relax and let go.   She had the uncanny knack of reducing a serious something into an insignificant nothing. Besides, he didn't want to steal her thunder by letting on that he had already seen the slur written about him.   Sally, who apparently did not want to lose anything in the translation, read him the piece in English: "It says that 'In colony after colony, from Boston to Newport to New York and Philadelphia, mobs are on the rampage, ravaging houses and terrorizing dissidents to protest the repugnant and unconstitutional Stamp Act, but all the while in New Jersey, quiet and tranquility prevail'."

"Like the eye of a tropical storm," Billy graphically but sarcastically inserted.

"Touché," she exclaimed, delighting in his wit but then immediately reproving him for interrupting.

"You mean there's more to this fable?"

She responded by rolling her eyes.

"Go on," he said, his seriousness all pretense.   "I'm all ears."

"It goes on to ridicule the members of your assembly for their apathy and moderation throughout this upheaval, but the clincher comes when the writer insinuates that you, my precious brother, have 'given them a Dose of Poppies and Laudanum'."

No sooner had she spit out the last half dozen words when they went into a fit of subdued laughter, ending as always in a prolonged, sidesplitting crying jag. Slowly the muted hysteria died down, leaving Billy as limp as a wet rag, but to his amazement, the dismal perspective he held upon rising had vanished, purged from his mind as cleanly and completely as a spring tonic of sulphur and molasses purifies the blood and bowel.

"My but it sounds like old times," Sammy cried as she

emerged from the kitchen carrying two plates stacked high with steaming buckwheat cakes and rashers of smoky bacon.

"I'm hungry as a woodcutter," Billy said in appreciation, knowing what it took to please. Mindful of her deformity, the ends of two fingers missing from a cider mill accident when she was a child, he said pardon moi, s'il vous plait to Sally and reached in front of her to take his plate. "I hope we didn't wake mother with our hilarity, Sammy; if so, I should be horsewhipped for being so inconsiderate."

"Amazin' what a difference a man around the house makes. She was sleepin' like a log when I came down. First decent night's rest she's had in a fortnight, harried as she is with all this fracas goin' on. Nothin's goin' to wake her this morning but those confounded drums."

"Papa's coming home in the spring," Sally hastened to say, abruptly leaping to her father's defense.

"Humph!" Sammy barked. "Seein's believin' I always say."

On the verge of tears, Sally snapped back, "Hold your sassy tongue! I'll stand for no such backbiting in my Papa's own house!"

"Thank you, Sammy.   That will be all," Billy signaled in a

conciliatory manner, shocked himself at his sister, who rarely flew

off the handle.   As much as he liked the maid, he did not approve

of her sleeping in the same room with his mother.   Benjamin

would scorn it too, if he knew, his maxim being, 'Never entreat a

servant to dwell with thee'.

"Mama's strong-willed," said Sally.   "I can tell you right

now that she's not going to leave her house and go to Burlington

with you.   What did you think of her 'fortifications'?" Sally

asked, toying with her food.

"I admit that I had that loaded flintlock at the ready early

this morning on my watch.   What worries me most, Sally, is that

if Mama's attacked, she'll fight to the finish.   You know, Sis,"

Billy said, tenderly cupping her trembling chin in his hand, "as

much as I hate to admit it, Sammy may be right.   The more I

think about it, the more I am convinced that Papa's place is here,

with you and mother, especially now.   These people mean

business."

Apparently not in the mood for a lecture, her nerves

noticeably raw and frayed, she removed his hand and continued her defense. "Mama will never have to fire that gun, Billy," she argued with youthful innocence, because Papa's friends in the White Oaks and Hearts of Oak will protect us."

"They mean well, but I'm afraid those men have their hands full guarding poor Mr. Hughs and his property."

"It's so sad. Ever since his appointment he's been ridiculed, harassed and threatened. You name it. To boot, he's been plagued with a carbuncle, and you know how excruciating that can be." Praising her mother for her compassion, she added, "Whenever she can, Mama goes over there to keep tabs on him." When her brother had no comment on their mother's neighborliness, she asked, "What's the matter?"

"Papa had no idea when he appointed John that he'd be in danger. I didn't either."

"Your stamp distributor resigned, too?"

"After receiving threats, William Coxe caved in," Billy confided, the corners of his mouth drooping further than usual with scorn. "I believe a man ought to finish what he starts, regardless of the consequences." He took his knife and fork and placed them just so across his empty plate.   "In retrospect, however, his dishonorable decision bought me some time."   His mouth curled into a self-satisfying grin.

"How's that?" Sally asked, listening intently.

"Because he received death threats, I went so far as to promise him military protection."

"The Sons of Liberty would have loved that."

"Nothing like cutting one's own throat, eh Sis?"

Sally smiled in agreement.

"As it stands now, my hands are tied, which puts me in the clear.   You see, I have no authority to appoint another stamp agent nor have I received instructions from Whitehall relative to the Act itself."

"In other words, you're in limbo."

"Somewhere between heaven and hell.   Yes, I'd say that sums it up in a nutshell."

"Seriously, Billy, what is your position on this legislation?"

"As I see it, 'for any man to set himself up as an advocate of the Stamp Act is a mere piece of Quixotism'."

"I think that's wise, brother.   Is there an antidote for this disease?"

"Repeal.   And it can't come too soon.   In the meantime, the epidemic is spreading to my very doorstep, and THIS," he exclaimed, crumpling the newspaper in his fist and shaking it in the air, is the deadly carrier."

A BRAND OF INFAMY

Chapter XV

It was midway to high noon when Billy's carriage arrived at Twickenham, Tho Wharton's massive stone country home situated northwest of Philadelphia in the next county. Billy had come here on his way home from his mother's to pick up his overseas mail, an inconvenience he had borne over the past few months, owing to the fact that some unprincipled underling was tampering with his correspondence.

"My God!" Sue Wharton cried, shifting the toddler straddling her hip to a more comfortable position. "Don't tell me the women stayed in Philadelphia alone!"

"Heaven knows I tried," Billy replied in his own defense, "but you know how stubborn and independent Mama is. Not even an act of Parliament could ferret her out of her burrow."

"'You can lead a horse to water, but you can't make him drink'," Tho chimed in, evidently overhearing his friend's lament as he approached them from the side yard.

"Thank goodness at least Sally's agreeable. She'll be along sometime next week. I made her promise on a stack of bibles that when Mrs. Parker, a close friend, returns to the city to stay with Mama, she'll pack up and come to Burlington."

"I just hope Deborah's not being too pigheaded for her own good," Sue warned as she deposited her squirming child into the governor's outstretched arms.

Billy shrugged his shoulders., not knowing what else to say. Instead, he focused his attention on their little toddler. Hoisting the boy high above his head, he spun him round and round evoking peals of genuine, unpretentious laughter, the kind that springs from the tips of the toes, the kind that does your heart good and makes you forget your troubles, the contagious kind, the kind reserved for the innocents. Feeling the little one had enough horseplay, Billy handed him to Tho. As he watched the happy trio clowning around, his heart suddenly filled with longing for Temple and hoped his mail would contain news from either

Straney or his father about his own son, who at the age of five was too young to join his grandfather at Craven Street and whose existence was still too much baggage for the neophyte governor to claim.

"If you and Benjamin have no objection, Sue and I would like to name this next baby Franklin."

"And who's to say it's a boy, Thomas Wharton," Sue quibbled, taking her husband to task for showing such out-and-out partiality.

"I'd be flattered, and I'm sure Papa would be as well."

"I'll write him tonight," Tho said, putting the tyke down to navigate on his own.

Billy declined an invitation to go inside while Tho got his mail, choosing instead to sit on the open porch in a rocking chair, Benjamin's newest contrivance, which Billy found to be a very relaxing pastime.

Presently, Tho returned with several envelopes in one hand and a broadside in the other.   "You'd better read this first," he said, clearing his throat.   "It was aired last night at the lodge."

Billy could tell by the set of his jaw and the intensity in his eyes that it concerned him and that it meant trouble.

As he skimmed the scorching indictment, his face turned bright red.   Withholding information?   Undue influence? Meddling in Pennsylvania politics?   Who's responsible for this libel?"

"Some local numbskull attorney read it.   I didn't recognize his name."

"A puppet of the Proprietary Party, no doubt, which, as you well know, is bent on making a laughingstock of me and my father."

"Demand a retraction!   Sue the bastard!"

"I know you mean well, Tho, but don't you see?   The damage is already done."   He got up slowly, suddenly feeling far older than his thirty-five years.   He grasped the railing and scanned the field of waving goldenrod, watching as a far-off thundercloud massed and cast its ugly shadow like a giant ink blot on the peaceful, verdant valley below, but, in essence, nothing registered.   All he really saw was the writing on the wall.

"Who's going to put any stock in these cockeyed accusations anyhow?   They're nothing but preposterous, pernicious lies, a maliciously calculated tactic aimed at tarnishing your image and discrediting Benjamin's reputation."

"You and I know that, but the question remains, will the populace believe it?   People with hungry mouths and empty pockets are seldom rational.   Reason, my friend, is a commodity in short supply these days."

"And the perpetrators of this rotten libel are feeding on it."

"Exactly.   They needed a butt to kick, and mine was the bullseye.   Anyone vaguely connected with executing the Stamp Act is a prime target."

"Imagine, accusing Dr. Franklin of stirring up this damned hornet's nest in the first place!   Why, those yellow-bellied, lily-livered sons of guns ought to be tar and feathered!   What do you intend to do?"

"Strike back.   Publish a public denial.   If I don't act fast to clear our names, they're apt to tear our houses down around our ears as they did Hutchinson's in Massachusetts."

"God forbid!"

"As to Papa, I will dare them to prove this grossly unwarranted falsehood regarding him."

"I see now why your father thinks the sun rises and sets in you."

Billy straightened, moved by the confidence.   "With respect to me," he continued, "their charges are flagrant lies, thus easily disproved.   To begin with, my speaker received the invitation to the Stamp Act Congress, not I, so how could I have possibly detained it as they charge?   In the second place, I learned of my Assembly's decision to send its regrets to Massachusetts Bay post factum, so how can I be accused of exerting undue influence?"

"Bob Ogden can vouch for that."

Not wanting to lose his train of thought, Billy hushed Tho until he finished pleading his case.   "And thirdly," he concluded, "I did not conspire in Pennsylvania politics with Joseph Galloway to sway the Bucks County delegates toward noncompliance in order to strengthen my hand at home."

"The culprits!" Tho lambasted.   "They're sick with envy and jealousy, resentful of the harmonious rapport that exists between you and the New Jerseyans."

Touchy from fatigue and unnerved by his friend's

misconception of the situation facing him back home, Billy got on

his high horse and testily shouted, "Just because the New Jerseyans

haven't run riot and attacked me or my possessions like mad dogs

doesn't mean their hackles aren't raised.   Why does everyone

think New Jersey is immune to the ghastly contagion spreading

throughout the Colonies or indifferent to the provocation that

caused the chaos in the first place?   Only by keeping the reins

slack, by averting authoritarian edicts and not flaunting royal

prominence have I managed to avoid open hostility.   Believe me

when I tell you that all is not harmony and bliss on the other shore.

I am skating on very thin ice and feel as though I'm being watched

like a hawk.   One wrong move and I'll be in the soup along with

the others.   Perhaps it's a blessing that we have no newspapers in

New Jersey to fan the flames," he added, looking weary and

drained.

     "Then conversely, take the *Pennsylvania Gazette*, which

publishes others' transgressions but kills stories about the goings-

on in Philadelphia that might taint our province.   Is it a noble

gesture designed to preserve the peace or a cowardly way out?"

Tho pondered.

"Whether Hall is wise or foolish, only time will tell.

Then again, that goes for all of us, doesn't it?"   Billy eyed the

storm brewing to the northwest.   "I must go," he said, tearing the

broadside into shreds.   "Please forgive me for sounding off."

"What are friends for?" he asked, patting Billy on the back.

Mingling with the cadenced clip-clop of the horses' hoofs,

the seesaw caw caw of a pair of glossy-black crows rose and fell,

putting Billy to sleep.   In his dream, Betsy discovered the cache

of hidden letters chronicling like a diary Master T's progressive

stages of development, his governess' unquestionable

qualifications and summary examples of his proper upbringing.

Separate but undeniably tied to the cover-up was Benjamin's strict

accounting of the cost of his grandson's upkeep, along with a

running tally of his son's burgeoning debt.   Billy awoke in a

sweat, and after reading two of his letters, tore them to bits and as

he ferried across the Delaware, inconspicuously seeded the water

with the evidence of his guilt.   More disturbing, the woman in his

dream was not his wife.   It was his old flame, Betsy Graeme.

Thursday, May 1, 1766

The workers had quit for the day, leaving their muddy traces behind.   From the waterfront, Billy could hear his wife fuming, her unmuffled voice carrying clearly through the unglazed windows.   "How in God's name will I ever clean up such a filthy mess?   It'll take a month of Sundays," she exclaimed.

Billy laughed off Betsy's womanly complaints, knowing that her worries would be over once her British maid arrived. According to Straney, who booked her passage, she was to sail with Captain Sparks on the brig Mary and Elizabeth and reach Philadelphia sometime during the latter half of July.

By the looks of things, Billy thought, roughly calculating the amount of work still to be completed on their three-story, brick mansion, she'll be here to take charge of the servants right in the thick of moving; that is, of course, he added skeptically, if the ship docks at the Crooked Billet Wharf on schedule.

Much to everyone's relief, English shipping had resumed since the repeal of the Stamp Act on March 18 when, with one stroke of the royal pen, the myriad miseries complicating Billy's life over the past few months evaporated into thin air.   He felt as light as the spring breeze that rippled the water at his back and swabbed his untroubled brow.

"It looks like things are beginning to pan out," he said aloud with a self-satisfying grin.

Ever since George Croghan, also known as the 'Wilderness Diplomat' after his triumphant return from the Illinois country, visited the governor in November, he could think of little else than the vast territory to the west, ripe for speculation and settlement. For the first time in his life, landed wealth was within his grasp, and he was determined to do everything in his power to keep it from slipping through his fingers. Moreover, in his mind's eye, he pictured himself as the new colony's first governor.

The ink was not yet dry on the Treaty of Paris when a land-mad craze swept England, with every schemer scrambling for dominance over the windfall acreage in America. America had her share of greedy opportunists as well. Leading the pack were William Franklin, Galloway, Colonial Administrator Sir William Johnson, Deputy Superintendent of Indian Affairs George Croghan and six others, all partners in the Illinois Company, a consortium, whose private Articles of Agreement, defined at numerous clandestine meetings held at the Galloway's High Street,

Philadelphia home throughout the past winter, were signed on March 29 and the formal petition readied for submission to Whitehall.

Circumspectly shielding himself from the scourge of scandal, Billy covered his tracks by not inking his name to the official document, nor did he plan to sign the transmittal letter, which he was in the process of composing.

"Yes," he mused, forgetting that he was here to stake out the location of the formal gardens and placement of the sycamore shade trees, "The Illinois Company has all the earmarks of success: influence, pull, money and aggrieved parties, but, in my judgment, the last item is the wildcard."

Billy was quick to acknowledge that the linchpin of his overall plan relied on one major ingredient—fur traders who stood to receive restitution in land from the savages for past offenses, a penance Croghan wrested from them on his recent missionary expedition as an emissary of the Crown.   For the most part, the fickle natives trusted the swashbuckling, barter-bearing conciliator and knuckled under to his redeeming proposition, offering 250,000 acres in western Virginia south of the Ohio River in reparations.

But every job has its drawbacks, and, as a consequence, Croghan took his share of lumps, one being a Kickapoo hatchet to the head. The fearless adventurer facetiously remarked, however, that his skull was too thick for it to enter.

In any event, talk about luck, the King unexpectedly announced that he was thinking of establishing a colony in and around Fort Chartres, a stone quadrangle built by the recently-ousted French on the banks of the Mississippi north of the Ohio. With all that virgin territory up for grabs, Billy convinced his cohorts to jump on the bandwagon and apply for a grant of 1.2 million acres. He advised them to strike while the iron was hot, before the Indians' repentant mood cooled. He figured that going in with their 250,000 free acres would give them a distinct advantage over other petitioners in that it was that much less the Crown had to buy. It was a bargaining chip he hoped would tip the scale in their favor.

Moreover, the treaty negotiated with the twenty-five tribes would set a precedent, a costly sentence for those whose only asset was land, and put the onus for keeping the peace squarely on the chieftains. At this point in time, safety was uppermost in the minds of migrators and merchants alike.   What an inducement for

wary settlers, Billy thought, dreaming up a fitting advertisement:

Come to safe, secure Illinois, the womb of the West.   Signed,

William Franklin, Governor.   Caught up in his orgasmic fantasy,

Billy started when Betsy called his name.   He looked up to see his

carriage approaching.

"What makes you such a poke today?" his wife called out

with mock sassiness.   "Why, you're slow as molasses."

"I'm finished, theoretically speaking," he hedged, fumbling

for his pocket watch.   Billy swung himself up into the closed

carriage unassisted.

"Giddyap!"   John slapped the reins smartly across the

horses' rumps, and they were off at a trot.

"Don't worry," Betsy said, placing her hand on his thigh.

"The packet won't sail without Papa's letter.   We've plenty of

time."

As they jounced along toward the wharf, Betsy slid over

close to her husband.   Being the sentient, tender man that he was,

Billy reacted warmly and eagerly to his wife's spontaneous, subtle

desire for affection.   Folding her in his arms, he kissed her parted lips. Judging from the irritation in his loins, he wished he hadn't labored so long over his father's letter the night before and turned in earlier. When it came to making love, Billy needed no coaxing, because he imagined his wife's physical needs were no less vital than his own.

For a brief moment, Billy prided himself on killing two birds with one stone, satisfying his wife's emotional needs and getting himself off the hook for daydreaming about his pie in the sky land deal, as skeptics labeled it, instead of attending to the business at hand, mainly, landscaping.

Betsy smoothed her bodice and adjusted the neckline of her low-cut dress to a more appropriate height, one that left more to the imagination. "So far," she whispered with impish devilment, "I've discovered two things about you, my darling. One, you're an exemplary lover and two, you're a proverbial dreamer." Although Betsy had the last laugh, Billy outdid her by far in volume.

"In the future, my love," he warned with a tomfoolish wag of the finger, "any advance will be suspect. Like a veteran angler, she feeds me the line. I, like a fool, run with the bait, and then, when I least expect it, WHAM, she jerks and catches me deep down in the gullet."

"And what a catch I made." She grasped his hand and pressed it covetously to her cheek.

"But I landed the prize!" Their eyes met. Words were not needed. With the backside of his finger, Billy grazed the curve of her chin and jaw, marveling at its velvety smoothness. The silky feel of it reminded him of his childhood, when his own skin had a similar texture, a time when accusing one's father of being wrong was unheard-of.

The errant thought, the loss of focus, broke the spell. Billy's hand faltered and fell; his gaze shifted.

Betsy seemed to surmise what was on his mind and asked, "In the final analysis, how did you answer Papa's criticism?"

"Here," he said, taking the unsealed envelope from his pocket and handing it to her. "Read it and tell me what you think."

She removed the several-page letter, unfolded it carefully and began reading to herself.

"Out loud, please. Skip the first couple of paragraphs.

Begin with 'I don't wonder at your disapproving, etcetera'."

"'I don't wonder at your disapproving my mentioning in my speech the villainous reports of the Proprietary officers.   It is impossible for you at so great a distance to be acquainted with every circumstance necessary to form a right judgment of the expediency or inexpediency of particular transactions'."

Hesitating, Betsy glanced up to gauge her husband's reaction, but seeing that he neither flinched nor batted an eyelid, she continued, enunciating every word as if the letter were an epistle: "'I have all the evidence the nature of the case will admit, that they had taken their measures so effectually with the Presbyterians and the Sons of Liberty in this Province, that had it not been for the paper I published in answer to the lodge paper, I should have had my house pulled down about my ears and all my effects destroyed.'"

"Not only our house!" Betsy cried.   "What about Papa's?" "Thanks to you his house is still standing.   Aren't you going to apprize him of that?"

"I don't want to worry him," he stated simply.

Shaking her head with annoyance, Betsy resumed reading:

"'I did not think the notice I took of this in my speech to be concerning myself with the affairs of Pennsylvania(;) all I intended by it was to fix a Brand of Infamy on the transactions of the officers of that government within this Province, and I should have done the same had the officers of New York, or any other Colony, given the like occasion.   All my friends in every part of the Province have approved my conduct, and I have ever since experienced the good effects of it; having, by thus removing the prejudices of the people, rendered abortive every successive attempt of my adversaries to hurt me.   For my part I always think it best to nip in the bud every report which may tend to hurt a man's character or interest and that no man should deem such reports below his notice...'"

"Go on."

"I can't."   She thrust the pages into his lap and stared into space.

"What's the matter?"

"It makes me sick.   That's all.   Papa should reward you for bravery, and what does he do?   Gives you a kick in the teeth."

"I told him to mind his own business, in so many words.

What should I do?   Pick a fight and have him disown me over a difference of opinion?   Papa's a pragmatist.   'Since human nature is capricious,' he says, 'why waste valuable time worrying about the shouts of those who will cry Hosanna today and crucify you tomorrow?   Instead, glory in the blessings of the impartial few, and insulate yourself from the brunt of brutal attacks with a clear conscience, just motives, and silence'."

"Go ahead.   Make excuses for him," she replied, mellowing.   "I do hope Papa realizes what a devoted, unselfish son he has!   If you ask me, Papa's an idealist."   Betsy tilted her husband's chin toward her until her eyes looked squarely into his.   "I hardly think your father will disown you over a difference of opinion."

"I remember on one occasion during our sojourn in England when I argued a contrary point to Papa's when we were in the company of his peers, and he took it very much to heart."

"You are who you are, William, a man with three masters, your King, country, and the people of your province.   That's a tall order for any man.   Papa needs to step aside and let you govern in your own way.   That's all I have to say."

They arrived at the wharf and sent the letter.

WHAT'S FAIR IS FAIR

Chapter XVI

Saturday, August 23, 1768

The two men stood at a comfortable distance, close enough to be heard over the humdrum drone of the river as it plunged headlong down the eight-foot drop comprising Trenton Falls yet far enough apart to keep their lines from tangling. George Washington's step-son, Jack, had positioned himself farther downstream.

Quite a tribute, having the old South River named in one's honor," the gentleman farmer from Virginia commented, recasting.

"De La Warr, your first royal governor. Lucky man," Billy concurred. There was safety in small talk, but he'd exhausted almost every topic since the travel-weary pair arrived unexpectedly on his doorstep the night before. The Franklins were well-known for their open-hearted hospitality, and in this instance, their Burlington mansion was a convenient half way house between Mt. Vernon and Kings College in New York City, Washington's final destination.   Any other time, Billy would have welcomed a visit from the esteemed member of the House of Burgesses, but in light of unfolding events, his misgivings were quite legitimate.   Simply put, the guest he was obliged to entertain was his arch business rival.

By way of explanation, Washington had a vested interest in a group formed in 1747 called the Ohio Company to speculate in lands west of the Appalachian Mountains.   Its roster included George's father, Augustine, and his brother, Lawrence, who were both now deceased.   Billy, the Whartons, Galloway and others formed the Burlington Company for the same purpose, to petition the Crown for land ceded by the Indians as a result of the late war. The ticklish problem was that the two groups were lobbying for the same tract of land, the former calling it the Ohio Company, the latter, Vandalia, for Queen Charlotte, a descendant of the Vandals.

It was because of this snag, therefore, that Billy's nerves were on edge and his conversation guarded.

"When did you say you were leaving for Fort Stanwix?" his visitor asked.

"The first thing Wednesday morning," Billy replied. Mentally mulling over the many loose ends that needed tying before his departure for the Indian powwow in New York, he was lost in thought when a whopping trout struck his bucktail fly. Unable to take up the slack fast enough, the catch of the day shook itself loose and got away.   Feeling somewhat better after muttering a string of unmentionable profanities, Billy turned his thoughts to fishing and the ensuing conversation.

"War or peace is hanging in the balance," Washington cautioned.

"A lot is riding on our success in forging this treaty and fixing a new, permanent boundary line."   Billy spoke openly of public trust and security, the need to stop infiltration and the avoidance of terrorism, all noble, well-intentioned reasons for making the three-month-long trek to the wilds of New York State. But brewing in the back of that designing brain was one ulterior motive, the hope of private gain.   His aim was to negotiate a personal land deal in the Lake Otsego area, about 50 miles due west of Albany, an acquisition that would become the basis of a Franklin real estate empire.   In other words, there was more to the cake than just the icing.

"Virginians are guilty of squatting on Indian lands," Washington admitted.   "And murdering warriors."

"New Jerseyans aren't lily-white either," Billy replied, thinking of the two he'd had executed for murdering the Oneida squaws.   "That's why Croghan and Johnson asked me to attend." He bit his tongue, fearing that mention of the Indian agent was treading on dangerous ground.   For God's sake, he said to himself, change the subject.   Talk about anything else, things we agree on.   Townshend's insufferable duties.   Tea.   Paper money.   Nonimportation.   No, we milked those issues dry last night.

Then, by divine providence, the orangy-yellow sun crept up behind them and cast its luminous rays into the shaded pool, sending the brown, speckled trout scurrying for a cooler, darker place to hide.   "I guess that does it for this morning," Billy said, eagerly pulling in his line and leaning his pole against a nearby tree trunk.

"Looks like it's going to be another scorcher," Washington said, following suit.

Being a typical, unbashful teen, Jack, presumably losing patience the minute he saw his lanky shadow, turned in his creel of fish to be gutted and fried by the servant who accompanied them, stripped and plunged into the choppy flow.

Seeing a perfect out and afraid of where merely batting the breeze might lead, Billy chanced a suggestion.   "This current can be awfully treacherous.   What do you say we keep him company."

"My sentiments exactly," Washington agreed, leading the way downstream.

Dinner was on the hearth by the time Billy got back to Burlington.   The sweet smell of savory stuffed turkey greeted him as he wheeled Thunderbolt past the open kitchen windows and around back to the stables.   Dismounting, he handed Ned the reins.   "Cool him down slowly.   I rode him hard."

"Yesir, Governor Franklin."   Ned looked puzzled, not about his instructions, because he was a first-rate stable hand.

Amused might be a better word.   Vociferant John would have cried, "Jumpin' Jehoshaphat, Governor Franklin, did you get waylaid or somethin'?"   But Ned was reticent, spoke when spoken to and stayed out of trouble.

Billy picked his steps carefully, being unaccustomed to walking barefooted out-of-doors.   "Yow!" he yelped, hopping on one foot, which only inflicted double punishment on the other. "Ow!   These cinders are hotter than hades.   More like a Fijian fire pit!"

His cries of distress brought the women rushing to his aid. Sally was visiting while her husband, Richard Bache, a "fortune hunter" in Billy's estimation was in Jamaica clearing up a few money matters.

"What in God's name happened to you?"

"Are you hurt?" Sally asked, trying not to laugh.

"Whose clothes are these?   They're not yours.   Where are your shoes and your wig?" Betsy asked, trying to hide her amusement.

"Never mind the questions.   Would somebody p l e a s e get me a pair of shoes!   Nona!"

"Whose dumb idea was it to put cinders on the drive anyhow?"

"Yours dear," Betsy replied with exaggerated innocence as she tried to shoulder a share of her husband's weight.

"What in the world happened?"   Unable to hold it in a minute longer, Sally let out a burst of pent-up laughter.

Despite his apprehension, Billy couldn't ignore the sparkle in his sister's eyes and felt like a snitch for writing his absentee father to complain about his brother-in-law's dire financial straits, desperately hoping Benjamin had burned the cursed letter after reading it.

Apparently hearing the commotion, Nona came out on the stoop to investigate.   "Lord o' mercy!" she exclaimed, shooing the ladies aside as she took charge.

"We were...you know...," Billy stammered, hemming and hawing.

"You were swimmin' in the altogether, and somebody stole your clothes," Nona said matter-of-factly, grinning like a Cheshire cat.

"Not exactly," Billy mumbled, "just down to our

undergarments." Turning to Betsy he added, "You know what a decent, modest man George W. is."

"'Whatcha don't see when you haven't got a barrel, said the foil to the comic'."

November 23, 1768

"God, it feels good to be back in my own bed," Billy said, yawning and stretching. "I've grown too soft for a lousy army cot."

"As long as that's all you missed." Betsy rolled over and pretended to give her husband the cold shoulder.

"Get over here, you temptress," he whispered, sliding her effortlessly across the sheets until their bodies meshed like two spoons. "I never want to be parted from you this long ever again. I couldn't bear it." His heart pounded in his chest and his breathing quickened.

Later in the night they lay awake, side by side, motionless, their fingers intertwined. "I still can't believe Sally's pregnant," Betsy said dreamily. "Can you?"

"It's hard for me to imagine my baby sister with a baby,"

Billy answered.   He hated himself for half hoping it was a false alarm; after all, maybe he was all wrong about Mr. Bache, but he doubted it.

"What kind of pie do you want for Thanksgiving, mincemeat or pumpkin?"

"No plum pudding?" he asked, trifling with her.

"No plum pudding?" she echoed, mimicking him.   "Of course.   Besides that."

"Apple."

"You're incorrigible, but I love you anyway, my Great Arbiter of Justice.   Say your name again in the Indian tongue."

"Sagorighweyoghsta."

"What a mouthful," she replied, laughing softly.   "But such a nice gesture, a novel way of thanking you for being fair."

"Ius est ars boni et aequi."

"Legal justice is the art of the good and the fair." Billy chuckled quietly.   "I know why they gave me a name."

"Why?" Betsy got up on one elbow and stared at him in the pitch-darkness.

"To show me they've finally forgiven me for refusing to eat

their squaws' maggot-infested venison stew that time."

"Ugh!" Betsy exclaimed.   "We'll discuss the Thanksgiving menu in the morning."   With that, she turned her back to him and went to sleep.

Billy turned over but did not go to sleep.   He had some disturbing news on his mind, a letter from Hillsborough that came when he was away.   It was a scathing rebuke that blasted the governor's actions over the past months, accused him of neglect of duty and questioned his principles.   Not wanting to upset his wife, he had bottled it up inside.

Bone tired from his journey but too upset (or angry) to rest, he slipped out of bed and crept downstairs to compose an immediate reply.   Lighting the lamp, he took pen in hand and began to write.   Six hours and thirty pages later, he straightened up, placed the quill in the ink holder and extinguished the light, for it was already dawn.   Weary from fatigue, like a barrister who has just pleaded the most important case of his career, he rubbed his eyes and went to the cupboard to pour himself a glass of brandy. Bothered by the acrid odor of last night's fire, he went to the window, opened it, and as he had seen his father do so often, drew deep, invigorating breaths of chilly, morning air, smelling of balsam fir, damp earth and pine.   He sipped slowly, marveling anew the squirrel's nest in the distant oak.   To the casual observer, it was flimsily constructed, capable of being whisked away by the slightest disturbance, but to the naturalist, it was as ingenious and durable as a spider web.

The light-handed approach I use to govern my province may appear flimsy to Hillsborough, Billy thought, drawing an analogy, but I survived the first ill wind far better than my counterparts with their rigid, ironhanded methods, and so, God willing, 'I will steer my little bark quietly through this one'.

Since I find that many of Hillsborough's assertions are based on mistaken information, Billy pondered, is he just a supercilious son of a bitch drunk with power, or is he deliberately trying to destroy me to get back at my father, he mused, stroking his chin.   This troubles me, and the longer I think about it, the more plausible the latter becomes.

Then suddenly everything clicked.   The answer is in Papa's last letter.   He crossed the room and took it from his desk drawer.   In it, his father mentioned that it had been rumored that he might be appointed undersecretary to Lord Hillsborough but went on to say that it was highly unlikely, since he was considered 'too much of an American'. His non-resident status was only a pretense. Because of his dual allegiance, he might, in fact, be stripped of his present job as deputy postmaster general also.

"Where is that paragraph?" He ran his finger down the pages. "Ah, here it is: '...a turn of a die may make a great difference in our affairs. We may be either promoted or discarded; one or the other seems likely soon to be the case, but 'tis hard to divine which'." Billy rolled the pronouns over his tongue several times. "Our...we." It is clear that my superiors have taken it for granted that Papa and I are of one mind. My fate appears to be tied to the same stake as his, and Hillsborough may be holding the torch.

Sitting, he picked up the missive he had written and reread it word for word as though it were his deposition. It was bold and forthright, a chronicle of his commendable service record as well as a personal, prophetic appraisal of the ministry's most recent blunder, the passage of the Townshend Acts, a measure that placed a duty on tea and glass, among other things.

'Mens Minds are sour'd,' he wrote, 'a sullen Discontent prevails, and, in my Opinion, no Force on Earth is sufficient to make the Assemblies acknowledge, by an Act of theirs, that the Parliament has a Right to impose Taxes on America ...As long as this Temper continues, they will do all in their Power, in their private Capacities, to prevent the Consumption of British Manufactures in the Colonies, that the Mother Country may thereby lose more in her Commerce than she can possibly gain by way of Revenue'.

Then bordering on open defiance, he argued for his assembly's right of petition: 'Petitioning the King is generally deemed an inherent Right of the Subject, provided the language be decent, and had I attempted to hinder the Assembly from exercising this supposed Right, without orders from my Superiors, I had Reason to apprehend that I should not only have been accused here of an unwarrantable Stretch of Power, but have been blamed by His Majesty and his Ministers'.

In short, the letter was a masterpiece of exoneration and recrimination, discrediting the self-destroying evidence and countering with charges of his own.   This may very well be the flint that lights the fire, he reflected.   God forbid.   Closing his

scratchy eyes, he leaned back and heaved a heavy sigh.

Then, dealing with the blow that pained him most, he wrote

an apology for any umbrage he may have caused the King, stating

that if his conduct was questioned by his monarch, '...Nothing

could affect me more sensibly, as I have long valued myself on a

strict Performance of my Duty, and the strongest Attachment to my

Sovereign'.

Finally, with a stroke of genius, he added a brief preamble,

taking the liberty to imply that since his Lordship was an impartial

man, he, also, would conclude, after being apprised of the facts,

that the censures made against the governor were biased and

unmerited.

With that, he affixed his signature to Letter No. 13.   Had

he signed his death warrant?   Only time would tell.

A BEAUTIFUL FRIENDSHIP

Chapter XVII

Burlington
Saturday, September 19, 1769

"Well, Lord Stirling, what do you think of my Strawberry Hill Farm?" Billy asked, trying hard not to sound smug or pretentious but knowing damn well that he was fishing for a compliment.   Inside he was bubbling with excitement, eager to show off his sizable acquisition: 600 acres of prime grazing meadows, cedar-fenced apple and peach orchards and shadowy pine forests, not to mention the imposing, Georgian-style manor house built of local fieldstone.

"You are much too modest, my friend," the surveyor-general replied, twisting in his saddle to cast a trained eye over the expansive property.   He was a good-looking man of 43 whose receding, dark hair betrayed the youthful face, made strikingly handsome by the contrast between his ruddy, outdoorsy complexion and dominant bedroom eyes.

Stirling's real name was William Alexander.   His claim as the 6th Earl of Stirling was denied in 1762, but he retained the title nonetheless.   Foes of Billy's, outraged by his appointment as governor in the first place, predicted that Alexander, who was a member of the New Jersey Provincial Council as well as a relative of the Penns, would be a prickly thorn in his side.   The naysayers were wrong again.   As it turned out, Lord and Lady Stirling and Betsy and Billy were the best of friends; in fact, the Franklins had spent the better part of the previous summer at The Buildings, Lord Stirling's opulent, country estate in Basking Ridge.

Friend or no friend, however, Billy had no intention of divulging the financial aspects of his land swaps and bargains with a man of Stirling's mathematical acumen.   In this instance he acquired this amazing 296-acre piece of property on Rancocas Creek, five miles south of Burlington, in exchange for 2,000 acres of his Otsego holdings.   The balance of his estate was acquired piece-meal.

With this in mind, Billy deftly directed his guest's attention to husbandry, a mutually-inviting hobby.   "Judge Read is beckoning to us.   I asked him to do me a favor and check my fruit trees for infestation."

"What's that the workers are sprinkling around them?"

"Walnut shells to ward off worms and horseradish for bugs."

"Does it work?" Lord Stirling asked.

"Like a charm.   Trust me.   Uncle Charles is a topnotch horticulturist.

"You must take after him for your interest in scientific farming."

"So long as I didn't inherit my great-uncle's temperament as well."   Billy laughed at the thought of being as fearful and high-strung as the judge.   Feeling a need to prove it, he collected his horse and squeezed his legs gently yet firmly against the stallion's sides, setting him into motion.   Gaining speed, he relaxed the reins as he approached the fence.   Then, leaning forward, he raised his butt to shift his weight to the stirrups and, in one fluid motion, vaulted cleanly over the obstacle.

Not to be outdone, Lord Stirling followed the governor's lead with an expert jump, thundering to a halt beside him and Charles Read, who was noticeably rattled by the young men's reckless daring.

"Why do you think they invented gates, you numbsculls?" the judge bellowed, his mouth twitching, his forefinger wagging, telltale signs that the man's spring was wound too tight.

"For people who are afraid of their own shadows," Billy wise-cracked, trying to release some of the tension.

At fifty-three, Judge Read looked and acted like a much older man.   His nerves were shot and it showed.   Poor health, an ailing wife and problems with his son, Jacob, contributed to his early decline.   His accomplishments in politics and business, nevertheless, were noteworthy, namely, state Supreme Court justice and owner of several iron ore foundries throughout New Jersey.

Industries were few and far between in the New World. In order to insure the Colonies' dependence on the Mother Country and to keep the well-heeled English merchants fat and happy, the King forbade manufacturing in the provinces.   To keep tabs on them, the governors were bound to report every business no matter how trifling.   Failure to comply was a major offense.   That was the reason why Billy found himself in hot water the year before when Hillsborough chastised him for neglect of duty.   Although New Jersey had few significant enterprises, the governor had dutifully filed an accounting of what there was: glassmaking, weaving, barrel making and so on, but as so often happened, his letter miscarried.   It is interesting to note that nearly a year after this flare-up, Billy's thirty-page letter remained unanswered.

"These trees are clean as a whistle," the judge countered, ignoring his grandnephew's flippant remark.

"Just what I wanted to hear!" Billy exclaimed, thanking him for his sagely appraisal.

"If that's all, I'll be on my way.   I've got no time to dillydally."

"How is Alice?" Billy asked, sensing something.

"She's taken a turn for the worse, I'm afraid."

"I'm sorry," Billy said, regretting his former callousness.

Then, leading their steeds, Lord Stirling and Billy walked

the judge to the gate, put down the rails and accompanied him to

the stable, commiserating with their friend over his wife's

incapacitation and expressing their regrets that he would not be

able to join them for the opening of the Burlington Fair later that

day.

Saturday, October 2, 1770

The annual Burlington Fair was held in the outdoor

waterfront marketplace beneath the hall where the Assembly met.

Day in and day out for an entire week farmers swarmed to barter

cows, pigs, chickens, butter, cheese or vegetables for necessities

such as coffee, tea, bonnets or calico.   Sprawled along the river

nearby were the brewhouses, bake houses, malthouses and timber

yards.

It was a beehive of activity, a yearly reunion for many

folks, a gabfest for others, a time for storytelling and news

swapping, a chance to hash over prevailing provincial problems

with the likes of Judge Read, Lord Stirling or the governor,

himself.   Everyone was there, everyone except Alice Read, that

is.   The Judge had buried his wife in St. Mary's cemetery last
November.

Personally, Billy liked the fair.   He used it as a barometer
to gauge not only the mood of the people but the level of his own
popularity as well.   As he sauntered along with his small party,
stopping here and there to engage in topical conversation, he was
mildly heartened to find a slight degree of optimism, reflecting, he
imagined, the salutary effect of Parliament's repeal this past spring
of the ill-advised Townshend Acts.

On the surface Billy regarded the move as a step in the
right direction but in the final analysis, judged it a bittersweet
victory, since the Mother Country, wielding an authoritative hand,
retained the tax on tea to remind her recalcitrant subjects exactly
who was boss.   In a recent letter, Benjamin bluntly expressed his
reaction this way: '...it is bad surgery to leave splinters in a
wound which must prevent its healing or in time occasion it to
open afresh'.

As a matter of principle, New Jersey's uncompromising,
unyielding Sons of Liberty had no intention of letting the wound
heal while the splinter remained.   Sticking to their guns, they

demanded an all-or-nothing revocation. Meanwhile, they continued to force the issue by extending the ban on British imports. For some unknown reason, Billy escaped their wrath, or perhaps their notice, when he wittingly imported an English farmer to oversee his farm and English-made Rotheran plows to work it.

But Betsy's smart, new, glittery Strass buckles didn't escape the eyes of the local women as she strolled along on her husband's arm. They were a luxury few of them could afford, even if they had the right connection abroad.

Lord Stirling stopped the cluster of dignitaries for a second to listen to a group of merchants who were bickering over the hardship the voluntary, nonimportation restriction was causing them. "Shame on you," he intruded, putting in his twopence worth. "Last Saturday we attended the graduation at Princeton, and the entire class was dressed in American-made homespun!"

"So what?" they retorted. "They have nothing to lose."

"They were acting in concert with the Sons of Liberty, which holds New York in contempt for resuming trade," Lord Stirling argued.

Billy grew uneasy with this explosive line of talk,

especially when other passers-by paused to eavesdrop, but why
flog a dead horse?   Didn't he have Hillsborough's assurance that
Parliament would design no new taxes against America?
Privately, he held that, given time, the wound would eventually
heal, but what about his father's splinter theory?   Evidently, he
chose to ignore it.   With accounts of the senseless massacre in
Boston still vivid in his memory, he knew he needed to defuse the
situation before it erupted into violence.

Thinking of the bloodshed inflicted by the British regulars
on March 5th, Billy suddenly realized that because of that incident,
his assembly was apt to discontinue its support of the King's troops
when it convened in Perth Amboy the following week.
Something tells me I may have a fight on my hands, he thought.
Maybe I'm just plain stupid to stay in this backwater province.
I'm the lowest-paid governor in the Colonies, with no pay hike in
sight.   Barbados!   Now that's where I'd really like to go.   Betsy
would have no objection, either, because she'd be going home.

"The Sons of Liberty call the New Yorkers traitors and
betrayers to their country," Lord Stirling harangued.

At this point, seeing an out, Billy jumped in, putting his

private concerns in the back of his mind for the time being.   "If I may interrupt, he casually intervened, walking over to where Sally was socializing with the women, "Perhaps you would all like to meet my nephew."   Lifting his thirteen-month-old godson from his perambulator and holding him on his arm, he proudly announced, "Ladies and gentlemen, meet Benjamin Franklin Bache."

A MICROCOSM

Chapter XVIII

Saturday, May 12, 1772

On the whole the year 1771 was politically peaceful for Billy, affording him free time to wheel and deal in his complex real estate ventures in upper New York State.   Legitimate but highly speculative, the transactions further entangled him with the slippery, double-dealing George Croghan, who, by capitalizing on the influential Franklin name and by exploiting the gullible governor's weaker tendencies, namely, blind faith and a voracious appetite for potential wealth, had, several years ago, wheedled him into securing a three-year, seven percent loan of £3,000 from a group of investors known as the Burlington Company.   The loan was now long overdue, and the sucker, William Franklin, was left holding the bag.

Everywhere Billy turned someone was crying for money. Benjamin's letters read like a lengthy bill of lading.   Always heading the list of debits was the sizable expenditure for Temple's education and upkeep.   Billy stalled for time by disputing his father's figures and gave him the putoff by pleading poverty until his lands were patented, which, at the rate things were going, could be never.

To make matters worse, Billy's research shed some disturbing new light on the legitimacy of the Virginians' claim to the disputed portion of Vandalia.   Concerned about it, he communicated his findings to William Trent and Sam Wharton, who the grantees had sent to London in '69 to lobby the ministry. Billy was galled when they chose to dismiss it, saying his discovery was old hat.

Trent and Wharton were too pumped up over Hillsborough's sudden renewed interest in the project to worry about minor technicalities, his lordship having suggested they apply for eighteen million acres.   This sweetening of the pot lured many London bigwigs to the nest like bees to honey, and at a December 1769 meeting in the Crown and Anchor Tavern, they drafted a revised petition, renaming the scheme the Grand Ohio

Company, eclipsing the Virginians' Ohio Company.

Billy was jarred.   He was leery of Hillsborough's motive

and furious that the emissaries had taken his warning with a grain

of salt.   Personally, he wanted everything aboveboard, on the up-

and-up, because unlike the others, his livelihood was linked to

these aristocrats, many of whom were members of the Privy

Council.   This lack of honesty soured Billy against Trent and

Wharton and caused him to doubt their competence and integrity.

The Following Week.

"What do you think of it?" Richard asked Billy as he turned

the key in the lock and ushered him through the door of the

Bache's recently-opened dry goods store on the south side of

Market.   The Penns had originally named this east-west

thoroughfare High Street, but the locals renamed it Market Street, a

defiant little gesture that symbolized a new-found autonomous

spirit.

Feeling somewhat embarrassed for having missed the

discourse immediately preceding the question, his mind having momentarily wandering shortly before Fourth and Market from his

brother-in-law's endless recital of the details of his London trip,

Billy submersed all anxious thoughts of Vandalia and the outcome

of the scheduled April vote by the Board of Trade, news Richard

had personally conveyed from Benjamin, and apologized.   "I'm

sorry, Richard.   What did you say?"

Vaulting up on the counter, presumably to take the weight

off his lame leg, which he had injured aboard ship en route to

England, Richard donned his spectacles and took a folded paper

from his coat pocket before answering.   "I said, do you think

Father will come home this summer?   He told Mother that he

planned to return to America 'for good and all'."

"If he cares about seeing mother alive," Billy replied

without mincing words.   "That stroke definitely set her back a

peg.   Surely you notice a difference in her after being away for

three months."   Billy studied the man his sister had married over

his vehement objection, who, by counting on Benjamin's pull and

the power of £1000 in his pocket, had set out across the sea to

snatch a public post.   But he was putty in the hands of the master,

caving in to Benjamin's proverb that 'He who has a trade has an office of profit and honor'.

When Sally learned from Richard that he was coming home empty-handed, she took it in stride as always and dutifully proceeded on her own to set up shop. Being less pliable than her husband, however, she balked at her father's suggestion that the store be located in the north room of the Franklin house and, with an admirable degree of pluck, rented the first floor of the Old House further east on Market Street next to Haddock's.

"Ah, yes, the poor soul," Richard replied, creasing the folds of the paper over and over again with his fingernail. "Her memory is failing, and she is having such trouble ambulating. Sally swears that if it weren't for Benny, Kingbird she calls him, mother would have died of melancholia this winter."

Irked by Richard's use of the maternal and paternal references, Billy turned to peruse the varied assortment of Chinese taffetas and nankeens, Irish linens and printed calicoes to conceal any trace of resentment that may have found expression in his face. Next, I suppose she'll be calling him son, he bitched to himself. The very thought of it rankles me, but I'll never let on. Why, he's moved in like he's flesh and blood! Regardless, from all indications, Papa's given his bankrupt son-in-law the official seal of approval, so that's that.   End of case.   (One might argue the point that Billy was guilty of 'the pot calling the kettle black'.) I've never been one for family squabbles anyway.   If only Betsy had the same rapport with mother that Richard has.   I realize they have nothing in common, but come to think of it, the same holds true for Betsy Graeme and mother, and they're bosom friends.

Early on, Billy had found it prudent to level with his wife about his former involvement with Miss Graeme, who, through lovesick gazes and longing eyes, wherever they happened to meet, at church, a dance or a party, conveyed an unbearable, unceasing desire for her once beloved fiancé.   The Graemes tried to snap their broken-hearted daughter out of her languishing emotional state by telling her that she was lucky to be rid of William Franklin.   When that didn't work, seeing clearly the futility of their daughter's hopeless yearning and evidently worried about her deteriorating emotional state, they shipped her off to England for a change of scene.

All at once something dawned on Billy.   He picked up the May 7th edition of the *Pennsylvania Gazette* off the counter and pretended to read Richard's 'For Cash Only' ad while he struggled

to recreate a mental picture of a winter day over six years ago:

Mother was boring us with a chronicle of her every visit and visitor

since we last saw her and unthinkingly boasted of seeing 'her'

Miss Graeme, who had arrived from England on the Mary and

Elizabeth the day after Christmas.   Now that I think of it, Betsy

left the room abruptly, apparently feeling somewhat like a

stepchild.   Hmm.

Billy erased the tableau from his mind and turned around to

face his relation.   "Good God," he said, dropping the newspaper,

"has anyone ever told you how much you resemble my father when

you're wearing spectacles?"

"How do you think I got Mother's blessing?   It was my

one unobjectionable trait."

Unable to help himself, Billy reeled back, laughing loudly.

He loved humor in a man!

Richard's smile, the responsive reflex of a telling blow,

quickly faded when his gaze fixed once more on the document in

his hand.   Noting this, Billy ventured to inquire, "Are you in need

of some legal advice on some matter?"

Taking a deep breath, Richard thrust the writ into Billy's hands like a process server with a summons, babbling all the while about time and proximity, reasons Father had supplied for giving him Power of Attorney.   "It's duly witnessed," he said, leaning over to point to Billy's cousin Sally's name.

"Oh, I'm sure it's perfectly legal.   Cut-and-dried I believe is the current expression," Billy replied as though in a trance.   He suddenly felt sick at heart, empty of spirit and totally shocked by his father's unthinkable action.   "And precisely what financial duties of my Father's am I to relinquish to you?" he asked, straightening to his full height as he awaited the next hit.

"Father wants me to take over the collection of all his outstanding debts in America."

"All of them?"

"All except yours, of course."

He clenched his fist but stopped short of punching Richard in the nose.   Needing to see it with his own eyes, he held it to the light to read the fine print.   There it was in black and white: '...empowers Deborah Franklin and Richard Bache to request and receive payment of all debts due me in America, except those owed me by William Franklin....'   One-handed, he crumpled the

Power into a wad, dropped it at Bache's feet and left, walking

briskly toward the river to lick his wounds in solitude.   His

private business was now a matter of public record.

Late that same evening, unable to unwind, Billy sat in his

Windsor chair holding Betsy in his arms before a hypnotic fire that

glowed from the recesses of the Franklin stove.

"Be glad you're out from under it," Betsy pointed out,

trying to coddle her husband into better spirits.   "Just think.

Settling Papa's lien against the Parker estate is in Richard's lap

now.   Tell me you're not pleased about that."

"You bet I am.   God, how I hated hounding that poor

widow for money, infirm as she is.   Don't get me wrong.   Being

replaced as Papa's fiduciary is no skin off my nose, but the thing

that galls me is why, after all these years, he suddenly finds it

necessary to hedge his bet and put into a legal document the fact

that I owe him money."

"Retaliation."

"For what?"

"For clipping his wings."

"By George, I never thought of that!"   Billy unfolded his legs so swiftly that he nearly dumped Betsy on the floor. "Whoops," he apologized, righting her.   "You may very well have struck on the reason for Papa's discontent," he pondered, giving her a bear hug.

"It certainly adds up: Your assembly appoints Papa agent for New Jersey.   Coincidentally, the ministry resolves that the appointment of said agent must be the concurrent act of the whole legislature AND the governor."

"Which goes against Papa's republican grain."

"Exactly.   What did he write and gripe about?   He complained that 'an agent under the government's thumb was relatively useless and that the Resolution would put an end to agencies altogether'.   You remember how belligerent he was."

"He got on his high horse and said, 'I am sure I should not like to be an Agent in such a suspicious situation, and shall therefore decline serving under every such appointment'."

"Well, has he declined?"

"Not to my knowledge.   It seems he's pulled in his horns,

because he continues to earn his pay."

"Just the same, having his son pitted against him in a duel over fundamental political principles, a contest he was bound to lose, must have been a bitter pill for Papa to swallow."

"I know the feeling."   Billy frowned, causing deep creases to form across his broad brow.   The biting exposé underlying the formality of the bland Power of Attorney emerged to gnaw at him anew.

"Forgive me, my darling.   I didn't mean to side with Papa."   She held him close, kissing him until the scowl vanished and the hurt look disappeared from his eyes.   "Come now," she coaxed.   "Stop brooding.   You did what you had to do."

"I tried to make light of the Resolution.   I wrote and told him that 'it really (made) no kind of Difference, and yet (would) satisfy the M(inistr)y as it (would) appear to be a point gained'."

Betsy placed her finger across his lips.   "The case is closed, counselor," she said in a hushed voice.   "Maybe retaliation wasn't Papa's motive after all.   You know as well as I that your father is a whiz at recruiting people to do his bidding, and, besides, you've got your hands full with your own affairs anyhow."

"That I do," Billy murmured, his terse yet cryptic remark and fiendish grin conveying a marked change of mood.   Rising with care, as though he were lifting a delicate china doll, Billy allayed all signs of anger and frustration and carried her up the flight of stairs to the front bedroom.

AN ILL WIND

Chapter XIX

New York City
July 28, 1773

The Franklins looked on their trip to New York as a cure-all

for both their physical as well as their financial ills.   Nearing

insolvency, Billy was forced to make a painful decision, rent his

Strawberry Hill Farm or lose it.   As it turned out, within a week

they succeeded on both counts.   They felt better than they had in

months, and, lo and behold, the son-in-law of their host, Governor

Tryon, offered to lease Franklin Park.

It was no wonder, then, that Billy's step was light as he left

the mansion house at Fort George on his way to Fraunces Tavern,

his heels clicking like castanets on the clean pavement in concert

with the solo performed nightly by the horde of bull frogs croaking along the river's edge.   The songs of the orioles, kingbirds, wrens

and robins that nested in the water beeches and flowering locusts

lining the well-lit streets were stilled by nightfall.

Sharp, cymbal like clashes of laughter descending from the

rooftop of a three-story brick house across the street where a

family sat cooling off and chitchatting on the balcony drew Billy's

attention and shifted his thoughts from financial to family matters.

The idea of Betsy living so close to New York once they

moved to the proprietors' house in Perth Amboy made him smile.

At least her wish would come true.   My wife will be in her glory,

he mused, and by the same token, Temple would probably enjoy

East Jersey, too.   I think I shall send for him.   It's time he

assumed his rightful place as my son.   He can sail with Papa

when he returns in the spring.

Over the years, Ben and Billy continuously haggled over

Temple's education, the elder Franklin favoring Elphinstone, a

reasonably-priced school and the younger Franklin partial to Eton,

Oxford and, ultimately, a law degree from the Inns of Court, his

alma mater.   In the end, it was a case of either put up or shut up,

so Temple was enrolled at Elphinstone as a boarding student, leaving to spend summers and holidays with his grandfather at Craven Street when he was abroad.

There, Billy exclaimed mutely, immensely pleased with himself for taking the initiative to retrieve his estranged 13-year-old. No more excuses. No more procrastination. He pledged on his sacred honor that the minute they returned home from Albany, the final and, hopefully, the most profitable leg of the journey, that he would write Papa and Straney and have them book Temple's passage.

Billy's optimism soared, permitting him to fabricate a dream. In it, he pictured Temple attending nearby King's College, Anglican-oriented and highly Tory. Benjamin, he imagined, would have something more conservative in mind, the Philadelphia Academy, for instance, where the boy would be at his beck and call. To override his father's preference, Billy needed money of windfall proportions. Although approval of Vandalia was imminent now that the stumbling block was removed (Hillsborough had resigned), Benjamin cautioned that '(they) had not yet killed the bear'. Once they had, Billy would be sitting pretty, but until then he was obliged to collect his piddling, outstanding debts, hence, the upcoming trek to Albany.   Since

Croghan defaulted on the Burlington Company loan, Billy, as the

sole backer of the folly, had been forced to buy out several

disgruntled investors' interests.   As a last resort, he advised

Croghan that he was at the end of his rope, that he was foreclosing

on the property he had put up as collateral for the loan and would

personally oversee its liquidation.

In the distance a steeple bell clanged the hour of nine.

Not wanting to keep his chief justice waiting, Billy quickened his

gait.   For the first time, he realized how burdensome the secret of

his paternity was, because the mere thought of being free of it

caused him to feel weightless and high-spirited.   Finally, the

disparate pieces of his personal life were falling neatly into place.

One ticklish issue remained, however, a minor loose end that Billy

chose to brush aside in his present mood.   How would he tell his

wife about his English-born, teenage son?

He passed the last row of unnumbered shops: the Sign of

the Mortar and Pestle, the Sign of the Table and the Sign of the

Spoon, without a glimpse inside.   Although the governor had

acquired an insatiable appetite for the imperial, surprisingly the silversmith's window would have interested him least, had he time to browse, because at his behest, Benjamin had recently shipped him a superbly-crafted, silver tea urn from England. When he found he needed twenty mahogany chairs for his spacious dining room, however, his financial condition was so pathetic that he condescended to commission a local artisan to make them, feeling the sacrifice would please his creditor.

Billy arrived at the corner of Broad and Pearl perspiring and panting a bit but on time. The tavern door gaped open, giving the trepid passerby a sampling of Fraunces, the most popular public house in the city. A draft of steamy air carrying noise, smoke and the rank smell of stale beer escaped but quickly neutralized when mixed with the fragrant, locust-scented air outside. Before he entered, Billy filled his lungs and held his breath, much as one would to frequent an outhouse. Although his recent ailment was happily behind him, disagreeable odors still offended his weak stomach. On that account and because he was anxious to bare his long-kept secret to Betsy before he lost his nerve, he decided the meeting would be short and sweet.

Frederick Smyth waved to the governor from a corner table

where he sat talking with the Colden boys, Alexander and David. Acknowledging him with a nod, Billy proceeded to nudge his way through the packed house, noticing as he progressed that his appearance sparked an uncommon amount of interest.   The clamor subsided, diminishing to a low rumble as here and there heads huddled together to whisper, a rudeness Billy found repugnant under any circumstance.

One thing is certain, he thought, bewildered but trying not to show it.   They know something that I don't but should.   A couple of possibilities crossed his mind: First, perhaps his 'little bark' had run aground during his absence from the helm.   He was aware that his assembly was balking at footing the bill for the British troops stationed in his province, and, of course, it was the royal governor's job to provide for them.   That's probably it, he reasoned.   On second thought, perhaps Betsy Graeme has made another spectacle of herself over me.   No, that is definitely out of the question, since she has recently married an Englishman named Henry Hugh Ferguson, a hapless man, in my estimation, nine years her junior.

Before he could speculate further, Billy felt someone grab

his arm.   He jerked it free before he realized that it was Frederick, who had come warily to his rescue.   "My carriage is outside," he said gravely.   "We can talk there."

They did not exchange words again until the coach was underway.   "What was that all about?"   Billy took out his handkerchief and wiped the beads of perspiration from his forehead.

"A rumor, nothing more.   Don't take it personally.   It's your office that evokes the distrust and uncertainty."

"What sort of gossip would arouse such mixed emotions? Compassion.   Contempt.   I read degrees of both extremes in their faces!   And the allegation?   Just what the hell is going on? Surely you know."

"Yes.   The armed schooner, the Gaspée, was shadowing a British warship in Narragansett Bay, its captain's duty being to enforce the navigation laws by searching vessels for illegal imports or exports.

"Ah, yes, the Gaspée.   Give me the details," Billy said, suddenly remembering the reason for their meeting.

"Well, on the night in question, the schooner, an armed

British customs revenue vessel was shadowing the British warship
Hannah, but the sloop ran aground seven miles out from
Providence.   The crew went ashore, their story was overheard by
an agitation movement, a group of men called the Committee of
Correspondence.   They went out, captured the crew and set the
vessel on fire, which soon exploded and sank."

"Did you apprehend the culprits?"

"The British formed a commission to investigate the
incident and offered a £500 reward, but no one would talk.   My
report is disappointing, I'm afraid.   We found nary a trace of the
devils," he exclaimed, accenting every word.   The rebellious lot
was to be shipped to England for trial, a provocative course of
action to begin with."

"This appears to be retaliation for the decision to pay the
judges of the Massachusetts Superior Court by using British
customs revenue in place of colonial funds.   I read that Sam
Adams was livid."

"No one would cooperate!" he hissed, stiffening with
rage.

"Rebel support is that widespread?"

"Alarmingly so."

"God help us." Billy shuddered, visibly uneasy about this latest turn of events.   "Where will it all end?" he asked, turning his eyes heavenward as a discharge of diffuse heat lightning to the southwest lit up the Common as they passed.

"Look there!" Smyth cried, pointing.   "Another Liberty Pole."

"I see it," Billy replied, squinting.

"Take a good gander, because it will be gone first thing in the morning."

A lone pine, hastily planted, stood like a beacon, a Pharos, a prophetic Jeremian symbol, its warning foolishly unheeded and the movement's adherents mistakenly underestimated by many on both sides of the ocean.

"It's becoming a daily ritual," said Frederick.   Each night the Sons of Liberty heel it in; at sunup, the British soldiers yank it out."

"A duel of wills," Billy sighed, shaking his head.

"A deadlock,"

Another smattering of brightness bathed the surrounding

hills and hollows, this time accompanied by the faint rumble of thunder, which spooked the horse.

"Would you mind taking me to the Fort?" Billy asked, noticing the leaves stirring.   "We're staying with Governor Tryon and his family."

"Not at all." Frederick so instructed his coachman.

For a judge, operating in the backwater province of New Jersey, Smyth was the exception rather than the rule.   Drawing pitiful salaries from the provincial assembly, a disgrace Billy worked vainly to rectify, a private carriage was a status symbol few could afford.   Being a bachelor, therefore, had a distinct advantage, his priorities and responsibilities differing significantly from his wedded counterparts.

An avalanche of thunder rumbled across the starless sky like an echo in a gorge, sparking shafts of lightning that, as in the blinking of an eye, brightened and darkened the countryside at will.   During one such spate, the imposing, equestrian statue of King George III loomed large and lifelike on the Bowling Green.

"Have you seen the monument up close?" Smyth asked. "Remarkable resemblance."

"Quit stalling, Frederick, and give me the lowdown."

"About what?"

"The rumor, for God's sake.   Would you please tell me what I'm supposed to have done!"

"Not you.   Your father."

Billy laughed as though Smyth had just introduced an element of comic relief into a Greek tragedy.   Seeing that his callous outburst disturbed the judge, he apologized and went on to explain.   "Surely you understand that, at times, a man in my father's position cannot avoid censure; it is one of the drawbacks of public service.

"I'm well aware of that, but I still think this could be serious, very serious indeed."   He hesitated.

"Go on," Billy prodded impatiently, competing with the mounting storm.   "What's the latest dirt?"

"Did you read the Hutchinson letters?" he asked in an equally elevated tone.

"You mean the ones printed in the *Massachusetts Spy* last month?"

"The same," Smyth replied.

"I did, but I fail to see what bearing they have on my father."

"Some say he stole them and sent them to the Massachusetts assembly; others say John Temple is responsible."

"Humph!   'Rumor is a pipe(,) Blown by surmises, jealousies, conjectures...'," Billy scoffed, quoting from Shakespeare's King Henry IV.

Not commenting, Smyth continued.   "I spoke to Hutchinson personally.   He's infuriated by the disclosure of his private letters to Thomas Whately, which were written before he was governor, and the consequent maltreatment he's received at the hands of the Bostonians.   It wouldn't surprise me if he returned to England."

"If what you say is true," Billy mumbled, turning white, "whoever engineered this wrongdoing is in hot water for sure."

"A lawsuit is more like it."

The carriage pulled up in front of the mansion, and Billy got out.   "Here," Smyth said, thrusting a note into the governor's hand.   "Read this and burn it, for I have no way of judging whether it is fact or fiction."

Blinding lightning bolts that turned night into day and

booming claps of thunder warned Billy to take cover, but needing a

few minutes of privacy, he risked getting drenched and strode from

the fort to read the message under the first street lamp:

"Hutchinson also told me that an adversary claimed he had

received certain letters from Dr. Franklin advising them to

insist on their Independency!"

"Jesus, Mary and Joseph," Billy muttered, covering his face

with both hands.

Presently, recovering from the initial shock, he began to

walk, keeping the wind at his back, hoping the churning of his

limbs, like the whirling sails of the upland windmills, would

restore the circulation to his numb body and energize his brain.

Ever so slowly, his legal mind began to function.   Logically and

analytically he examined the two counts against his father,

beginning with the Hutchinson letters:

Should correspondence between a public official and a

friend, in this case the chief justice of Massachusetts and an ex-

treasurer of the British government, in which accounts of public

events and controversial issues are discussed be considered private papers?

Damn right it should, Billy blasted inwardly, his ire stemming from the suspicion that his mail to and from Benjamin was being blatantly intercepted, opened and read.

In reaching the above conclusion, Billy overlooked the fact that although it was true that Whately was a private citizen during the interval when the letters were written, Hutchinson had picked a very unpopular shoulder to cry on, since it was he who had drafted the odious Stamp Act.

Secondly, were the letters incendiary, he questioned?   As I recall, they advocated that the governor's salary be paid by the Crown; opposition to nonimportation; protection for customs commissioners and a call for British troops to restore and maintain order.

Naturally, the firebrands find these views atrocious, but I do not see them as particularly heinous, perhaps because they mirror some of my own private, innermost beliefs.

"Wait a minute," Billy exclaimed, stopping in his tracks. "Why am I getting so hot and bothered over groundless rumors? Papa's mentioned none of this in any of his letters to me.   Besides having no access to the late Thomas Whately's possessions, he had no motive. Papa believes in promoting reconciliation not fostering strife. John Temple, on the other hand, a more likely suspect, had the perfect motive. With Hutchinson out of the way, he may have had a shot at the governorship. In any event, he concluded, moving on, to satisfy my curiosity, I shall write Papa before the sloop departs tomorrow and confront him outright.

Billy looked up and saw to his surprise that he'd walked clear back to Fraunces Tavern. Having worked up a sweat, he sat on the steps to take a breather. There wasn't another soul on the porch, a one-story shed roof appendage that ran the entire length of the four-story landmark. Glancing inside, he was equally surprised to see that the place was deserted, its patrons, he imagined, having scurried home like scared rabbits after the first crack of thunder.

The humidity continued to build like a relentless fever in a sick child. Studying the sky, Billy noted that the breeze had shifted and was pushing the clouds offshore, which meant there was no relief in store for the city that night.

Dry as a bone, Billy decided to go in for a nightcap.

"Another teaser," he said to the West Indian proprietor, making small talk.

The owner shrugged his shoulders indifferently, ending the conversation.

Billy got the message.

"What'll ya have?"

"Beer, please."

He tipped a keg, giving Billy the dregs.

"Thanks." Billy guzzled it down without complaint.   Then taking the note, he held it over the opening in the blackened chimney until it caught fire and burned.

The shuffling of many feet and the murmur of men's voices directly overhead aroused Billy's suspicion.   He was almost sure he had discovered a secret meeting place of the outlaw rabble-rousers, the Sons of Liberty.

"Fill it up," he said, wanting to stick around a while.

"Sorry, I'm closed," the owner stated uncivilly, blowing out the lamp.   He walked to the door and held it open for the governor to leave.

Billy dropped money on the bar and left.

'TO ERR IS HUMAN, TO FORGIVE DIVINE'
Alexander Pope

Chapter XX

New York City – Monday, July 29

The following morning Billy delivered the mail to the packet himself.   It would no doubt be well into October before Benjamin's side of the story reached him, but giving little credence to the slanderous rumors after sleeping on them, he decided they were trumped-up charges with no basis in fact and not worth dwelling on.   Indeed, in his letter his father's alleged transgression and the hearsay regarding his radical change of heart took a backseat to questions and concerns about Vandalia, which was the key to his financial independence.   Why wasn't the charter granted in May as Wharton advised it would be, he complained?

As you see, money matters were uppermost in his mind.

His father's asserted misdeeds were secondary.   He was tempted
to try again to enlist Benjamin's help in his quest to have
Parliament pay his salary, but he figured it was no use.   The elder
Franklin had already flatly refused to intercede with Lord
Dartmouth, the new secretary, arguing that it was the sacred right
of the Colonists to provide for a royal governor.   Furthermore,
Benjamin feared it would 'embroil his son with his people' if he
intervened.

Bidding the captain bon voyage, Billy mounted his horse,
whipped him smartly on the behind and galloped off along the East
River.   After putting a couple of furlongs between himself and the
wharf, he drew rein and laughed freely as he pictured the
clandestine tamperer, somewhere between New York and Craven
Street, searching futilely through the mail sacks for a letter in his
typical handwriting.   As a safeguard he took great pleasure in
outfoxing the fox by conspiring with his father to disguise their
handwriting and alter their seals.

Having dealt swiftly and decisively with the unpleasantries
of the past day, Billy's time was now his own to enjoy.   He
spurred his mount and cantered across town to meet Betsy at the

appointed hour in St. Paul's Chapel, a church dear to their hearts,

because it reminded them of St. Martin's-in-the Field, London.

Its fourteen Waterford crystal chandeliers glistened in the

summer sun as they made their way down the center aisle past

pairs of graceful columns whose hollows, Billy had been told, were

filled with solid oak tree trunks to add support to the roof.   At the

front of the nave, the couple genuflected reverently before

proceeding down the north aisle to the canopied pew reserved for

the royal governor of New York.   Kneeling together, they blessed

themselves in the name of the Holy Trinity and presented their

petitions and prayers of thanksgiving:

"Heavenly father," Betsy read, from the Book of Common

Prayer, "you have blessed us with the joy and care of a child.

Bless Temple wherever he may be, keeping him unspotted from

the world.   Strengthen him when he stands.   Comfort him when

discouraged or sorrowful.   Raise him up if he falls, and in his

heart, may thy peace, which passeth all understanding, abide all the

days of his life.   Amen."

"In thy boundless mercy, O Lord, deliver Papa and Temple

safely home to us.   Amen," Billy added.   Then, placing his hand over his wife's, he looked her in the eye and paid homage to her by quoting a passage from Sophocles, feminizing the last word to fit his present state of grace: "'Numberless are the world's wonders, but none more wonderful than woman'."

By the time they reached the narthex, the realization that one day soon she would be the mother of a half-grown schoolboy apparently struck home, and Betsy's composure collapsed. Moved by her tears of joy, Billy gathered her in his arms and rocked her gently until the sobbing ceased.   "Here," he said, taking out his handkerchief, "let me blot your eyes before the rector appears and accuses me of browbeating my beautiful wife."

"Does Sally know?   Deborah?"   Billy shook his head no to both queries.   "Who then?"

"Papa and Straney," he replied, coming clean.   He felt it was neither the time nor the place to divulge that Polly and Mrs. Stevenson also knew, so to avoid further interrogation, he resorted to vanity.   "Hold still," he scolded, tilting her chin but avoiding her eyes.   "Your powder's all streaks."

"Never mind.   It doesn't matter," she replied, brushing his hand aside.   "May I tell Sally?   Please!   She'll be so surprised.

Not more than I was, of course," she mocked him good-naturedly, yet with a tinge of scornful reproach.   "Won't it be wonderful?" she exclaimed.   "Sally and Richard have Benny and baby Will, and we'll have Temple.   All boys.   Isn't that something!"

"William Temple," Billy said, correcting her.

"What shall I buy him?   I must go shopping right away."

"The packet sailed already," Billy parried, thanking God for small favors.

"I'll send it from Philadelphia."

"Why didn't I think of that," he mumbled, tacitly acceding. In a move to duck an expectant invitation to join her, Billy offered to go over to the John Street Theater and purchase their tickets for the *Tempest*.

But a tempest of quite another sort greeted them as they opened the door to the portico.   The air was tainted with the acrid smell of smoke, and it seemed that the entire male population of the city, carrying buckets, brooms or makeshift flails, was pouring into the street, running at full tilt toward a black, ugly pillar rising above the fort.

"My God," Billy cried with solemn dread.   "What's

burning?" he shouted over and over again to the locals but to no avail.

"They say it's the governor's palace," a high-pitched voice answered bashfully.

Billy caught sight of a young negro lad with a scrubbed face and close-cropped hair, a mere slip of a boy, peering around a brownstone quoin.   Billy approached him, and the frightened child shrank in the face of authority, plastering his small frame against the foliated schist of St. Paul's.   Before the governor could show his thanks, the child took off on a run down Fulton Street. Billy turned to Betsy and said, "Go quickly.   Have John take you to the Brannon tea garden.   I'll meet you there as soon as I can."

"Be careful, my darling."

Billy could tell by the massive belches of black smoke and flames shooting high above the fort that it was a fire of major proportions but was totally unprepared for the drama that was unfolding as he muscled his way to the forefront.   The Tryon's nine-year-old daughter, Margaret, was trapped inside.   She and her faithful nursemaid, Luci, clung together, waiting for someone to rescue them from an upstairs window.   The throng gasped as

the greedy blaze ate through the roof, and from the blackened hole,

a flaming torch spewed upward like a fountain.   Tongues of fire

shot from every crevice and crack, licking the dry exterior, which

burned like tinder.   Time and time again, the firemen tried to

ladder the wall but were forced back by blistering heat and dense

smoke.

At center stage, Billy picked out the Tryons, Margaret and

William, pressed together to steady one another.   To his relief,

they appeared unharmed but were suffering immeasurable mental

anguish, he imagined, as they looked on helplessly as their child, a

son having died in infancy, faced mortal danger.

Suddenly, Governor Tryon broke away from his wife and

began to take charge, evidently knowing there wasn't a minute to

lose.   Scavenging through a pile of household articles that had

been hastily salvaged, he found a large panel of heavy damask.

Billy, along with a flock of others, ran out to take hold of the jury-

rig.

"Jump!" the father shouted, his voice pleading.

Terror-stricken, the child turned away, hiding her face in

Luci's skirts.

Then, despite the dousing it received by the volunteers manning the city's three fire trucks, a sizable portion of the roof collapsed, spewing ashes and sparks from here to kingdom come. The spectators scattered and scrambled to safer ground, but the mother ran forward, defying the manly warnings to keep back. She rushed to the net and ordered Luci to pick Margaret up and drop her out of the window. Obeying, the courageous woman did as she was told before saving herself.

The onlookers clapped and cheered, openly thankful that human tragedy had been averted. For a moment, Billy's legs felt like two cordwood sticks with dry rot, but he soon recovered and bolted into action. Seeing that the Tryons and Luci were safely away from the conflagration, he offered to fetch their carriage from the stable.

On his way through the grounds, he passed a mound of familiar objects smoldering on the grass and recoiled: the governor's walnut tree writing desk, Mrs. Tryon's rosewood writing table, the mahogany chairs with horsehair seats, the elaborate centerpiece that Betsy so admired, and books, volumes of

Rapin's "History of England," the works of Jonathan Swift and Locke's essays, to name only a few.   Moving on quickly he nearly choked when he encountered the charred remains of Governor Tryon's treasured portraits of King William and Queen Anne, King George I and II and King George III and Queen Charlotte, thinking how wretched he would feel if his own fine collection of personal belongings went up in smoke.

Tearing off one of his shirtsleeves, he blindfolded the panic-stricken horse before he attempted to attach the traces to the whiffletree, talking softly and calmly to the animal all the while.

Viewing the ruins and assessing the damage, Billy considered it a stroke of luck that he and Betsy had sent the bulk of their baggage on ahead to Albany the day before.

A bit smudgy but presentable, Billy met Betsy at the Brannon's tea garden as arranged.   It was a beautiful out-of-the-way spot located in view of Hudson's River on the west side of the island.   He found the coolness and quiet a welcome relief to the inferno and hubbub at Fort George.

The incredible story Billy recounted was just as dramatic at second hand.   "What a miracle no one was hurt," Betsy

exclaimed, fanning herself furiously.   "Do they have any idea

what caused the blaze?"

"From all indications, it started in the council meeting

room.   I spoke briefly with Governor Tryon who said that when

the carpenters remodeled the fireplace recently, they extended the

paneling down slightly over the firebox, far enough, he surmises,

for a spark to have lodged behind it."

"But who would light a fire in this weather?"

"After yesterday's meeting, rubbish was burned.   The

spark probably smoldered all night and ignited the paneling

sometime this morning.   By the time it was discovered, it had

burned up through the partition to the second floor."

"How dreadful!   Where are the Tryons now?   Is there

anything we can do to help?"

"They've gone to the Colden's home on Long Island.

We've been invited to stay there also."

"Wouldn't that be imposing?"

"Yes, I suppose so, yet I did want to conclude my state

business with the governor before leaving.   In all candor, however, I hardly think our boundary dispute dire enough to trouble the poor man about during such a trying time."

"I was under the impression that the dispute was settled, in New York's favor, I might add."

"You're right, my dear.   That issue is pretty much cut-and-dried, but, remember, Staten Island is still up for grabs. Nevertheless, the assembly is still smarting over our loss of that big chunk of land across our northern border to the New Yorkers so is, understandably, hesitant about engaging in another territorial squabble on the heels of this latest defeat.   Besides, as I said, Governor Tryon has his hands full at the moment, and I'm sure any loose ends we need to iron out can be done by mail."

"That's why I love you so, my darling.   You are so compassionate," she said, squeezing his hand.   "Now," she added, finishing her tea, "we'd better compile a list of the things we lost in the fire and decide where we are going to stay tonight.   What about the King's Arms on Crown Street?   I think that's the nicest, don't you?"

"By all means, my sweet," Billy replied, keeping the sudden discomfort of a sour stomach to himself.

October 12, 1774.   NUMB. 2590.

The PENNSYLVANIA GAZETTE.

Containing the Freſheſt Ad-   vices, Foreign and Domeſtic.

merchandize of them, or tranſact any buſineſs for them, nor after them to try ſell any for us, but will wholly abſtain from them, and leave them to the confiſcation of peddling; and contemplating the ruinous moments of Britiſh induſtry and American ſlavery, which they would inevitably aim to to themſelves for ſo baſe and wicked purpoſes; and ſhall conſider in the free light, and treat in a like manner, every Perſon that ſhall purchaſe any ſuch goods of them, or do buſineſs for them, or employ them in their buſineſs.

Reſolved, That the committee of correſpondence for the ſeveral towns we repreſent, be deſired to make diligent enquiry after the perſons who have ordered goods as aforeſaid, and inform the next county an colony meeting

Suſſex County, Repreſentatives, Thomas Robinſon, John Clowes, Boaz Manlove, Benjamin Burton, David Hall, James Rench, *Sheriffs,* Dorman Loſſard, Rhoads Shankland, *Coroners,* Littleton Townſend, Peter White.

On friday next the GENERAL ASSEMBLY of this Province meets here.

We have authority to aſſure the Public, that the reports which have been circulated reſpecting a neighbouring Governor having wrote to the Miniſtry, recommending certain hoſtile meaſures againſt America, are without any juſt foundation.

We hear that the Univerſity of Edinburgh have conferred the degree of DOCTOR OF DIVINITY upon the Rev. Mr. JOHN EWING, of this city.

B. FRANKLIN'S CREED ON NEGLECT:

'…for want of a nail the shoe was lost;
for want of a shoe the horse was lost;
for want of a horse the rider was lost.'

Poor Richard's Almanac

Chapter XXI

Friday, October 7, 1774

To Billy, the short ride from Philadelphia to Twickenham seemed endless today, probably because it was no social call, no christening, no detour to pick up his mail, no casual visit to relax in a front porch rocker and chew the fat with Tho.   Instead, Billy was here to attend his own funeral, his former friend having arranged an inquisition, replete with witnesses, two for each side. The purpose was to delve into published charges, an excerpt quoted word for word from a private letter to Straney, dated May 21, 1774, wherein Billy revealed his true colors, that Governor William Franklin was aligning himself with the British government.

In all fairness, Strachan no doubt felt he was doing the governor a favor by publishing it, thereby distancing him from his contentious father, who was mired in conflict in London.

As the carriage rumbled along, Billy's seconds, Richard Bache and long-time family friend, Captain Nathaniel Falconer, sat opposite him in stony silence, withdrawn and unsociable, but Billy didn't mind; he was too busy soul-searching.

Rolling back time, he recalled the revolutionary events of the past year in sequence and reexamined his own posture regarding them, beginning with the day he received the shocking letter from his father, confessing that he was guilty of acquiring and transmitting the notorious Hutchinson letters.

Thank God Papa owned up to it in time to prevent a second duel between JohnTemple and the late Thomas Whately's brother, William, because instead of nursing a sword wound, Whately might be pushing up daisies about now.   Let me take a good look at Papa's reasoning for exposing the letters.   Was he justified? According to his open statement published in *The London Chronicle* last Christmas, he maintained that the letters, written by public officers to persons in public station, on public affairs, and intended to procure public measures', tended to widen the breach between England and her colonies.

That's not how I see it.   As a man of law, I, like Hutchinson, am bound to guard the English constitution, 'to watch, to check, and to avert every dangerous innovation'.   The man was merely doing his civic duty by reporting the illegal smuggling, the lawlessness, the turmoil and the social upheaval.   I, in a way, am doing the same thing by secretly relaying to Lord Dartmouth accounts of the proceedings of the illicit Continental Congress, which has been sitting at Carpenter's Hall in Philadelphia since the fifth of September.   To Papa's way of thinking, my source, Joseph Galloway, would be considered a mole and I a traitor.

It seemed that Ben and Billy agreed on nothing relative to the Hutchinson letters except motive: They both championed reconciliation as the only salvation.   Benjamin risked everything by staking his job, his honor and his good name on one last-ditch effort to throw the blame for the coercive measures imposed on Boston from the Ministry to Hutchinson, a native-born, full-blooded American.   He gambled '...that when they saw the measures they complained of took their rise in a great degree from the representations and recommendations of their own countrymen, their resentment against Britain on account of those measures might abate...'.

Actually, the direct opposite occurred. It backfired. Contrary to his expectations, Benjamin was the devil in British eyes, not the good Samaritan - the incendiary, the warmonger, not the peacemaker.

On January 29 before a packed house, the Privy Council had convened at the Cockpit, so named in the days of Henry VIII when it was used for cockfighting, to hear the petition presented by Dr. Franklin as agent for the Massachusetts Assembly to remove Hutchinson from office in order to restore order and harmony. To begin with, neither the Chairman, Lord Gower, nor the thirty-five councilors was in a particularly conciliatory frame of mind after learning the news just in of the Bostonians' latest mischief, that of turning the waters of Boston Harbor into tea!

The silver-tongued Alexander Wedderburn, solicitor general to the King, defended Hutchinson, washing him whiter than snow, but in the process, shot Benjamin's petition all to hell. Then with unprecedented latitude, unchecked by the bench, he improperly turned his wrath on Dr. Franklin personally, reducing the Massachusetts Bay courier to a wily, dishonest, designing, seditious caballer.

Billy winced, heartsick that his father, who had given so many years of his life to the cause of unity, ended up as the scapegoat for the Sons of Liberty, a band of ruffians in Billy's judgment.

Impropriety prevented Benjamin from defending himself. A concurrent law suit, filed in Chancery Court by William Whately, charging him with purloining his brother's letters was pending. Billy learned from one source 'that his father stood silently before his peers, taking blow after blow from Wedderburn, his hands clasped loosely behind his back'. Not surprisingly, the Massachusetts petition was dismissed for lack of evidence.

Even though Billy sided with Hutchinson in this sticky mess, deploring his father's shameful, political misdeed, the blood tie that bound them was as constant as ever. His gut knotted as he remembered the terse, unemotional, bitter letter his father wrote him only four days after his humiliating ordeal. He knew it by heart:

'...my Office of Deputy-Postmaster is taken from me. As there is no Prospect of your being ever promoted to a better Government, and That you hold has never defrayed its Expenses, I wish you were well settled in your Farm ...You will hear from others the Treatment I have received. I leave you to your own Reflections and determinations upon it...'

Hardheaded but not hardhearted, Billy fought back the convulsive sobs that strained for utterance. His two companions, who had dozed off miles back, stirred, changed positions and resumed their napping.

Supposing he would get no sympathy from 'a thorough government man', the label Benjamin had given Billy the previous autumn when they disagreed over the elder Franklin's radical view that the King and the provincial assemblies and not the King and Parliament should legislate for the colonies, Benjamin punished his son by keeping him in the dark regarding the details of the ghastly spectacle at the Cockpit.

As a consequence, Billy had to scrounge for information like a quidnunc, extracting bits and pieces from outsiders until on April 20th a fuller account appeared in *The Pennsylvania Gazette*.

Reading it tore him apart. Deservedly or not, seeing his father's character assassinated pained him greatly, but because he was legal-minded, what worried him even more was the upcoming trial. If Benjamin was convicted of theft, he would most assuredly land in Newgate prison! God forbid, he silently prayed. The thought was so horrid that he nearly cried out in mental anguish.

Having more ground to cover and less time to contemplate, he moved on to another issue: 'Papa's awareness of the situation here is derived from a nearsighted perspective, mine through a magnifying glass. The powerful winds of discord I see, hear and feel somehow diminish in the transmission'.

Papa's sentiment is that if we all hang together and not consume British goods, we will bring the Ministry to its knees by strangulation. Outbullied, the Ministry will sheepishly back down and remove the obnoxious blockade from the Boston Port. I find this belief naive and this course precipitous!

As I see it, tea is the key to unblocking the harbor. The Bostonians ought first to do justice before they ask it of others by making satisfaction to the East India Company for the 342 chests they wantonly destroyed that night. Papa was so astounded by the imprudent act that he agreed with me at first; in fact, he advised voluntary reparation but quickly changed his tune when England returned an equal injury and closed the port.

Papa's indignant about it and berates me for seeing everything through government eyes, but I know which side my bread is buttered on and act accordingly.   Look where I'd be now if I followed his line of thinking.   I'd be in the quicksand along with him!   Let me think.   What did Papa say in *Poor Richard?* 'He may well win the race that runs by himself'.   That was it.

John slowed the team to a trot as he veered into the long driveway leading to the Wharton house.   It didn't look the same with Sue gone.   The baby, Franklin, was dead, too, died of the bloody flux long before he was weaned.   The epidemic claimed six-year-old Joseph as well.   Billy glanced up at the sidehill. Tears stung his eyes as he recalled the sunny August day he wept with his friends beside the two small graves.

Richard and Nathaniel stretched and yawned, ending their awkward silence.   "First off," his brother-in-law snapped, "let Wharton produce the evidence or we turn around and walk out."

"I intend to," Billy replied, gritting his teeth.   He couldn't elaborate, because he and Richard were worrying about two different matters.   It was bad enough that his pro-government stance was out in the open but disastrous if his London friend had double-crossed him and leaked to the press any of his confidential criticisms of the Ministry.   There was probably no man more loyal to his station or more unswerving from his duty than William Franklin, and he assured the Ministry of this fact more than once, but on the day in question, May 21, frustrated by Parliament's continual inaction and major misconception of the seriousness of the American crisis, he let the body politic have it.

As the colonies drifted closer and closer to war, Billy had not sat idly by twiddling his thumbs, however.   Powerless to stop the mass county meetings in his province aimed at the selection of deputies to the Continental Congress in Philadelphia, he wielded what influence he had with Dartmouth by suggesting that a Congress be authorized by His Majesty to supplant the illegal one then being formed.   It should consist of the governors, provincial council and assembly representatives, and a few commissioners from Great Britain.   To drive his point home, he reminded the Earl that 'There (had) been, indeed, an Instance of Commissioners being sent over to settle Matters of far less Importance to the

British Interest than those now agitated, which (are), perhaps,

worthy of more Attention and Consideration than any Thing that

(has) ever before concerned Great Britain'.

But Billy's recommendation fell on deaf ears, and his

prophetic warning was totally ignored.   As things stood, it was a

case of the tail wagging the dog.

The coach stopped before the stone house, and the men

alighted according to rank.   Leaving the autumnal warmth and

splendor of Indian summer behind, they entered the chilly foyer at

the maid's bidding and followed her to the library where Billy's

three adversaries awaited.

Since introductions were unnecessary and cordialities and

formalities unfitting, Tho wasted no time but lit into Billy tooth

and nail.   "'You certainly must be lost to every principle which

(your) aged and honoured father has been for years supporting',"

he shouted, his voice cracking with disappointment and anger.

Playing it close to the chest until he knew the extent of the

damage, Billy winced but held his tongue while Richard demanded

to see the letter.   It was quickly produced and read by William

West.

Billy could feel everyone's eyes upon him.   He grimaced at the outset as the brand of 'Tory' was applied, as the umbilical connection to his beloved father was irreparably severed, but at the finish, satisfied that Straney had not stabbed him in the back by revealing anything derogatory about the Ministry, he showed his concealed relief with a faint smile.   His tacit reaction left no doubt in anyone's mind exactly where he stood.   His allegiance was apparent.

Infuriated, Tho lambasted him again, pointing out the error of his ways.

"You accuse me of 'betraying the place of (my) Nativity, yet you, my friend, think nothing of being disloyal to me by (making) such a letter public without first advising (me) of its contents'," Billy argued, fighting back.

"Did your father consult Hutchinson?"

"Our circumstances are different.   Papa is an agent."

"'If the liberties of America (are) to be injured it (is) no matter whether Hutchinson or (you do) it, but whoever (does) it ought to be known'."

Billy's shoulders slumped with despair. "Please give the children my love," he said to Tho with automatic politeness. He turned on his heel and stormed out of the house. Brushing the rocker as he passed, he intentionally set it in motion without missing a stride. He flung open the gate and strode by his own carriage and down the drive, feeling it would be a waste of time at this juncture to defend himself or, for that matter, to belabor conciliation further, to cite its numerous benefits and obvious advantages, because with the defeat of Galloway's Plan of Union by the slim margin of 6-5 at Carpenter's Hall on September 28[th,] he would only be flogging a dead horse. Framing a constitution, the majority argued, was out of their jurisdiction, beyond their delegated authority; obtaining redress of Colonial grievances by peaceful means was their sole mandate.

Billy respected the legitimacy of the latter, fundamental point. It was not only the prerogative of those who conceived themselves aggrieved to petition the King but 'a Duty they owe(d) themselves, their Country, and their Posterity'. What he objected to, what he could not condone in his present capacity, was their mode of proceeding, subverting the English Constitution by ganging up on the Mother Country and piping their complaints

through the extralegal Congress now sitting in Philadelphia.

What he feared was reprisal from abroad.   The King would not

spare the rod and spoil the child.   Of this he was certain.

"For Lord's sake, Billy, 'restore (your) good name by

publishing a certified copy of (your) letter in the papers of this

city'," Tho yelled after him, the plea brought on by an apparent,

sudden pang of remorse.

"Go to hell!" he replied under his breath and kept booking.

Exiting close behind, Bache and Falconer stopped long

enough to steady the rocker, then boarded the carriage hastily.

Without needing to be told, John kept a respectable distance

between the carriage and the governor.

Flushed and perspiring, Billy tore off his coat and pitched

it.   His head was throbbing, his throat parched, but he needed to

walk off his anger, his disillusionment, his heartbreak.   "The lot

of them can't see further than their noses," he snarled.   "Have they

all gone mad?   They decry compromise, denounce give-and-take

and, by fighting fire with fire, are creating a dangerous deadlock,

leaving no room for negotiation.   Mark my word, those hotheads are going to plunge us headlong into a bloody war!   And I, mind

you, I, who spent half my summer slaving with Galloway to

hammer out a mutually acceptable Plan of Union, have 'injured the

liberties of America'.   The audacity!"

Little by little, Billy mellowed out, lapsing momentarily

into the indulgent fantasy of woolgathering.   Maybe if Papa had

been here to help us frame a plan of accommodation, to plead our

case, they would have listened to reason, he lamented.   He was all

for it.   Galloway showed me his letter: 'I wish most sincerely

with you that a Constitution was formed and settled for America',

he said, 'that we might know what we are and what we have, what

our Rights and what our Duties, in the Judgment of this Country as

well as in our own.   Till such a Constitution is settled, different

Sentiments, will ever occasion Misunderstandings'.   We had his

blessing but needed his presence.

By association, an image of his mother flashed before his

eyes, old, feeble, heartsick and lonely, brought on by years of

spousal neglect.   Billy's personal and global cares vanished as he

turned his thoughts to Deborah's plight.   Her rapid decline worries

me, especially since she told me she never expects to see Papa unless he returns this winter.   Is disappointment merely preying

on her spirits, or does she really have a premonition of dying?   I

must tell Bache to notify me at once if there is any dire change in

her condition.   What on earth is keeping Papa abroad anyhow?

There, he is censured and disgraced; here, he is loved and revered.

On October 12th, 1774, *The Pennsylvania Gazette* carried a

notice which read: 'We have authority to assure the Public, that

the reports which have been circulated respecting a neighboring

Governor having wrote to the Ministry, recommending certain

hostile measures against America, are without any just foundation'.

Philadelphia – The Front Bedroom
Saturday, December 24th

Billy got up, put on a robe and went to stoke the fire and

add some kindling.   A skim of ice covered the water in the

washbasin, so he placed the bowl beside the hearth to thaw while

he wrote the letter.   This was the first opportunity he'd had to

fulfill his sad duty, to tell his Papa the unpleasant news of

Deborah's death, what with the steady stream of callers since they

laid her to rest in Christ Church burial ground on Thursday

afternoon.

He was glad Betsy had stayed in Perth Amboy, because a pervasive somberness filled the house, which not even Sally's lively youngsters nor the advent of Christmas could expunge. Outside, the world was sunny and bright, whitewashed by the severe snowstorm that had nearly kept him from reaching Philadelphia in time for the funeral.

Knowing full well that it was his responsibility and not Bache's to convey the dreadful news to Benjamin, he still procrastinated a while longer, allowing himself to be distracted from the blank sheet of paper before him while he watched a pair of titmice scrapping over a piece of suet. Then, from out of nowhere, a thievish old black crow swooped down and put an end to the squabble.

Finally, he picked up the quill, dipped it in the inkstand and began the difficult and unpleasant task of dispensing blame and censuring his father for his repeated postponements.

After conveying the pertinent details, Billy brought pressure to bear, intimating that Benjamin's absence contributed to his mother's decline. He went on to substantiate a case for his immediate return: his fall from grace, the danger he was in because of his political misconduct, his advanced age and the rigor of another sea voyage.   Not letting up, he brought up the Continental Congress, how Benjamin may have been the great conciliator, had he been present.

Letting his anguish flow, he concluded: 'However mad you may think the Measures of the Ministry are, yet I trust you have Candor enough to acknowledge that we are no ways behind hand with them in Instances of Madness on this Side (of) the water.   However, it is a disagreeable Subject, and I'll drop it'.

Throwing down the pen, he went to wash his face.   "Is there no middle ground?" he moaned, searching the mirror.   "May God help us!"

DIVIDE AND CONQUER

Chapter XXII

Proprietary House, Perth Amboy
Monday, April 24, 1775

Billy paced back and forth, from one end of the green-wallpapered study to the other, clutching an olive branch in his right hand and a quiver of arrows in his left.   "That fool, Gage!" he grumbled, slapping the sickening message just in from Massachusetts Bay down hard on his desk.   "Clashing with the Colonial militia at Lexington and Concord!   Inflicting casualties! Oh, what a blunder!" he moaned.   "AND what lousy timing! Here's exactly what we've been waiting and praying for, a peace proposal from Whitehall, but I'm afraid it has arrived too late." His right arm dropped and hung limply at his side.

"What is it?   What's happened?" Betsy cried appearing in

the doorway.   Her face was ghostly white, her voice shaky and

her legs unsteady.

Billy thrust Prime Minister North's communique in the

direction of his desk and ran to catch his wife before she collapsed

in a heap on the floor.   "You shouldn't be out of bed yet; you're

not strong enough."

"Please don't take me back upstairs.   I need to be where I

can see you."   Her frail arms knotted about his neck and her

hollow eyes pleaded.

Taking pity, Billy rang for a servant and carried her

through the palatial center hall and into the cheerful yellow

drawing room, neither one appreciating the mural of the Passayak

and Cohoes Falls, 'an innovational depiction resembling an

imitation copperplate, the effect having been produced by applying

the design in black and white on buff-painted walls'.   "Promise

me you'll stay put on the settee and let Nona wait on you hand and

foot or up to bed you go," he said with fake sternness as he

propped her up against the silk damask pillows to ease her

breathing.

"So here you is!" Nona exclaimed, hustling in with her tray

of medicinal hodge-podge and wide assortment of brandies.   "I's

been scouring every nook and cranny for you, Missy."   Taking

note of the use of the pet name, a habit Nona had recently

developed whenever Betsy took sick, the Franklins let her fuss and

fret to her heart's content.   "I told you this morning you wasn't

ready to come downstairs.   How did you get down here anyway

without breaking your neck as weak as you is?"   She bustled

about shutting windows, fluffing pillows and hauling out a

coverlet.   "What she needs is a good spring tonic of sulphur and

molasses, Governor Franklin."

At this point Betsy broke silence and protested, making a

face like a child who is gearing up for a spoonful of cod liver oil.

"You're an old fogy, Nona," she teased, laughing faintly.

"I may be an old stick-in-the-mud, but I's been carin' for

folks since you was kneehigh to a grasshopper.   Don't you forget

that."

"I think an ounce of peach brandy might do the trick," Billy

said softly but firmly, coming to his wife's rescue.

"Yessir," she replied, mumbling under her breath.

At that moment, Margaret, the fastidious English overseer

Billy imported in '66, arrived empty-handed and inquired, "You rang?"

"Better late than never," Nona grumbled as she tilted her large frame forward to serve the brandy.

Standing straight as a flagpole, with collar and cuffs as stiff as a cleric's, Margaret nearly swallowed her tonsils when she saw Nona's red-and-white-check apron and matching bandana.   The fabric was a spitting image of the new dining parlor curtains.

Seeing the scowl on Margaret's face, Billy flashed a reproachful glance and dismissed them both.

"Please open a window," Betsy said, the color slowly returning to her cheeks.   "I want to smell the lilacs."

"Nona just shut them so you wouldn't be in a draft.   Just keep the coverlet up over your chest or she'll be fuming again," Billy replied as he granted her request.

"Now, my darling," she said, motioning for him to come and sit beside her, "tell me what provoked you so."

Friday, May 10, 1775
9:30 a.m.

In the weeks that followed, tensions mounted as the provinces prepared to defend themselves against any eventuality. Men marched at the slightest rumor of provocation, and those connected with government lived in constant fear of reprisals since the skirmish at Lexington and Concord.

This particular day began as a very ordinary one at Proprietary House. Billy sat at his desk working on the critical speech he would deliver at the upcoming assembly meeting he had called for the fifteenth in Burlington. Betsy was upstairs in the blue room with Margaret planning her next social function, and the remaining servants were busy with their daily, routine chores.

All of a sudden, faintly at first, Billy heard something ominous. He put down his pen and went to the open window. The foreboding sound increased, the familiar, unmistakable cadent beat of drums and the penetrating, high-pitched sound of fifes. His blood ran cold as he thought of the possible consequences. Could they be coming for me, he wondered? "I have that idiot Gage to thank for this," he growled. Going quickly back to his desk, he scribbled a note, summoned John and ordered him to ride bareback to Chief Justice Smyth's house and wait for a reply.

"Billy, where are you?" Betsy called from the top of the stairs, gripping the railing.   Although she had regained a modicum of physical strength, her nerves were extremely jittery.

"I'm right here, my dear," he answered, poking his head out of the study to reassure her.

"Do you hear that?"

"Yes, I hear it."

"Are we at war?"

"I wish I knew," Billy murmured to himself.   "I dispatched John to Judge Smyth's to find out what's going on.   Please Betsy, return…"   Before he could complete the sentence, she had skimmed the stairs and was in his arms.   Wherever he went, she went, like a shadow.   From window to window and door to door they darted, trying to get a glimpse of the forward echelon or, more important, of their messenger.   The music grew louder; the marchers were closing in.   And still there was no sign of John. At this point, aware of his wife's unstable emotional state, Billy decided to keep his thoughts to himself:

Perhaps I have stirred up resentment for scheduling this meeting to consider Lord North's peace proposal.   Colden feels that at present 'New Yorkers' minds are too much heated and

inflamed to weigh it objectively'.   That may be true here also, but

trying and failing is one thing.   Not trying is unpardonable.   We

must not slam the door of reconciliation shut because of timidity!

Billy's eyes reflected inner consternation that his lips did

not convey.   "Come," he said, forcing a smile as he took his

wife's trembling hand.   "Let's go up to our bedroom.   We'll have

a bird's-eye view from there.   It's probably nothing more than a

show of force to kick off the first day of the Second Continental

Congress."

"You can bluff all you want, William Franklin," Betsy said,

getting hold of herself.   "I may be a nervous wreck, but I'm not

oblivious.   The prevailing attitude out there is: All who are not

friends are foes.   Your fidelity to King and Country puts you in

imminent danger."

The Minutemen made their way down Kearny Avenue

toward Proprietary House.

"Oh, my God," she cried, evidently thinking the worst.

"Are they coming to take you away from me?   I couldn't bear

living without you."

"There, there," he whispered, comforting her.   "You'll make yourself sick again."

Acceding, she accompanied him meekly up the broad staircase, neither of them hesitating as they usually did to enjoy their prized imitation copperplate on the stairway wall.   Filing past the door to the crimson bedchamber, they entered their own, which Billy had decorated with a fine grade of English blue-and-white striped wallpaper.   He opened the door to the balcony, a modest cantilever that protruded directly over the front entrance, and, together, they stepped out into the warm sunlight.

The leafy maples at roadside, abounding in new growth, provided them with a screen-like shield that concealed them from the curiosity seekers as well as the unidentified henchmen en route.

The converts, who had nothing to fear, greeted the militia with, "Huzzah! Huzzah!"

By contrast, the friends of government, the holdouts, those who disapproved of the edicts of the Continental Congress, huddled in dark doorways or pried from upstairs windows, not knowing what to expect.

Billy clenched his teeth, not daring to utter what was on his mind: He pictured himself being arrested and 'led (away) like a Bear through the Country to some (detestable) Place of Confinement in New England'.

The appearance of the colours through a key-hole size clearing not ten yards from the Franklin drive caused Betsy to start. Then the fifers, who had taken a breather, broke into a popular, patriotic song called 'America, Commerce and Freedom'.

Billy shuddered at first sight of the motley crew, about thirty in number, citizen soldiers wearing cocked hats and dressed in everyday clothes, with a firelock resting on every shoulder, whether a boy of sixteen or a grown man of fifty the only sign of uniformity.

Betsy slumped slightly, her knees buckling from relief when no order was given to halt.   The red flag was down and another crisis past.

"You see?" Billy said, pressing the back of her hand to his lips.   "They meant no harm."   He repressed the urge to embrace her for fear she would feel the pounding of his heart.

"This time," she replied with savvy foreboding.

At that moment, Judge Smyth, driving somebody else's gig,

barreled into the drive, drawing up abruptly beside the front steps.

Seeing them, he called out, "Sorry for the delay.   My horse is

being shod, so I borrowed Doc Lawrence's.   The skittish mare, its

head bobbing up and down, refused to stand still.

"What happened to John?"

"There was mail for you at the Inn.   I told him I'd deliver

the message."

Dying to know the lowdown, Betsy and Billy leaned over

the wooden railing and fired questions at him left and right.

"Whoa!" he shouted, his command aimed directly at the

unruly horse and indirectly at the Franklins.

Amused by his predicament, they backed off and waited,

all ears.

"It was a contingent from Freehold," Frederick proceeded.

"It seems that 'a rumor...circulated...(there) that a man of war was

lying off Sandy Hook and that ...' (The horse reared and nearly

dumped him out backwards.) 'the British planned to sneak ashore

at night, raid the secretary's office at Amboy, rifle the public funds

and take off with the records'.   (The nag whinnied, snorted,

pawed the ground, then bolted, nearly sending the judge flying into the whiffletree.)   "Anyhow, 'it was a false alarm'."

I could have told them there was no man-of-war off Sandy
Hook, Billy sniped to himself, enjoying a delightful chuckle.   As
Papa would probably say, 'He laughs best who laughs last'."   All
kidding aside, he mused, having a British sloop stationed in
Raritan Bay is a gem of an idea.   I'd feel a hell of a lot easier if I
had a place of refuge, a way of escape in case of an emergency.
I'll write Dartmouth first thing and push for it.   As things now
stand, I am entirely at their mercy.

Betsy's lighthearted gaiety, stemming from Smyth's comic
dilemma, caused Billy to abandon his present train of thought.
"Didn't you know Doc Lawrence's Dorothy mare is a one-man
horse?" he jested.

"How do you rate?" Betsy bantered, getting in on the fun.
"From what I hear, Doc wouldn't loan her to the pope."

"He d..doesn't know I b..borrowed her," Smyth stammered,
his confession coming in fits and starts, matching the up-and-
down, stop-and-go motion of the rig.

"Get wise to her, judge," Billy coached.   "Get out and
walk."

"By golly, you may have something there," the judge replied, jumping to the ground.

Acting like a different animal, one who'd been freed from a choky bellyband, Dorothy simmered down just as nicely as you please and without further fuss, plodded down the avenue from whence she'd come with the judge walking meekly beside her.

They laughed so hard they cried.   It did Billy's heart good to see his wife so relaxed for a change.

They were still holding their sides when strait-laced Margaret's decorous knock sounded.

"What is it?" Billy snapped, annoyed by the interruption that would cut short his wife's brief interlude of high spirits.

"A letter from Philadelphia, Sir," the maid replied with customary formality.

"And why didn't John deliver it to me?"

"He was so dusty that I wouldn't allow him past the kitchen door."

"Aaaa yes," Billy replied knowingly.   Well, bring it here, and then you may go."

"John said it came by stage."

"That will be all, Margaret," he muttered, shooing her out with a backhanded motion.

"I hope Sally hasn't miscarried," Betsy gasped.

Billy made no comment but shook his head no, for at first glance, he recognized his Papa's disguised handwriting.   "Papa's home," he mumbled in disbelief.   His stomach flipped as he broke open the seal.   Aside from a copy of Lord Chatham's plan for reconciliation and a brief, unsatisfying sympathy note promising to detail, when leisure permitted, his recent involvement in negotiations with regard to the misunderstandings between Great Britain and America, Billy had not had a single word from his father in months.   It was no wonder.   Ordinarily, it was Benjamin who chewed Billy out for something or other: 'running behindhand with (him)' or not 'disengaging' himself from an office that might prove uncomfortable 'in the (present) state of American affairs', but last December, out of grief, anger and frustration, Billy had taken it upon himself to condemn his father for staying away without cause and went so far as to suggest that his absence had contributed substantially to his mother's deterioration and ultimate death.   Benjamin was not one to defend himself against public censure, preferring, rather, to sit back and let unfolding events speak for themselves, but this was a horse of another color.   His ever dutiful son had accused him of forsaking them, and that was without precedent.

Betsy, apparently bursting with curiosity, snatched the note from his hand, condensing its contents: "Temple came," she cried, her face brightening like a lighted chandelier.   "Papa and Temple are really home."

Billy nodded, too stunned to speak.   He had gained his son but had he alienated his father?

"They arrived by Osborne," she continued.   "The evening of the fifth.   In six weeks.   Peter, too.   Papa was immediately appointed a delegate to the Continental Congress so has been very busy."   Then her voice faltered, losing its vivacity.   "He wants to see you, Billy.   Either you go to Philadelphia or he will come to Burlington, whichever is more convenient for you."

"Yes," he replied hazily.   "I shall cancel my plans to confer with Governor Colden and go directly to Philadelphia at the conclusion of the assembly meeting."

Steadying their gazes upon one another, they stood in a

pool of sunlight, surrounded by a cloud of uncertainty.

TROUBLED WATERS

Chapter XXIII

Trevose – 6:00 o'clock
Saturday, May 20, 1775

Not seeing the Franklin carriage drawn up at the entrance,
Billy was surprised to find his father already inside waiting to greet
him.   At first sight, he filled with remorse, and for a few fleeting
moments their animosities and differences seemed to float away,
leaving them free to follow the dictates of their hearts.   "Papa," he
said, swallowing the lump in his throat.

"Son," the other responded, appearing equally touched.

Meeting one another halfway, they embraced, letting tears
of joy streamed down their faces, neither of them needing to feel
embarrassed or ashamed in front of such an old friend as Joseph
Galloway.

While the exchange of letters during the intervening years served to convey and confirm shifts in his father's political thinking, it had done little to prepare him for the physical changes time had wrought.   The aging process had definitely taken its toll. Noticeably diminished was the protuberant paunch, reduced by the necessity of having to gum his food, Billy assumed.   Beyond that, the missing teeth altered the familiar facial contour, hollowing out his cheeks and leaving them sunken, like two empty sockets. Sadder still, was the hobble he'd developed, brought on, no doubt, by periodic, crippling bouts of gout.   All in all, despite the many doting fosterers Benjamin bragged of having in England, he looked all of his sixty-nine years.   Like a vine of ivy in autumn, outwardly he was similarly withering away.

"How did you get here?" Billy asked, regaining his emotional composure at last.   "Had I thought, I could have stopped by the house and picked you up."

"Temple would never have forgiven you if you simply ate and ran, so to speak.   He's so eager to spend some time with you."

"And I with him," Billy replied wistfully.

"Besides, Mr. Galloway was kind enough to send his

carriage for me earlier in the day."

"Joseph, forgive me.   As always, it's good to see you."
Extending his hand, he gave his fraternal brother the Masonic
hand-shake, a long-established habit stemming from his twenty-
odd-year membership in freemasonry.

"Happy you could make it, Governor.   I realize you've had
a hectic week."   They exchanged knowing glances.   "Why don't
we go into the library and celebrate this reunion with a bottle of
Madeira."

"If God made anything better than Madeira, he kept it for
himself," Billy quipped, hoping to lure Benjamin into a nonhostile
topic of conversation, one that might possibly prolong the
pervading sociable and congenial atmosphere of the moment.

But Benjamin didn't bite.   Instead, as soon as they were
seated and the wine flowing, the good Doctor dove headlong into
the business of his detainment in London by picking up the 96-
page letter that lay on the table beside him and reading it to them
word for word.   He began:

‘On board the Pennsylvania Packet, Capt. Osborne,
bound to Philadelphia

March 22, 1775

Dear Son',

Billy raised his eyebrows, shocked that the massive journal was addressed to him personally.

Benjamin paused briefly, sneaking a peek over the rim of his glasses.   Obviously satisfied that he had attained the intended result, he returned to the text.

From the outset, it was clear to Billy that those few, cryptic remarks he'd written after the funeral had hit home.   Perhaps for the first time in his life, Benjamin was on the defensive, testifying on his own behalf, 'arguing that since last fall, at the urgent behest of several British nobles, he had agreed to act as a go-between and play a crucial role in secret negotiations aimed at arbitrating the present crisis and trying to reach an accommodation of differences between the Mother Country and the American Colonies'.

Then, without notice, the crafty advocate peered a second time over the rim of his glasses.   Looking Billy straight in the eye, he asked, "Given the same opportunity, would you have done differently?"

"Hell no!" Billy shot back, the zealous response fired by his intense desire to reach a compromise.   But no sooner had the words escaped his lips than he realized what his father was up to, the sage was fishing for exoneration, pleading no contest, and Billy, being caught off guard, had vindicated him, falling for the artifice hook, line and sinker.

Billy thought of all the arguments he had rehearsed. Commitment.   Obligation.   Duty.   But somehow, five months after the fact, it seemed best to 'let sleeping dogs lie'.   As the saying goes, 'Time is an herb that cures all diseases', grief, bitterness and sorrow included.

Seeing that Billy was letting the matter ride, Joseph got up to refill the wine glasses, obviously sensing that round one was over.   Judging from the governor's next remark, he figured right. Round two was underway.

"But I don't get it, Papa," Billy said, scratching his head. One minute you're in such disfavor that you divorce yourself from the Ohio Company for fear you're an albatross, and the next minute the great conciliator, Lord Chatham, seeks you out when he is writing his plan of reconciliation, stating that 'He was not so confident of his own Judgment but that he came to set it right by (yours) as Men set their Watches by a Regulator'. To put it bluntly and succinctly, Papa, what happened to restore your credibility?"

Mumbling something about stuffiness, Joseph cleared his throat and got up to open another window and in so doing was able to give Billy the high sign, reminding him to stay cool-headed.

Benjamin removed his smudged spectacles, steamed them with his hot breath and, taking a handkerchief from his pocket, stroked the wire-framed lenses between its folds in a methodical motion, taking his good old sweet time to answer. At length he said, "From what I could gather, they were ashamed of the way I was treated at the Cockpit."

Billy denoted triumph in the set of his jaw. Probing further he asked, "By they, do you mean Dartmouth and North?" The governor slid to the very edge of his seat.

"My feeling is that the secretary and the prime minister were too embarrassed to deal directly with me. Why, I hadn't attended one of Dartmouth's levees in over a year. In any event, Chatham, Barclay and Hyde led me to believe that the *Hints* I prepared for them would be reviewed at the top. As for my sudden conversion, perhaps you could shed some light on that, my son."

"Me?" Easing back in his chair, Billy replied cautiously. "Explain yourself, Papa."

"Well, for months the Britons doubted our resolve, to remain firm and united, that is.   It seemed that someone on this side of the Atlantic was painting them a different picture than the one I was conveying."

Well I'll be, Billy exclaimed angrily to himself behind a mask of innocence.   So much for secret communications. Maybe when Dartmouth receives my head on a silver platter, he'll know I meant business when I told him how vulnerable I would be should my dispatches be published.   And he said I could rely on him!

"A governor's duty is to report on the state of affairs within his province," Billy replied, speaking in generalities.   His measured response, the fact, no more, no less, gave the library the formal feel of a courtroom.   What was more, the Doctor had artfully turned the tables and put his son on the witness stand.

"What goes around, comes around," Benjamin commented

wryly, apparently satisfied that his 'if the shoe fits, wear it' tactic had worked. Then picking up where he left off, he continued. 'But the unanimity and firmness shown by the Continental Congress seemed to force the Ministry to sit up and take notice, to get off its high horse, demanding only to save face, to preserve the dignity of the Crown. So I, the idealist, the dreamer, believing resolutely that 'There never was a good war or a bad peace,' grasped for the olive branch'.

"Hear! Hear!" Joseph saluted. "Bottoms up!"

The three clicked their glasses and drained them.

Up to this point, Joseph sat stoically along the sidelines, unnaturally withdrawn, like a child who is to be seen and not heard, leaving Billy to believe that a heated exchange had taken place before his arrival.

"I'm glad we're all in agreement thus far," Benjamin said, his eyes not straying from Galloway's face as he painstakingly searched his facial expression for some clue that would either betray a professed innocence or expose a hidden guilt.

Billy had a pretty good idea what they may have quarreled about. First and foremost, on May 12th Joseph, Benjamin's close friend and old political ally, jumped ship and quit the Continental Congress, a desertion he would not take lying down.   In his view, the split would send a negative signal abroad, proving Billy's reports that there were chinks in the Colonial armor.   Benjamin had become the standard-bearer of unity.   It was his rallying cry, his watchword, his motto.   John Dickinson captured this growing sentiment in the words of his *Liberty Song*, "By uniting we stand, by dividing we fall."

Billy squirmed in his chair, his palms clammy, thinking about the second possibility.   Maybe Benjamin had wormed the truth out of Galloway about his leaking of confidential intelligence regarding the Congress to me.

Joseph, of course, did not realize at the time that the governor was then funneling it on to Dartmouth.   When a rumor circulated in London that the Pennsylvania delegate was the pipe, Benjamin dutifully wrote to Joseph, saying that he didn't believe a word of it.   Nevertheless, because of Galloway's action of the 12th, Benjamin was having second thoughts regarding his host's involvement and the accusation that Joseph was a 'Friend to Government', too.   Of course, the gossipers were half-right.

Joseph was the funnel and Billy the conduit.

To avoid the opening of Pandora's box, Billy began to stretch and yawn, signaling Galloway to call a recess.

"Everyone must be famished," he said, taking the hint.

Billy had no stomach for haggling with his father over right and wrong, obligation or even treason.   One thing and one thing alone guided his thoughts and actions, DUTY!   As a colonial agent, Benjamin informed on the British, and as a royal governor, Billy weaseled on the radicals, the irony being that both men, in their own separate ways, were striving for the same end, peace and harmony with Great Britain.

Or were they?   Billy had read Galloway's letter and was sure his father had not meant it when he lashed out angrily at England, referring to her as 'this old rotten State' and lamenting that 'To unite us intimately, will only be to corrupt and poison us also'.   Having written it after the Cockpit incident, Billy dismissed it as mere backlash.

In any case, the letter didn't end there as Billy recalled. Backing down, Benjamin finished on a nobler note: 'However, I would try anything, and bear anything that can be borne with

Safety to our just Liberties rather than engage in a War with such near Relations, unless compelled to it by dire Necessity in our own Defense'.

Joseph yanked the bell sash nearest him which summoned two menservants. Without being told, one went immediately to a cupboard, removed a large chamber pot and proceeded to pass it around. Then he returned it to the cupboard where it was emptied from the opposite side. The Franklins got up to stretch their legs while the table was being spread. Giving them a moment alone, Joseph excused himself, claiming he needed to have a few words with his wife and daughter.

"Please give Grace my best," Billy said cordially, "and tell Elizabeth if she's up bright and early, I'll take her riding with me."

"If I do, she won't sleep a wink all night waiting for daybreak," he replied, smiling for the first time all evening.

Billy tossed back his head and let out an effusive laugh, crying that he had a feeling he would eat those words in the morning. The eruption, however ill-timed, had a neutralizing effect that tended to clear the innuendo-laden air, much as a dab of sherbet cleanses the palate between the courses of a heavy meal.

"Tell me about Temple, Papa," Billy inquired, once they were alone. "Is he impetuous and outgoing or reserved and shy?"

"He's more of an introvert than an extrovert, although he does take after you for elocution, not his grandfather, thank goodness."

"I'm flattered," Billy responded, surprised by the unexpected compliment. "Perhaps he'll follow in my footsteps and become a lawyer."

"I favor that course myself."

"What does Temple say?"

"You know how fickle-minded a 15-year-old can be."

"He's a chip off the old block," Billy retorted, poking fun at his own capricious youth.

It was evident by the watery look of his father's eyes that Benjamin was reliving the day in '48 when he fetched his own son from the deck of a privateer bound for war against the French. But oddly enough, he did not pursue the past, acting more and more like a man with an urgent mission, a driven man who would not be sidetracked. "One day he talks of nothing but becoming a surgeon, the next, a painter. He draws very well, you know.

Between that and his dog, he was fully occupied during the entire
crossing."

"His dog?" Billy hadn't bargained for a dog.   He hated
dogs.   His province was crawling with the bothersome, rabid
critters.

"Pompey.   She's a little mite, a lap dog, actually."

"That should be tolerable," Billy replied, groveling.

Benjamin ambled to the open window, positioning himself
with his back to his son.   He inhaled deeply, filling his lungs with
the sweet-scented air of spring and then, swiftly, went for the
jugular.   "All the more reason for you to enroll the boy in the
Academy of Philadelphia," he said quietly.

"Over my dead body!" Billy blared, throwing caution to the
wind as he pitted himself for confrontation.   "I have given
Temple's future considerable thought and have decided to send him
to King's College in New York."

"With what, may I ask?" Benjamin bared his open palms in
exasperation.

Billy glowered.   A flush of anger reddened his face as he
strained to harbor the spiteful accusation that flooded his mind, the

imputation of blame his lips could not utter: Had you kept your nose clean, our lands might be patented by now, and I would have money to burn.   Yet, when he fixed his eyes on the figure before him, the hair gray and thinning, the frame smaller than he remembered, love triumphed over enmity, and Billy marveled that in spite of all outward appearances, his father's brain was, without question, wholly unimpaired.   That weasel, he mused.   He knows he's got me over a barrel.   "Croghan promises..."

"Croghan!   Bah!"   Benjamin grumbled, wheeling around to make the pin.   "You're in over your head as it is!   Be sensible, son.   Think of all the money you'll save if Temple lives with us during the school term and spends his summer vacations in Perth Amboy."

Billy knew from experience that his father had him whipped.   "I guess that's that," he conceded, retreating to the solace of his glass of Madeira.   He swirled the remainder slowly, as a connoisseur would and announced out of the blue, "Did I tell you that I am naming my son after me?   William Temple Franklin."   Commendable or not, Billy derived a modicum of consolation by getting in the last lick.

As soon as the evening repast was finished, the dishes cleared and the drop leaf table folded and restored to its place against the wall, Benjamin picked up his lengthy letter and took up where he had left off.

A captive audience, the two mavericks listened passively to Benjamin's seemingly unending recollection of the sequent political maneuvers, the backdoor diplomacy that had postponed his departure and prevented his return to America in time to see his wife alive.

While his father droned on, a startling realization struck, becoming clearer and clearer to Billy as the merry-go-round of clandestine meetings unfolded and drew to a climax.   He strained hard to hold his tongue, waiting for the appropriate opening. However, when Benjamin came to the part where he was wrongly singled out by Lord Sandwich in the House of Lords (Dr. Franklin was attending at the personal invitation of Lord Chatham) as being the author of the elder statesman's Plan of Reconciliation and labeled 'one of the bitterest and most mischievous Enemies (England has) ever known', Billy exploded, "My God, Papa!

Couldn't you tell they were trying to detain you?"

"Hear me out!"

"Answer me, damn it!"

"Hold your horses," Joseph prompted.   "Let him finish. You'll have your say."

Benjamin continued as though he had not been so rudely interrupted, passing over his own chastisement, except to say that 'as (he) had no Inducement to take it to (himself), (he) kept (his) Countenance as immoveable as if (his) Features had been made of Wood'.   "What I could not stomach was their malevolent treatment of Lord Chatham, their honorable peer and patriarch. 'Like an aged cedar of Lebanon, he was cut down and his plan blackballed, pulverized by their vile tongues, which were unloosed by ignorance, prejudice and passion'."

My friends, I watched helplessly as the weak ones, your Lord Dartmouth chief among them," Benjamin testified, eyeballing the two doubting Thomases, "after a brief spurt of lukewarm resistance, were easily swayed by the overbearing force of the opposition and soundly trounced."

Billy and Joseph jumped to their feet, decrying such

sacrilege.

Without batting an eye or faltering, Benjamin concluded his tirade. "Like Adam's, my eyes were suddenly opened, and I saw the naked truth: These lawmakers are warmongers and 'appear to have scarce Discretion enough to govern a Herd of Swine'!"

Joseph lunged for the door that stood ajar, Billy the open windows. After slamming them shut, he accosted his father in an articulate, scathing whisper. "For God's sake, Papa, THINK! Do you realize what you are saying? You speak SEDITION!"

"I speak THE TRUTH."

Wringing his hands, Billy paced back and forth as he launched his now untempered, verbal attack. "And you believe seditionists here are less onerous? Tell him, Joseph. Tell him what two of his virtuous, sensible Americans did to you!"

Joseph pulled his chair up close and put his hand over his old friend's. "It happened in February," he began. "I was staying in Philadelphia to attend our assembly debates on the First Congress, where my opposition to and repudiation of the Congress's unlawful measures gained me the reputation of being the 'notorious dissenter'."

"Get on with it," Billy cued, anxious to take the advantage.

Joseph got up and turned away.   "'Late in the Evening a Box was left at my Lodgings nail'd & directed to me'.   In it was a hangman's noose and a letter threatening my life."

Billy stared at his father, ready to blurt out who did it, who the conspirators were, wanting to have the satisfaction of telling him they were two of his old cronies, but contrarily, Benjamin didn't ask, Galloway's tale of intimidation bouncing off him as though he was cast in iron.

Benjamin wore a faraway look, and when he did react, he simply said, "Tis easy to see, hard to foresee."

Billy went limp, feeling like the wind had been knocked out of him.   "You can't be serious, Papa.   It's as plain as the nose on your face.   These nuts are maniacs!"

"What would you call those who advocate making eunuchs of American males to reduce our numbers and to discourage further emigration from England, SAINTS?"

Billy paled and reached for his glass of wine; Joseph gagged and sat his down.

"Now that we have established that neither side has a

corner on wanton atrocities, please sit down, gentlemen, and allow me to finish."

Before complying, Joseph poured another round and moved his chair back to its remote position.   Too teed off to be complaisant, Billy stood where he was, tall and defiant.

Overlooking his son's insolence, Benjamin proceeded, lapsing into a soliloquy as he relived the backdoor diplomacy that filled his last days in London.   "I tried everything in my power to strike a bargain, offering, as a last resort, to engage to pay for the tea myself."

"Good grief!" Joseph exclaimed.   "I know it's none of my business, but weren't you biting off a little more than you could chew?"

"New wine in an old bottle.   Right, Papa?   Tell Mr. Galloway what you demanded in return."

"I was going for broke."

"Repeal of the Boston Port Act?"

"Repeal of ALL the Massachusetts Acts."

"A nervy gesture."

"But totally unacceptable.   I refused to give ground, and it

was then that the most revolting thing happened.   They tried to
BRIBE me."

Billy exploded.   When put to the test, blood was thicker
than water.   "What did they take you for anyway?"

"Obviously, something I was not."

"A plenipotentiary?" Joseph suggested, the seven-syllable
word difficult to form after nearly that many glasses of wine.

Benjamin nodded.   "Where they got such a far-fetched
notion, I have no idea, for I had received no secret instructions to
act on my own."

His curiosity getting the better of him, Billy asked, "What
did they offer?"

"Restoration of my old job, anything my heart desired."
His mouth turning down in contempt, he concluded, "'The
Ministry, I am sure, would rather have given me a place in a cart to
Tyburn, than any other place whatever'."

"Papa calls bribery 'spitting in the soup'," Billy explained to
Joseph on the side.

"Gross but fitting," Joseph remarked, stifling his
amusement.

"When temptation failed," Benjamin went on, ignoring their petty asides, "my seaport properties were subtly threatened with destruction, but I countered that they could torch them whenever they saw fit, because, in good time, they would be obligated to pay me for 'Damages with interest'."

"Oh, Papa," Billy sighed, his mind's eye pitting the ragtag soldiers that had marched through Perth Amboy against the red-coated regulars of the British army.

"I hate to butt in, Dr. Franklin," Joseph said, picking unconsciously at a hangnail, "but let's stop to look at the picture here in America.   Anarchy exists.   Dissension is not tolerated. Dissidents are subdued and converted by painfully intimidating methods, like tar and feathering and arson."

"For the most part, Papa, 'the tightly-woven fabric of unity you tout is, in reality, an airy cut of cheesecloth patterned of coercion'," Billy chided, trying to reinforce Galloway's argument.

"I see your point," Benjamin replied, drifting again into the recesses of his mind.   "It seems that we are jumping from the frying pan into the fire, but," he added, taking the floor, "I hold to my belief that 'those who would give up essential Liberty to

Purchase a little temporary safety, deserve neither LIBERTY NOR

SAFETY'."

"And I hold," Billy shouted, pounding his fist on the table,

"that 'the Tyranny of the mob is the worst of all tyrannies,

involving all in one common ruin'!"

Joseph struggled to his feet to intercede.   "Aren't we

jumping the gun, my friends?   Have you forgotten Lord North's

peace proposal?"

"That!" Benjamin sneered.   "A divisive contrivance if I

ever saw one."

"Beggars can't be choosers," Billy sniped stubbornly.

"'It seems to me the Language of a Highwayman, who with

a Pistol in your Face says, Give me your Purse, and then I will not

put my Hand into your Pocket.   But give me all your Money or

I'll shoot you thro' the Head'," Benjamin retaliated.

"I admit that the idea is far from flawless, but it is a start,"

Joseph contended, exerting whatever influence he had to the hilt.

A lengthy silence akin to the prolonged pause at the end of

Handel's *Hallelujah Chorus* followed as the two sticklers waited

with bated breath to hear the verdict, to see whether they had been convincing enough to sway the prominent patriarch.

Benjamin shuffled his papers together, stashed them under his arm and turned to render his decision. His eyes were moist, his lip quivering. "Gentlemen," he said with chilling somberness, "I fear we do not see eye to eye."

THE GREAT DISPUTE

Chapter XXIV

Perth Amboy
Thursday, August 30, 1775

As father and son galloped side by side along the deserted beach, the naked summer sun inched higher above the horizon and in no time at all stole the few precious hours that remained for them be alone.

Soon Benjamin would be arriving to take Billy away from his overindulgent parents, back to Philadelphia and the Academy, to the world of Greek and Latin, French and mathematics.   Just as Dr. Franklin unrelentingly drove himself, working day after day from dawn to dusk, he never missed an opportunity to prod his grandson to do the same.   For instance, the young man had no sooner stepped foot in Perth Amboy when he received a letter from his grandfather telling him to 'Take Time by the Forelock', which meant to bone up over the summer, get a head start and don't fritter away your entire three-month vacation.

But happily for the debonair newcomer, Betsy and Billy had their own ideas about rearing a child.   Although studying had its place, holidays were not to be dull or monotonous.   In some respects, his lenient part-time guardians were more grandparental playmates than parental taskmasters.   Billy took him swimming, taught him to ride, and when they were not doing either of these, they were off somewhere sketching landscapes.   Anxious to show off her suave, lovable stepson, Betsy did her part by proudly introducing him to all their friends, who, in turn, welcomed him with open arms, filling his social calendar with scads of picnics and parties all season long.   There was no doubt about it. William Temple Franklin was the talk of Perth Amboy.

Overnight, the governor and his first lady, two middle-aged socialites, had become instant parents, catering to a talented and precocious, yet considerate and polished teenage adolescent.   And the truth of the matter was that they were loving every minute of it.

"It wouldn't hurt to take German, too," Billy counseled as

they walked in stride from the stables to the mansion.   "If your

grandfather agrees, that is."

"I would much rather take fencing or dancing lessons,

father."

"In that case," Billy replied, giving his son an affirmative

wink, "while we're at it, we'll ask him to consent to those classes as

well."

"Oh, father, I do love you.   I love you both," he cried,

stopping impulsively and clutching Billy about the middle in a

gripping bear hug.   "I never dreamed I would ever be so happy."

"Nor we," Billy confided, savoring the moment.   He

tousled the boy's sun-streaked hair and held him tight, treasuring

the bond that had grown between them during these past few

months.

Peering over Billy's head, the governor saw in the distance

the outline of the British garrison, manned by its few remaining

loyalists who stubbornly resisted the radical wave of change and

refused to join the swelling ranks of the new provincial militia.

But since fervor is no match for fear, he knew it would only be a

matter of time before they, too, would capitulate.   All along, he had been powerless to stop the exodus. Deserters flocked from the royal to the colonial standard just as sand freely flows from one half of an hourglass to the other. Yet, in spite of this dilution of royal authority, Perth Amboy was still known as 'Tory' territory, a fitting epithet for a town described as 'almost the only spot in America where a friend to American liberty (is) a disgraceful character'. Billy shuddered.

"What is it, father?"

"It's nothing, son. I was just thinking about your grandfather." Betsy spared him a further explanation by coming out of the house carrying Pompey. As soon as the pooch spotted her master, she leaped to the ground and began running circles around him.

With his arms folded across his chest, Billy stood back to watch the rumpus, delighting mostly in his wife's delight, moved by her motherly mannerisms and amused by her sudden liking for canines. It was into this heartwarming setting that Benjamin arrived.

As was the Franklin custom, they all rallied about his carriage ready to give him a royal reception.

"How are you, father?   Here, let me help you down."

"Come in, Papa," Betsy said.   "It's good to see you."

Benjamin grudgingly accepted his son's offer but completely snubbed him otherwise, directing his queries and comments to his daughter-in-law instead.   "The boy seems happy as a dog with two tails."

"He's such a pleasure.   I don't know what I'll do without him between now and Christmas."

Billy wasn't the least bit surprised by Benjamin's standoffish behavior.   After all, their parley at Trevose three months earlier ended on a pretty sour note with Benjamin leaving in a huff after having failed to win over his two closest companions to his way of thinking.   Had he come to try again?   Billy wondered.

"Look, grandfather," Billy yelled, drawing his attention. He threw a stick halfway across the yard.   On command, the puppy obediently retrieved it, dropping it playfully at Benjamin's feet.

"Good dog, Pompey," he exclaimed, patting her on the head.

"Come and see my horse, grandfather," Billy coaxed.

"Later, son," Billy said, stepping in.   "After your

grandfather has washed up and had some refreshment, I'm sure he

would like to see Tallyho."

Miraculously, two days passed without a flareup, not

because there weren't plenty of provocative issues to debate.   For

starters, the Congress had rejected the North Peace Plan and

officially declared war following the Battle at Breed's Hill,

appointing George Washington General of the Army.   The

Franklins' intervening letters mentioned neither of these historic

events, their correspondence dealing strictly with personal matters,

mainly Billy's schooling and Vandalia.   Billy did, however, make

reference to the political unrest when he conveyed Walpole's

current optimism to his father that 'as soon as the present Great

Dispute is settled our Grant shall be perfected'.

Later, as Ben and Billy strolled down Kearney Street in the

dazzling mid-morning sunshine, they were discussing the pros and

cons of selling off the suffering traders' portion of the Vandalia

tract.   "Take off the blinders, Billy.   My advice is to get while the getting's good."

"My concern is that we may take a piece and forfeit the pie."

"Why are you being so wishy-washy about this? It's legally yours. The aborigines needed no royal authority to dispose of their own lands."

"In your opinion."

"The money would come in handy, wouldn't it?" Benjamin volleyed, delivering the clincher. He kept his eyes downcast, apparently not wanting to rub it in.

Billy took a slow, deep breath. "All right," he said, letting it gush out. "I'll go along. But mind you, it's against my better judgment."

"That settles that."

"Not quite."

Benjamin looked up.

"Have you forgotten, Papa? I'm persona non grata in Philadelphia."

"That is undeniably true, I'm afraid, or I wouldn't be here in Perth Amboy today." Benjamin sighed, looking dejectedly at his feet again.

Billy flinched as though he'd been flogged with a cat-o-nine-tails. In silence, they turned down Gordon Street in the direction of the water. At the juncture of Rector Street, they passed St. Peter's, the Anglican church where the governor and Mrs. Franklin attended regularly. By way of transcendental imagery, Billy knelt before the red-draped altar of Pentecost and asked that the power of the Holy Ghost descend upon him and fill him with tolerance, patience and forgiveness but, above all, grant him the will and the wisdom to keep his frigging mouth shut.

"Suppose you give me your power of attorney," Benjamin suggested. "I'll be glad to attend the Grand Ohio Company meetings and act on your behalf."

"That's very generous of you, Papa." Billy couched his suspicions under a show of affable backslapping. Then, all of a sudden something struck him funny, and he broke into uproarious laughter.

"What's the joke? Your notoriety is certainly no laughing matter."

"It just occurred to me that in the place of my nativity, I am both famous and infamous at the same time."

"I find it rather sad, myself."

"Yes, it is," Billy responded, looking glum. "Sad that my friends Charles Thomson and Tho Wharton suffer from myopia and that I have failed so miserably to reverse it." Instantly realizing that he had opened the floodgate, Billy kicked savagely at a piece of driftwood that lay mired in the mud. You numskull, he cried inaudibly, bawling himself out.

"Don't be too hard on yourself, son. Somebody had to break the ice. A fester's got to come to a head sooner or later." Benjamin pointed to a spot down along the shore where they might stop and rest.

It was the brown wooden hulk of a battered skiff half buried beneath the tidal sand with her port side bared to the elements and her starboard side kissing the ground. Stories varied as to how and when she was beached, but judging from her mossy exterior, she had been there quite some time.

They walked the short distance in stilted silence.

"We must talk, Billy," Benjamin said grimly, leaning against the exposed bow. "I am very worried about you, son."

"And I about you, Papa."

"Time is running out."

"I know."

"But it's still not too late."

"Are you saying there's a chance the Ministry will send over a commissioner to settle this mess?" Billy asked, totally misconstruing the occult meaning behind his father's measured response.   He searched his face for a sign of hope.

Noticeably flustered, Benjamin turned abruptly away and picked nervously at a patch of crusty barnacles grappled to the vessel's rotting hull.   Whether he was upset because his initial volleys had backfired or whether his son's poignant question put him on the spot was not clear.   "The idea was entertained," he admitted, hedging.

"Then my suggestion was proposed?"   Billy's eyes bulged with excitement.

"Yes, according to secondhand information."

"When?"

"Shortly before I left England."

"Why didn't you tell me this at Trevose?"

"Don't you remember?   I didn't get to finish my story," he retorted, passing the buck and thereby ducking the blame.

Billy drew in his horns, not wanting to start a quarrel over a blame game.   There was too much at stake.   "So, tell me, Papa. Where do we stand?   Is an envoy coming soon?   I have received no formal word of this."

"I wouldn't hold my breath if I were you.   It may have been a ploy to induce me to make concessions, for after 'they threw me away as an orange that would yield no juice, and therefore not worth more squeezing', the motion appeared to suffer a similar demise."

"Damn!" Billy cursed, kicking a spray of sand out to sea.

Benjamin checked the time and suggested they continue their conversation on the way back to Proprietary House.   "Let me ask you this," he pursued, picking at a scaly patch of psoriasis on the back of his hand.   "What stock do you put in the Congress' Olive Branch Petition?"

"The King will view it with contempt, as he should."

"What if it is our final appeal?"

"Then the die is cast.   Wait a minute," Billy cried,

stopping short. "Go back to where you said it was still not too late. If it had nothing to do with an emissary, what is it? Do you have some brilliant plan of reconciliation up your sleeve?"

"I wish I had, my son, but I fear the 'Golden Opportunity' is lost. Recent events and resolves have dashed our united longing for a swift and negotiated settlement of this 'Great Dispute'. So, what is left for us to do? I for one will continue to leave no stone unturned in my diligent search for peace and harmony, but, on the other hand," he added, his caustic tone a clear indication of his adamance, "I shall work tirelessly to build a defense against those who are determined to rob us of our inalienable rights and essential liberties. Remember, 'Make yourselves sheep and the wolves will eat you'."

"Enough, Papa!" Billy exploded, throwing up his hands. "Enough philosophizing! I know what you're up to, what you're pushing. It took a while, but I've finally doped it out and put two and two together. JOIN or DIE. That's it, isn't it?"

"For your own sake and that of your family, you must act quickly," Benjamin pleaded, "before it's too late."

"Never mind ME! I'm on the winning side," he shouted.

"What about YOU?"   Billy pictured the shrunken skulls of ex-revolutionists impaled on spikes over the entrance to London's Temple Bar, a ghastly, gruesome sight he was never likely to forget.

"Spoken like a true, dyed-in-the-wool royalist," Benjamin scoffed.   "'If you think they can bring us to our knees, you know neither (this) people nor (this) country'," he sneered, his boisterous remarks drawing the attention of several passersby across the street.

"Have you lost your marbles, Papa?   No fools in their right minds would take on the might of the British Empire, much less expect to win."

"'There is no little enemy'."

"Adages, adages.   I'm sick to death of your adages," he blared, not caring who heard him.

"Where there's a will, there's a way."

Billy's eyes darted menacingly in his father's direction.

"And I'm tired of your doomsday predictions," Benjamin fired back curtly.   "Let's let the numbers speak for themselves: So far, 1500 British killed vs. 150 Yankees.   The cost to them in dollars?   Two million for a measly half mile of territory gained.

Agonizing not over the disparity in the lopsided figures but over his father's inordinate blindness, Billy cried out in pity, "What can I say, Papa, to bring you to your senses?"

"Me?" Benjamin shouted, obviously feeling that the shoe should be on the other foot.

"Yes, you!   WE HAVE NO NAVY!   England is invincible!   Her fleet's artillery could smash our seacoast towns to smithereens!"

"I'll concede that the seacoast is indefensible, but the interior, never!"   Benjamin's face was red with rage, his expression resolute, showing no signs of wavering.

Seeing that he was up against a stone wall, Billy tried a different approach.   "Damn it, Papa, listen to me.   Listen to reason.   Those lunatic rebels in Philadelphia are fomenting a civil war.   You know what that will mean: neighbor against neighbor, friend against friend, brother against brother..."

"Son against father."

Billy's breath caught in his throat at the painful prospect. "Those bastards would do well to adopt the old adage..."   He hesitated.

"What adage is that?"

"'Those who do not carry a big stick are advised to speak softly'," he whispered.

"We did speak softly, but England didn't listen."

Utterly fed up and frustrated by their complete lack of accord, Billy clammed up, but when they reached the front steps he turned on his father and snarled, "Do you know what our problem is, Papa?"

"Yes.   You're too headstrong for your own good."

"The problem is," he persisted, ignoring the reproach, "that we have parallel points of view, so even if we argued this issue from now 'til kingdom come, our positions would never converge."

Down but not out, Benjamin came back with the old one-two, delivering a nasty blow below the belt in the vulnerable vicinity of Billy's pocketbook, a reliable target he had used to his advantage time and time again.   "What will you do for money if the assembly cuts off your salary?"

"I'll deal with that when and if the time comes."   Billy

wasn't altogether sure where his father's questioning was leading, but to an ear so perfectly attuned to the wile and guile of the master instigator, it had the distinct ring of a bargain in the making.

There being no immediate rebuff from Benjamin's corner, Billy opened the door and motioned for his father to precede him into the foyer.   Billy knew from experience that he'd not heard the end of it, that his father's silence was no guarantee that he'd thrown in the towel, not by a long shot, because as any farmer worth his salt would tell you, rain only lets up to get a better hold.

"There you are, father," young Billy called from the top of the stairs.   "I've been looking all over for you."

"What is it, son?"

"I put your perspective glass back where I found it.   I'm not taking it with me after all."

"Why not?   I said you could borrow it."

"When would I find time to use it?"

"That's true," Billy laughed stiffly.   "You do have quite a heavy schedule.   If you've finished packing, have Thomas bring down your bags.   Your grandfather wants to be on his way shortly after dinner."

"Very well, father."

As soon as the brief exchange ended, Benjamin took Billy by the elbow and steered him into the privacy of the adjoining drawing room.   Shutting the door, he began to pepper Billy with a deluge of pointed questions.   "When will the assembly vote on your salary?"

"The first of next month."

"Do you expect the appropriation to pass?"

"I doubt it."

"What then?   Do you have a contingency plan?"

"No."

"You should," Benjamin warned.

"I'll ask the Ministry for help."

"'God helps those who help themselves'."

"I will not leave my post, Papa!"

"Fine time you pick to become a martyr!"

"Look who's talking.   The quintessential optimist."

"Fighting is getting us nowhere," Benjamin said, rubbing his temples as though he were soothing a splitting headache.

A knock at the door evoked a momentary cease-fire.   Billy

made a swift retreat to open it, grateful for the well-timed interruption. "What is it, Margaret?" he asked with unusual tolerance.

"Dinner is served, governor."

"It will have to wait," Benjamin replied coldly.

"But Papa!" Billy protested.

"Don't you understand? THIS CANNOT WAIT! Close the door."

"I will not. Let all who need to hear, hear."

Arm in arm, Betsy and young Billy entered from the hallway, their jubilation quickly fading when they confronted the two warring members.

"Come on, you two," she said, making light of their apparent set-to. We're not going to have a family feud on young Billy's last day in Perth Amboy," Betsy railed, trying her best to make light of the situation by treating the quarrel in progress as a petty squabble and attempting to shame her husband and father-in-law into an immediate truce.

"Maybe you can talk some sense into this pigheaded husband of yours, Betsy. I can't," Benjamin growled, looking

Billy straight in the eyes.

"Maybe it would help if I knew what you two were fighting about."

"Papa wants me to turn traitor!"

"Patriot!"

Betsy gasped.   Young Billy put his arm around his mother's shoulder to steady her.

"Papa has the cockeyed notion that the rebels can win this war."

"But England is all-powerful!" Betsy cried.

"And her ministers bungling fools!" Benjamin countered, showing no sign of contrition whatsoever over his forthright denunciation of the lofty British hierarchy.

"I shall never leave my post."   Billy doggedly repeated, not giving an inch.

"Hah!   '(You) can no more bear the light of truth, it seems, than Owls can endure the light of the sun'."

"Stop it, both of you," Betsy cried, trembling.

Ignoring her plea, Benjamin continued, speaking softly now, like that of a man who has emptied his heart and soul and still lost. "'Independence (is) more honorable than any service.' Besides, it is highly probable that you will be forced to leave your post anyhow."

Benjamin's soft-spoken remark jabbed Billy like a dagger. "Are you hinting that the current rumor is true, that there is a plan afoot to replace all royal governors and set up a ...a republic?" The word was so repugnant to him, that it literally stuck in his throat.

"All I'm saying is this."

"JOIN or DIE."

"Or die?" young Billy cried.

"Not in the mortal sense, son. Don't be alarmed."

"Join and you may be able to continue as governor is what I started to say."

"Aren't you forgetting my solemn oath?"

"What about Jonathan Trumbull?"

"He must live with his conscience and I with mine. The Connecticut governor is supporting the rebel cause," Billy coached, seeing his son's look of bewilderment. "Furthermore, Papa, what assurance do I have that the assembly wouldn't dismiss me anyway?"

"You've been a popular leader.   Why should they?"

"It hasn't been easy serving two masters."

"You're in the thick of it, Papa.   Can't you do something to end this nightmare?"   Betsy pleaded, sobbing from despair.

"It's in Whitehall's hands now, my dear," Benjamin replied with a shrug.

Ranting and raving like a wild man, Billy rushed to a nearby table piled high with newspapers and began rummaging through them, flinging the unwanted ones clear across the room. Finally finding what he was looking for, an August 17th edition of *Drapier's Massachusetts Gazette*, he grabbed it in his fist and shook it in his father's face.   "John Adams, a member of your so-called Congress, admitted that it was he who wrote these letters," he began, gritting his teeth.   "Are you aware of this man's sentiments on independence?   If nine-tenths of the delegates oppose independence, as we are led to believe, why hasn't someone called for Mr. Adams' expulsion or censure?"

Not giving the elder Franklin a chance to say aye, yes or no, young Billy shocked everyone present by lighting into

Benjamin with a vengeance.   "What kind of grandfather are you,"

he demanded to know, "breaking up the family that has just been

united?"   Then, being the perfect gentleman that he was, he took

his mother's arm and escorted her in to dinner.   Speechless, the

two combatants followed humbly behind.

THE POINT OF NO RETURN

Chapter XXV

Perth Amboy
Tuesday, November 7, 1775

It was two months between visits, a span sufficient in length for the foliage along Kearney Street to turn, fade and die and time enough for word to reach America that King George had rejected the Olive Branch Petition and declared the Colonies in rebellion.   Whether it was time enough to heal the wound inflicted by the Franklins' last clash, remained to be seen.

Apparently refusing to give up on his 'Tory' son, as he now called him, Benjamin decided to drop by on his way home from a nine-day-conference with General Washington in Cambridge, bringing with him living proof that the Colonial side was the right side.   En route from Massachusetts, he had detoured to the little

Rhode Island town of Warwick to pick up his sister, Jane Mecom,

who had been forced to evacuate Boston four months earlier and

leave her comfortable home to the likes of General Gage and the

ransacking redcoats.   There was a third passenger in the Franklin

carriage when it arrived at Proprietary House on that clear, brisk

autumn day.   It was a promising ten-year-old named Ray, the son

of close family friends, Caty and William Greene, who generously

opened their home to Aunt Jane for a four-month stay when she

had nowhere else to go.   Benjamin was repaying the debt

somewhat by taking their boy to Philadelphia, where he would

attend the Academy with Temple.

Utterly floored by the unexpected stopover, Betsy and Billy

were equally overjoyed; hence, in keeping with the time-honored

custom at the governor's home, the happy pair spread the welcome

mat and greeted the three weary travelers with open arms.

Although Benjamin had a standing invitation to visit whenever he

pleased, after their last confrontation, Billy was shocked that his

father would condescend to sleep under his roof again.

More surprising, Benjamin was all smiles when he stepped

from the coach, because, unbeknown to Billy, his twofold sojourn to New England had been an enormous success. It was militarily productive in that many procurement and policy stipulations contained in the Congress' Articles of War were addressed and ironed out and monetarily rewarding because, miracle of miracles, his constituents in the Massachusetts Assembly, free of a royal veto, came across with his agent's salary, retroactive from 1770. As a result, he had a wad of money in his pocket, £1,851 to be exact, less the piddling sum he had spent to buy a new team and carriage before starting out on his homeward journey.

Not one for family feuds in the first place, Billy was happy to bury the hatchet and begin his father's visit with a clean slate, for his Aunt Jane's sake if for no other reason. The poor woman had already borne her share of grief, her son, Josiah, having been killed in the battle for Breed's Hill.

"God be praised," she exclaimed, preceding her escorts into the foyer. "We're here at last, safe and sound. Are you sure we're not imposing?"

"I never would have forgiven you if you hadn't come. My favorite aunt never needs an engraved invitation to visit her favorite nephew," Billy cajoled, using soft soap to erase any trace of uneasiness she may have been feeling.

"Speaking of invitations, your Papa said you offered to take me in after I was displaced."

"The minute I heard of your plight, I wrote.   Papa told me in August that you didn't receive my letter."

"Maybe it went astray, because I haven't had a line from you in ages, William."

In spite of the delicate dig, Billy had to laugh.   "That's what I love about you, Aunt Jane," he chaffed, giving her an affectionate kiss on the cheek.   "You chew a person out with such finesse."

"In all seriousness, it's a horrible feeling to be homeless.   I thank God every day for this boy's good mama and papa.   It seems their hearts are open to all who arrive at their door in need of refuge, taking in a dozen people at a time.   They're close as my own kin.   Isn't that true, Ray?"

"Yes, Granmah."   Ray tugged at the hem of Jane's black cape.   She bent down, and he whispered something in her ear.

"It isn't polite to whisper," Benjamin said, correcting him on the spot.

"I'm told I have a grandnephew in Philadelphia with impeccably flawless manners, who will set a perfect example for young Ray," Jane countered, boldly unveiling the secret of Temple's existence.

Ray tugged again, this time with a little more urgency.

"He needs to use the commode," Jane said softly, stepping aside to tell Betsy privately.   "The last stop we made was in Belleville, or was that Ringwood, Ray?"

"It wasn't Ringwood.   Doncha remember?   That's where I met Captain Erskine."   Turning to Betsy he added, "And he showed me a real iron mine."

The men's ears perked up like foxhound's when Robert Erskine's name was mentioned.   A Scot from Dunfirmline, he was the son of a celebrated preacher hired by a London syndicate in 1771 to manage The American Company, Hasenclever's bankrupt iron ore mines at Ringwood.   An engineer and inventor, Erskine was a fellow at the prestigious Royal Society, one of his sponsors being none other than the distinguished Dr. Benjamin Franklin.

Billy was very familiar with the turncoat, Erskine.   It was he who assembled the first company of rebel troops in northern

New Jersey, fitting them out at his own expense.   His generosity earned him the rank of captain, and the soldiers under his command were ordered by the Continental Congress to guard the iron works at Ringwood from Tory attacks.   What the governor did *not* know was that this secure, little out-of-the-way hamlet, nestled in the foothills of the Ramapo Mountains, was being used as a sanctuary to store hoards of gunpowder and other army scarcities right under his very nose.

In an effort to divert the conversation away from New Jersey's iron and copper mines, Benjamin grasped his newly-acquired charge around the shoulders, needling him with a mirthful, "I told you so."

"He gorged himself when we stopped along the Passayak River to water the horses," Jane offered, filling in the details.

"Out of the mouth of babes," Billy muttered in Benjamin's ear, taunting him.

Ray crossed his legs when the word water was mentioned.

"I declare," said Betsy.   "Ray Greene will think we New Jerseyans have no manners at all.   Please.   Go in the parlor, everyone, and make yourselves at home.   John, who was standing in the great hall ready to take their wraps, was instructed to see that the youngster was made comfortable at once."

"Oh, how magnificent," Jane exclaimed, studying the mural that covered the entire wall in the grand hallway.

"This one is Cohoes, and that one is the Passayck Falls," Billy explained, pointing them out.

"I can't wait to see the rest of the house."

"Wait for me," Ray called over his shoulder.

"Governor Franklin will take you and your Granmah for a grand tour the minute you get back, won't you dear?"

Billy was far from being your typical henpecked husband, but the threatening, sidelong look and his wife's unnaturally commanding tone convinced him that she meant business.   As plainly as the circumstances allowed, she was telling him to get the frown off his face and forget about starting another row with Benjamin.

All went well through dinner.   Afterwards, the family gathered in the yellow drawing room where a fire blazed and tallow candles flickered, mellowing hearts and soothing tensions.

Giving in to the sandman, Ray pushed two chairs together and curled up with his head in his Granmah's lap, having already heard the account of her travail ten times over.

"If you're going to sleep, young man, you'd better go to bed," she said.

"I'm not sleeping, Granmah.   I'm just resting my eyes."

Betsy took a white coverlet embroidered with delicate yellow narcissus from the back of the settee and covered him.

"Thank the Lord he's no older," Jane sighed, brushing the hair back from his face.   "The horror I witnessed watching our brave men and boys return from the battle at Lexington depressed me so that I couldn't sleep for days on end."

The image of the grisly scene and the sickening fact that some of the dead and wounded were probably boys only slightly older than Temple affirmed Billy's belief that his decision to take the bull by the horns and make a last-ditch effort to avert civil war, in his own province at least, by pleading his case for reconciliation before the assembly when it convened in Burlington the following week was crucial.   The mere fact that they agreed to meet at all was a feat in itself, because, by this time, all the other royal governors had either fled to safety or, as in Trumbull's case, defected.

Having been lost in his own thoughts for a moment, Billy picked up the conversation as his Aunt Jane lamented, "'...while the Ministry have been distressing poor New England in such a Cruel Manner.'"

"Now sister," Benjamin said, consoling her, "what did I advise you on that head?"

"'To keep up my courage and that foul weather does not last always in any country'."

Billy gulped so hard that he almost swallowed his Adam's apple.   Has Papa forgotten his history?   What about the Hundred Year's War?

"Believe me," Jane continued, holding the floor, "it took a heap of courage to smuggle as much as I did past Gage's cold-hearted plunderers without being caught."

"How did you do that?" Betsy asked wide-eyed.

"I packed 'em in my bedding and apparel," she replied matter-of-factly but with a roguish grin.   Then, obviously afraid that her nephew, the lawyer, might accuse her of doing something

illegal, she stated defiantly, "It was no contraband.   They were
<u>my</u> things, bought and paid for."

To the contrary, Billy cried, "Bravo, Aunt Jane!" praising
her for her pluck and daring.   The thought of all those little old
ladies putting something over on that gauche horse's ass, General
Gage, tickled him silly.

Amid the shouting and applauding, Margaret arrived with
the tea.

"Ah, at last," Betsy said, getting up to do the honors.

Grimacing, her houseguests stiffened in their chairs,
reacting as though some terribly vulgar profanity had been spoken,
with brother staring at sister and sister at brother.

Punctilious to a fault, the maid set the gleaming silver-
plated urn on the table, laid out the tea service and left the room.

While Betsy was pouring, Jane roused Ray and announced
that she was extremely tired and was going to bed.

After Jane's unceremonious exit, Benjamin turned to his
daughter-in-law and, just as brusquely, asked if she would mind
leaving so he might have a word with his son.

"Please wait for me in the parlor, Papa," Billy said sternly, seeing the dismayed look on his wife's face.

As soon as they were alone, Betsy cried, "What an unthinkable blunder.   I've spent the entire day trying to keep you from stirring up a hornet's nest, and look what I do.   Offer them tea!"

"Never mind, my darling," he said, taking her in his arms. "The masquerade had to end sooner or later.   We've been walking on eggs all day.   Why don't you have the tea taken to our room. I'll be up in a little while.   I promise."

"Please don't fight with Papa again."

"That I cannot promise.   Don't you understand?   The man is toying with treason.   And I love him so..."   Tears came where words would not.

"I do understand," she answered, pressing his wet cheek to hers.   "But..."

"But what?   What kind of son would I be...how could I live with myself if I didn't do my utmost to extricate him from such a hellish entanglement?   Pulling himself together, he whispered, "I must go before he up and leaves."

"Just remember one thing," she warned with a faint smile,

holding fast to the tips of his fingers.   "Our son isn't here to

referee."

Billy acknowledged his wife's caution with a wink and a

nod.

Although the parlor was comparatively lighted and heated,

the lackadaisical mood of early evening was conspicuously

missing.   Billy expected to find his father pacing fiercely back

and forth wearing out the rug but was surprised to find him

standing motionless before the full-length portrait of George III, a

Ramsey painting drawn at the time of the coronation.

"I've been wrong, Billy."

"About what, Papa?"   His pulse raced.

"He's had me fooled all along."

"Who in God's name are you talking about?"

Benjamin pointed an accusing finger at the British monarch

in the gilded frame.

"God Almighty!" Billy exclaimed, plopping into an easy

chair.   He thrust his head back against the doily-covered headrest

and closed his eyes, trying to contain himself.

Benjamin wheeled around to face him squarely.   "If you think this is easy for me to admit, you've got another thought coming."   His voice waned and faltered.   "'It was always less painful to blame the mangling hands of bungling ministers or inept, bloodthirsty officers for our miseries than my honorable and trusted sovereign.   But, more and more, I am convinced that they, like puppets, have been responding to manipulation from above, acting by instruction and currying favor by such and such conduct. You know as well as I do that 'a fish smells from the head down'!"

Billy's eyes sprung open.   His fingernails dug into the arms of the wing chair to prevent him from lunging at his father. "Watch what you say in this house, Papa," he said, seething with wrath.

"This *Tory* house you mean," Benjamin fired back, twisting the lion's tail.   "Deny that the King has singled out America and is setting her up as an example before the rest of his dominions. Submit or suffer the consequences.   Is that our lot?   Go ahead. Deny it."

Unable to, Billy leaped to his feet to defend the King's motive.   "What he's doing is crushing a damned uprising and, at the same time, sending a warning signal to all his subjects, whether in Tobago, Senegal, Minorca, Pennsylvania or Massachusetts Bay, to either respect the laws and uphold the constitution or else."

Inside, however, Billy was fighting a separate hell, a struggle between love for his father and attachment to his King. In his desk drawer, under lock and key, lay secret information that might affect not only the safety of Philadelphia at large but, more selfishly, the lives of his pregnant sister, Sally, his nephews, Benny and little Will (the infant Hercules, according to his grandfather) and, of course, his own son and Benjamin.   The confidential intelligence sent to him from Whitehall revealed anticipated British fleet strength and specific deployment locations.   One squadron, potentially, was being ordered to Delaware Bay.

"Then he's a tyrant!" Benjamin blared wild-eyed.

"And you're a traitor!"   'The ugly word fell freely from his mouth like a drop of blood from a cut lip, almost as though it had been incubating for months and needed the proper temper and climate to hatch'.   Without forethought, the accusation tumbled from his tongue, giving credence to the saying coined by the ancient Roman poet, Horace, that 'Once a word has been allowed to escape, it cannot be recalled'.

Benjamin's eyes narrowed.   "'Rebellion to tyranny is

Obedience to God.'   In my book, that makes *you* the traitor."

Billy swallowed hard and took his lumps like a veteran.

His feelings were immaterial.   What mattered was that he keep

his father from making the mistake of his life.   Somehow he had

to get through to him, to convince him that he was mixed up with a

bad bunch, designing men, powerfully ambitious men, who would

stop at nothing to achieve their end, the complete separation of

America from the Mother Country.   What maddened him most

was his developing notion that the radicals in the Congress were

plotting this treachery behind the people's backs, knowing full well

they did not have their consent to lobby for independence.   What

was more, Billy believed the people back home would throw the

instigators out like the moneychangers in the temple if the truth

was known, but he was consumed with a growing sense of dread

that 'the Design (would) be carried on by such degrees, and under

such pretenses, as not to be perceived by the People in general till

too late for Resistance'.

"The pot calling the kettle black," Billy lashed back,

neutralizing his father's attack.   "And since you brought it up, speaking of tyranny, what do you call silencing the opposition by mob rule, using hatchet men called the Sons of Liberty to do your dirty work, tar and feathering dissenters and roughing them up so badly that one man I know of will be nearly blind for the rest of his days?   Answer me that."   Billy knew he'd struck home by the wooden expression on his father's face, but a stranger never would have guessed it, because the experienced whipping boy never batted an eye.

"Any abuse is insufferable, but UNITY is our strength and must be guarded," Benjamin stated with dogmatic sureness, paraphrasing the famed fabler, Aesop.

"Your prize UNANIMITY is skin-deep.   Superficial. Attained by heavy-handed tactics."

"However distasteful, the end justifies the means, and, furthermore, how dare you talk to me about tactics.   Was there any justification for General Howe's barbarous attack when he shelled and burned Charlestown, where the sick and aged who could not be carried off in time perished in the flames?   You tell me!   Is that brutality the act of a legitimate government?"

"The ravages and havoc of such a war will likely be inflicted by both sides, I'm afraid," Billy sighed.

But his doomsday prediction went unheard as Benjamin fought back hot and heavy, hammering away at the royal plan to divide and conquer.   "North's Plan pits colony against colony. Another strategy encourages slaves to murder their masters and Indians to attack our innocent back settlers.   What will they think of next?"

Without commenting one way or the other, Billy fired off his final volley.   "And I heard that one of your eminent delegates at the Congress has suggested that New Jersey Tories who do not disarm should be executed.   What do you say to that?"

Benjamin's eyes dropped but said nothing.   He shifted his weight from his swollen foot and, leaning heavily on his cane, limped to the window to stare out into the pitch-black night.

"Sit here, Papa, and put your feet up on the Ottoman."

Without changing position, he shook his head.   At length he said, "To those of little faith, we must appear crazed, like David taking on Goliath.   Severing the bands that bind us is a painful process but a necessary one.   If we only had representation in parliament, taxation would be more palatable."

Billy raised his head slowly, not quite believing his ears. Did he detect a ray of doubt, a degree of uncertainty, the will to negotiate?   Until he had more to go on, he answered with caution. "Not go from the frying pan into the fire," he said with a watchful eye, not wanting to appear lacking in give-and-take.

But instead of surrendering, Benjamin turned on Billy with a vengeance.   "Contrary to your stubborn, misguided belief, these congressmen are not warmongering insurgents but gifted, patriotic visionaries."

Billy plumped into the chair, feeling like all the wind had been knocked out of him.   It was all too evident that his father had been taken in by the anarchists' seditious rhetoric and mindless propaganda, hood-winked by the dreamers in Philadelphia, by amateur politicians drunk with power.   Having taken all he could, he covered his ears and moaned, "They're false prophets, wolves in sheep's clothing.   Can't you see that, Papa?"

"You're dead wrong, you hardheaded royalist."   Groping for the clincher, Benjamin crossed the room and eased himself into the chair next to Billy.   "How can I convince you that our way is the only one left open to us." He lifted his spectacles and rubbed the bridge of his nose, seemingly hoping a genie would appear to supply the magic words.

"For starters," Billy interjected, "tell me the Congress is not planning a coup d'état." For emphasis, Billy pounded his fist on the table width that stood between them.

"Our powers are derived from the people," Benjamin stated simply, replacing his eyeglasses.

Billy scowled. "I ask for a straight answer and you give me subterfuge! Laboring, he lifted himself slowly out of the chair and shuffled over to a side table where a display of brandies and an assortment of fine spirits were laid out. Without asking, he poured two cognacs. When Benjamin refused his with a wave of the hand, Billy downed one and then the other.

"Nothing but the best, I see. Shouldn't you be drinking it more sparingly?"

Billy gave his father a searing look out of the corner of his eye. Although he was at the end of his rope, he refused to lose sight of his inherent duty as a son, to rescue his father from the clutches of an elusive enemy whose fanatical extremes were leading America and its people to the shores of the Rubicon.

Then, like an ugly sea serpent, another bugaboo surfaced in

his mind.   Was his father becoming senile?   After all, in a couple

of months he would turn seventy.   Funny.   Billy had never

thought in terms of his Papa's mortality and could not imagine life

without him.   The scary prospect caused a sinking feeling in his

chest, evoking a more temperate response.   "Sometimes I don't

understand you, Papa.   Here we are in the throes of a damned

civil war, and you sit here lecturing me on thrift and frugality.

What's your point?"

"My point is this.   Without a salary coming in, how are

you going to swing it?   Face it.   You're an obsessive spender.

Isn't that so?"

"What are you getting at, Papa?"   Billy had ample reason

to be wary whenever the question of money was raised, because he

had been stung before.   It was a red flag that he approached with

great caution.

Uneasily, Benjamin stood up.   "I've come into some

money, back pay.   It's yours for the asking, a sort of bread-and-

butter stopgap if you will.   Consider it an advance on your inheritance."

"An outright gift?" he asked, stupefied by the charitable offer.   Something was fishy.   The sudden transformation set the wheels of thought in motion.   What's the catch?   What's his motive, Billy wondered, shying away from a hurried answer? Speak in haste, repent at leisure, he mused, tailoring a hackneyed phrase to fit his present circumstance.

"Well?"

"First, tell me what's on the other side of the coin," Billy said, being exceedingly cagey.

Apparently feeling a chill, Benjamin went to stand with his back to the fire, its red-hot coals casting a long shadow across the room.   After a pause, pregnant with suspense, he broke the deadly silence and proceeded to lay the groundwork for what he had in mind.   "It's time we stopped splitting hairs, patched up our petty differences and formed a family coalition, a united front."

"Stop beating around the bush, Papa."

"All right.   I'll lay it on the line.   America is going to win this conflict.   Why?   Because our cause is just.   'God will protect and prosper it; you will only exclude your(self) from any share in it if you don't commit yourself tonight to our valiant

struggle against this unwarranted aggressor, these ruthless invaders

who hate and despise us, who think of us as an inferior species'."

Billy saw red.   "Do you know what you're doing, Papa?

You're offering me a bribe.   A filthy dirty bribe!"   Mortified,

Billy teetered from the shock and had to grasp the table edge to

steady himself.   "You told me the last time we met that I didn't

know this people or this country.   Well, Papa, it is unequivocally

evident that you know your son even less."

"Don't you see?   I'm trying to save you."

"It wasn't long ago, as I recall, that you were 'too much

attached to that fine and noble china vase the British Empire to

smash it'."

Benjamin was quick to add the justifying qualification to

his sentimental epithet.   "Except as a last resort," he sighed.

Billy's mind was a sea of confusion where love, hate, duty,

honor, pride, prejudice, failure, futility, compassion and anger all

swam together.   This can't be happening, he cried to himself as

though in a daze.   You are not only my father but my dearest

friend.   Then, lashing back, he attacked not his father but the dastardly liberty cult that had corrupted so fine a character.

"Denounce them! Please, Papa, make a pledge: For King and Country. Do it, Papa. Renounce them!"

"I renounce one thing and one thing only," Benjamin replied, his tone spiritless and husky with remorse, "and that is my one and only son." He walked toward the door, shoulders drooping, looking like a man who had just received the licking of his life. "We'll be leaving first thing in the morning," he stated bluntly.

"Papa?" Billy called.

Benjamin hesitated.

"I hope that if you 'design to set the Colonies in a flame (that you take care to) run away by the light of it.'" His voice, too, like that of a beaten combatant, was calm and contrite, with no discernible sign of haughtiness or hostility.

'PRO REGE ET PATRIA'

Chapter XXVI

Perth Amboy
Sunday, January 7, 1776

For William Franklin, the closing months of the old year culminated in two dramatic events.   First, behind his back, his friend and colleague, William Alexander (the Earl of Stirling), accepted a colonelship in the New Jersey militia.   Unwilling to believe the hearsay at first, the governor instructed the council secretary to add a postscript to Alexander's meeting notice, asking him point-blank whether it was true.

It was, Lord Stirling wrote back, revealing his true colors, but he was sure the governor would approve, having heard him say on several occasions that the 'Rights of the people and the prerogative of the Crown were equally dear to (him)'.

Fit to be tied, Billy fired back a scorching reply informing the Earl that he was suspended from the council and reminding his lordship of his frequent statement that 'a man ought to be damned who would take up arms against his Sovereign'. Given the same chance in private, Billy would have called his erstwhile friend every name under the sun, from an abominable, hypocritical renegade to a treasonous, two-faced son-of-a-bitch! But Lord Stirling was a shrewd cookie and kept his distance.

The second event concerned the governor's whopping success in convening the province's legal assembly on the 15th of November in Burlington, a stone's throw away from the extralegal seat of Colonial power. By hook or by crook, he rounded up a quorum of moderates and nearly pulled off a bombshell, that of splintering the cohesive, united colonies by having New Jersey make a separate peace with England.

Billy's timing was perfect, coinciding with a general public outcry against the Congress' imposition of higher taxes and stringent military requirements. As a result, the chamber room was packed. There to speak their minds were everyday countryfolk, Quakers, tillers of the soil, hard-working, peace-loving men whose rancor against the assembly and its abuse of power had brought them to Burlington to stand up and be counted.

It was a red-letter day for the governor, because the malcontents' anti-war/pro-peace sentiments played right into his hand.   When the dust settled, a petition had been drafted and a decision made to send the appeal directly to the Crown, bypassing the Congress.

Billy's euphoria was short-lived, however.   News of New Jersey's defection carried down river to Philadelphia, causing great alarm in the congressional chamber of that city.   Three topnotch arm twisters were dispatched posthaste to suture the breach.

When Dickinson of Pennsylvania, Jay of New York and Wythe of Virginia arrived and demanded admittance and permission to speak, Billy was livid.   He argued that it was against the law, that only New Jerseyans who paid taxes had the right of access.   Beyond delivering his opening address and subsequent prepared statements, even *he* was barred from the assembly's deliberations.   Nevertheless, after much ado, Speaker Cortlandt Skinner, caving in to pressure, allowed them to enter and gave them the floor.

Getting even, Skinner unwisely took notes, which he passed along to his friend, Governor Franklin. His report disclosed that, altogether, the spokesmen harangued the assemblage for about an hour, bludgeoning the legislators with guilt by convincing them that by acting alone, they were proving what England had thus far failed to prove, that the Colonies were nothing more than a 'rope of sand'. After all was said and done, the petition was withdrawn and, in Billy's view, another 'golden opportunity' lost.

The governor returned to East Jersey with his tail between his legs, finding little consolation in the one personal triumph he had achieved early on in the session: The assembly voted to fund his salary for yet another year. Had an on-the-spot poll been conducted, however, his foes would have cried 'foul', undoubtedly claiming the dole was granted with a £100,000 string attached, a reference to the sum total of the letters of credit the King had authorized New Jersey to issue. Despite the fact that the lawmakers had waited over a decade for such a windfall, Billy belatedly announced the Loan Bill in his opening address, a measure Parliament had approved way back in February.

Keeping it under wraps, he had saved the unveiling for the

opportune moment.

At the time he reveled in success and celebrated his brief

hour of glory, but it was a hollow, empty victory, for there would

be no chance to gloat.   Temple was sent to spend the holidays in

Perth Amboy, but he brought no Christmas greetings or

congratulations from the head of the Philadelphia household.

When the festivities were over, grateful that he was still

gainfully employed, Billy sat down on January 5th to write

Dartmouth an account of the late assembly proceedings.   Trusting

no one, least of all his secretary, Petit, whose family tie to

Washington's personal secretary made him suspect, he copied the

letter himself and enclosed it in a packet along with some

newspapers and a letter from Skinner to his brother.   After

mapping out a circuitous route, he summoned a courier, a

neighbor's son, to deliver the parcel to Staten Island.   Hoping to

avoid suspicion, he had him ferry across the Arthur Kill at

Elizabeth Town Point, sixteen miles north of Perth Amboy in the

very heart of rebel territory and only minutes away from Lord

Stirling's headquarters, but before the young man could step foot aboard the boat, he found himself looking down the long barrel of

a flintlock rifle.   Unable to give the colonel's patrol the slip, he

was taken into custody and searched.

Lord Stirling had netted the big fish.   Armed with positive

proof that William Franklin was an 'unworthy American' siding

with Britain and backed up by a recent Continental Congress

resolution which authorized the apprehension of 'the more

dangerous among them', the colonel gave the fatal order: Arrest

Governor Franklin at Proprietary House in Perth Amboy.   The

betrayal was complete.

Was his action a manifestation of military prowess or was it

retaliation?   After all, it was the governor's faction in the

assembly that had moved to seize many of the Colonel's land-

holdings for back taxes; furthermore, if the legislature had

reconvened on January 3rd as originally planned, a motion was in

the works to investigate Lord Stirling's shady financial dealings.

In all likelihood, it was a combination of the two.

St. Peter's Church

Shortly before the 8 o'clock service was to begin, the parish priest went to the Franklin pew and asked the governor whether he might have a few words with him in private.   Being one of the pillars of the church, this was nothing strange, yet to a lady whose nerves were as taut as an overtight violin string, every overture became a threat, every nuance another treachery.   Betsy's shaky hand clutched the sleeve of her husband's coat.

"It's all right," he whispered, comforting her.   Reassured, she relaxed her grip, enabling him to free himself and follow the pastor into the sacristy.

"Cortlandt! What on earth are you doing here?"

"Shh!" The speaker shut the door behind them.

"Cortlandt has learned that Lord Stirling intercepted your mail and that you and he are to be arrested.   A regiment from Elizabeth Town is on the march as we speak."

"I was afraid this might happen."

"It should be here by noon.   There's no time to waste. I've arranged for a boatman to take us to Staten Island.   From there, we will take refuge on one of the King's ships in the harbor."

Billy shook his head wildly.   "I will not quit!"

"Go with him, William."

"What about Mrs. Franklin and Billy, Reverend Preston? What about Mrs. Skinner and your thirteen children, Cortlandt?"

"I'm doing this for them."

It was a small room with a window to match.   Billy walked over and rested his elbows on the wide stone sill.   His hot breath steamed the cold panes and obstructed his view of the adjacent, snow-covered graveyard, not that he saw anything but the inner workings of his own troubled mind.

As the church bell sounded summoning Anglicans to worship, Billy turned to render his decision: "I will do all in my power to remove my wife and my son from this danger, but, gentlemen, if I were to abdicate, I would be falling right into their trap by giving them an excuse to set up a Republican government in this colony.   The same would be true if I took up arms against them.   No, my best bet is to sit tight, do my duty, and leave my destiny to Providence."

"May God bless you both."

"Thank you, Reverend."

"'Pro Rege et Patria'," said Cortlandt, shaking Billy's hand.

"'Pro Rege et Patria.'   Farewell, my friend."

Proprietary House
January 8, 1776 – 2:00 a.m.

Thump! Thump! Thump! Bang! Bang! Bang!

Too furious to be frightened, Billy bolted out of bed and ran to the window to see who had the gall to pound on his door at such an ungodly hour.   Betsy sprang upright after the first Thump, nearly jumping out of her skin.   She clutched Billy's pillow and began to whimper uncontrollably.

"It's that scoundrel Lord Stirling's doing," he seethed, his teeth clenched from fury and cold.   A contingent of soldiers had surrounded the house.   Drenched in moonlight, their incongruous shapes were silhouetted against a background of sparkling winter white.   "Has the man no sense of human decency?"

After signaling John Billy went to his hysterical wife's side. "Don't go," she cried.   "Please, don't leave me.   They can't take you away from me.   I can't bear it.   Please, Billy, please."

Gently enfolding her in his strong, sinewy arms, he buried his face in her graying hair, trying to soothe away her fears and anxiety with soft, tender words and the nearness of his body.   But her distress was too great, her constitution too frail.   She went limp and collapsed.   Thinking she had died, Billy began to shake

her.   "You can't die," he cried.   "I won't let you die."

All the while, the racket outside continued.

"Governor Franklin?" Thomas called through the closed

door.

"John!   Get Nona!   Fast!   Then go answer the damned

door!"

"Nona's right here, Governor Franklin."   Without waiting

for an official invitation, she burst into the bed chamber carrying a

candle and her customary tray of medicinal paraphernalia.

"I think she's died from fright, Nona."   Billy was as white

as the bed linen.

"No," Nona replied with her usual cocksureness.   "She's

just fainted from fright, and it's no wonder.   Whoever dat is ought

to be strung up, scarin' people plumb out of their wits in the middle

of the night.   I never did see such ugly goins-on.   A whiff of

spirits of hartshorn and she'll come around in a jiffy."   Uncorking

a small vial, she waved it several times under Betsy's nose.   In no

time her eyelids began to flutter and her flaccid body regained its

natural flexibility.

Billy coughed as a whiff of spirits went up his nose and down his throat.

"Make them go away," she muttered.   "I'm so tired."

"Sleep, my darling, sleep," he cooed, laying her down with painstaking care.

Suddenly all was quiet.   Billy tiptoed to the window.

"Has they gone?"

"No.   They haven't budged."

He grabbed his robe from the back of the chair and put it on when he heard John's hurried footsteps on the stairs.   Nona's brow clouded with a look of foreboding.

"Billy knelt beside his wisp of a wife.   "I begged you to go back to England or to Barbados," he said, talking to his sleeping wife as though he were half out of his mind.

"It'll kill her to be separated from you, Governor Franklin." Nona muffled her sobs and mopped her eyes with a scrap of flannel that she kept in her apron pocket.

"If I'm gone when she wakes," Billy said huskily, not hearing a word the wise woman said, "tell her I'm sorry.   Will you do that for me, Nona?"

"Yesir.   I'll tell her," she said, sniffling.

John stood fidgeting in the open doorway.   Tearing

himself away, Billy got up, covered Nona's sagging shoulders with

a throw from the bottom of the bed and went to meet his fate.

"So who is this unfeeling bastard, John?" the governor

asked as they descended the stairs.

"An armed man delivering a letter from his superior, a

Lieutenant Colonel Winds.   He says it requires an immediate

reply, Sir."

"It does, does it."   A ray of hope crept into Billy's soul.

Had it been an unconditional demand for his immediate capture, no

response would have been requested.   Once inside the study, he

took the note, tore it open and holding it up to the lamp that John

was lighting on his desk, digested its contents in one sweeping

glance.   In short, it said that Wind feared the governor might be a

flight risk after learning that his correspondence had been

impounded and forwarded to the Continental Congress.   What he

required was the governor's promise to stay put until the will of

Congress was known.

Billy sat down and composed a brief reply, saying that

since the letters were routine, he had no intention of leaving,

except if he were banished bodily.   'Were I to act otherwise,' he

concluded, 'it would not be consistent with my Declarations to the

Assembly, nor my Regard for the good People of the Province'.

Having completed his mission, the subordinate returned to

Proprietary House, posted a sentry at the front gate as well as

several others at strategic locations around the house and withdrew

his troops.   Seeing this, Billy dashed off a threatening letter to

Winds protesting his imprisonment and ordering him to remove the

guards or suffer the consequences.

Throughout the night he kept his vigil.   At the break of

dawn, the sentries left, leaving behind the lone man at the gate.

Not knowing if and when they might return, Billy set to work

apprising Dartmouth of his present predicament and reaffirming

his allegiance to the King 'which has been the Pride of my Life to

demonstrate upon all Occasions', he wrote.

Nevertheless, like a recurring nightmare, they returned later

in the day in force.

"You're under arrest, Governor Franklin," said the young

whippersnapper.   "I have orders to take you into custody and transport you to Elizabeth Town where you will stay at the home of Elias Boudinot."

"You may force me, but you shall never frighten me out of the Province," Billy told his captors in a brassy, belligerent tone; howver, being outnumbered one hundred to one, he was compelled to surrender.

After an emotional good-bye, he left his distraught wife in Nona's capable hands and went to board his carriage.

The procession had proceeded only a short distance when it was halted by another of Wind's officers, accompanied by Frederick Smyth.   The chief justice had been working without letup to countermand the order, relying on instilling fear of reprisal into the minds of the military if they seized one of the King's men. Fortunately, the scare tactic worked, leaving Billy free to return to Proprietary House.

The days that followed the aborted arrest taxed the governor's patience and stamina.   Even more worrisome than the uncertainty of his tenure was Mrs. Franklin's continual nervousness.   She would fly into a dither at the slightest sound, however innocuous, be it the clatter of dishes, the banging of a shutter or the rumble of a visitor's coach.

Since misery loves company, Billy waited day in and day out for a sympathetic note from the Philadelphia clan.   Finally, on the 22nd, after receiving a letter from Temple that failed to even mention the dreadful incident, Billy dashed off a snippy reply, bawling his family out for abandoning Betsy in her hour of need. All apologies, Temple wrote back to clear himself, swearing that he knew nothing about it.   Likewise, Sally absolved herself by announcing the recent birth of her new baby girl.   Although no tangible consolation came from the head of the household, Benjamin may have done his bit in his own nebulous way, for when Lord Stirling's incriminating evidence was brought before the Congress, a select committee ruled that Cortlandt Skinner was to be seized and questioned, but nothing was to be done about William Franklin.

Proprietary House
Monday, April 1, 1776

The dreary, socially uneventful Perth Amboy winter wended slowly into spring, bringing with it a bright spot on the Franklin's empty calendar, Temple's mini school vacation. As Alexander Pope sagely said, 'Hope springs eternal in the human breast'. With a sixteen-year-old to tend and pamper, Betsy perked up like a bed of droopy impatiens after a rain shower. For Billy as well, the boy was a godsend, providing a welcome distraction in the realm of his humdrum, workaday world.

"Well, chum, what do you think? Will this be a bumper crop or not?" Billy asked, stopping now and again to inspect the budding apple trees.

"The trees look perfectly healthy, father, but will they produce fruit that isn't wormy or knotted? That's what's important."

"Is something troubling you, son? You sound a little down in the dumps this morning."

"I don't mean to add to your worries, Sir, but ever since grandfather left for Canada, my treatment at school has changed."

"In what way?" Billy stopped short.

"No fistfights. Only verbal abuse. They taunt me

constantly about being a Tory, like you, father."

Billy gave a ferocious jerk on an overhanging branch, snapping it off in his hand. Those heartless ignoramuses, he chafed to himself. Can't they see that the young man is caught in the middle, like a crenel between two merlons of a battlement?

"What should I do?"

"Just keep a stiff upper lip, and don't provoke them in any way," Billy counseled, putting his arm around his shoulder.

Temple was standing on shaky ground. He was like a book between two bookends, the loss of one or the other would seriously affect the stability and security of his world.

"When does your grandfather plan to return?"

"Not before the end of the term, sometime in June, I believe."

"It's absurd that a man Papa's age would undertake such an arduous trip. When I learned he was going, I thought of trying to dissuade him, but it wouldn't have done any good. He's as stubborn as a mule."

"Didn't grandfather stop to say good-bye? I overheard him say he and the commissioners were passing through

Brunswick en route to New York."

"No, Billy, he didn't."   Benjamin's son experienced a
severe tightness in his chest, one brought on by the suppression of
intense, pent-up emotion.

However potent Billy's feelings of anxiety were for his
father's health and well-being, they had not deterred him from
squealing on the good will ambassadors in the name of duty.
When he learned that they had traveled through Woodbridge, a
scant five miles from his doorstep, in a rash moment of
spitefulness and self-pity, he jotted a postscript to the report he was
about to send to his new boss, Lord Germain.   By naming names
and outlining the mission, to lure Canada into the colonial alliance,
Billy had signed his father's death warrant and guaranteed him a
place in line at the gallows, should England win the war.   On the
other hand, should his letter fall into the wrong hands, it was *his*
life on the line.

Then again, since Benjamin always '(made) it a Rule not to
mix personal Resentments with Public Business', perhaps it was
instinct that guided his hand rather than impulse.   Like father like
son?

Proprietary House
Monday, June 17, 1776

Tension mounted in the governor's mansion as the days and weeks slipped by, causing Billy to become almost as high-strung as his wife.   In his letters to Temple, he found fault with everything from his wasteful spending habits to his tardiness at mailing the dozen copies of Paine's *Common Sense* (which he asked him to send on the sly) and other periodicals he'd requested.

To keep abreast of Congress' shenanigans and the latest developments outside his own bailiwick, he read anything and everything he could get his hands on.   The combination of voraciousness and exalted rank served him well, affording him a fair sense of the overall picture on both sides of the water.

Biding his time, he rode the waves of good news and bad, smiling when word arrived that Lord Howe had set sail for America on a peacemaking expedition.

So the Ministry has finally heeded my advice, he gloated in private, vaingloriously floating on a swell of personal accomplishment.   His spirits were soon dampened, however, when he read that the Continental Congress had passed a resolution

on May 15th recommending that the Colonies overthrow royal rule

and replace it with a popular government.   Billy couldn't help but

wonder how his father would have influenced the vote had he been

present.   It seemed that both he and Temple were vulnerable to

attack without Benjamin's repellent protection.

Be that as it may, Billy realized that things were rapidly

coming to a head, and unless he reversed the tide quickly, his

goose was cooked.   Studying the Resolution with the eagle eye of

an attorney, he discovered a subtle technicality: 'resolved: That

it be recommended to the respective Assemblies ...where no

government sufficient to the exigencies of their affairs has been

hitherto established, to adopt such government...'

The lame duck governor interpreted the resolve as an open

invitation to call the legitimate assembly into session to consider

the proposal.   In a daring move, he placed a notice in the

Pennsylvania Gazette on June 5th calling for a meeting in Perth

Amboy on Thursday, June 20th.   The ad stated that he had

'matters of great importance' to convey to the assembly.

Needless to say, he had an ulterior motive in mind: to provide a forum where the British peace initiative could be announced and discussed, thereby discouraging and staving off the planned coup. It was a long shot, but he was out of trumps.

Same Day – 9:30 a.m.

Billy was on pins and needles.   The past twelve days had seemed like an eternity as he waited for a protest to materialize. He put the finishing touches on his speech and set it aside, glad that it was finished.   It did have meat: The envoy would be investing him with power to issue pardons.

A knock sounded at the study door, startling him.   "What is it?"

"Two men to see you, Sir," said John, "Colonel Heard and Jonathan Deere."

Billy froze.   "What do they want?"

"They insist on talking to you personally, Sir."

His heart sank.   "Very well."   Locking his papers in his desk drawer for safekeeping, he went to see for himself.

"What is your business here?" he asked with icy contempt.

"To present you with your parole.   You will be held at

either Princeton, Bordentown or your farm on Rancocas Creek.

Please make your choice, fill in the blank and sign."

"On what authority?" Billy indignantly asked.

"The Provincial Congress of New Jersey."   Heard handed

him two other documents.

The further Billy read, the madder he got.   "This is insane!

For calling a meeting of the people's representatives, I am 'an

Enemy to the Liberties of my Country'?   By so doing, I violated

the May 15th resolve of the Continental Congress?   Asinine!

Anyone with an ounce of sense could see that I was literally

following the dictates of the resolution."   Openly admitting that

he had obeyed the will of the extralegal Congress when he so

vehemently denied its jurisdiction or, in fact, its very existence,

made him sick to his stomach, but desperation, like misery and

politics, makes strange bedfellows.

Hypocritical or not, it was his only alternative.   How else

could he gather a forum to push Howe's peace initiative?   It was a

long shot but, in his mind, his last chance to save his province from

certain ruin.

"And I see they are stopping my salary.   So this is the

thanks I get for thirteen years of faithful service.   Gentlemen, I do

not intend to lower myself by putting this in explicit language, but

I believe you know what you can do with this parole."   Billy

glowered at them as the documents fluttered to their feet.   He

banged the door in their faces and returned to his study to begin

writing his defense.

He hadn't gotten far when he heard the cadence of

marching feet.   Dropping his pen on the unfinished text, he raced

from the room to find his wife.   He met Nona storming down the

upstairs corridor, crying like a baby.   "Thank the Lord you's here,

Governor Franklin.   Mrs. Franklin's a bundle of nerves, shakin'

and shiverin' to beat the band.   That poor woman's not gonna last

long if this misery don't let up soon."

"The days ahead are going to be very trying.   Please stand

by her, Nona."

"Yesir.   You can count on me."

Too choked up to thank her audibly, Billy patted her arm

and entered the blue-striped bedroom.   He was surprised to find

Betsy standing at the window, watching and waiting.   He walked

up behind her and ever so gently clasped his arms around her trembling body.   She dug the back of her head into his chest and closed her eyes, as though she wanted to remember this moment for the rest of her days.   Without opening them she slowly pivoted, craving the feel of his lips.

All the while the soldiers advanced, peeling off to completely surround Proprietary House.   It was plain to see that the governor was under house arrest.

"Where will they take you?" she asked, sounding as though she were in a trance.

"Somewhere for questioning, I would imagine."

Since signing the parole was out of the question in the first place, he considered it unnecessary to mention that three choices of residence had been offered, one of them their own Strawberry Hill Farm on Rancocas Creek.   Signing it would have tied his hands, kept him from leaving the province and made it impossible for him to help the British cause in any way.

"Can't Papa do something?"

"In one respect, maybe he did.   My name is Franklin. Remember, Cortlandt Skinner was taken before the Committee of Safety of the Continental Congress and questioned.   I was not.

"Also, darling, Papa's been extremely ill ever since he returned from Canada."

"There is one consolation, I suppose."

"What's that?"

"Being away, Papa had no hand in passing the treasonous Resolve."

But the question is, had Papa been present, would he have lifted a finger to stop it?　Billy wondered.

For two endless days, the governor was left to stew in his own juice.　Then on the afternoon of Wednesday, the 19th, Heard came thundering through the gate at the head of the cavalry to take his prisoner to Burlington, where he was to have his day in court.

Arriving in the West Jersey capital before nightfall, Billy was able to see the three-story brick mansion he and Betsy had built ten years before jutting up along the waterfront, its airy rooms now empty, its geometrically-designed gardens overgrown with brambles and weeds.　His eyes teared at the thought of her, as he relived their last kiss, their final act of love.

All too soon the carriage stopped and he was ordered out.

Testy and tired to begin with, Billy was outraged when he saw that he was standing before Josiah Franklin Davenport's house, the cousin he took under his wing when Benjamin washed his hands of him.   Now down-and-out, Josiah was Billy's keeper, validating his prediction that conflicting loyalties would become commonplace in countless Colonial families.

The following morning, waspish and ill-tempered, Billy was led under guard to the courthouse to face the music.   There to try him sat thirteen judges.   The most notable among them were Provincial President Samuel Tucker, Princeton President Rev. John Witherspoon and Provincial Secretary William Paterson.

After declaring his innocence and stating his grievances, the governor fell silent, stubbornly refusing to answer any questions put to him by what he termed 'this illegal Assembly, which has usurped the Government of the King'.   His aloofness and resentful, insolent attitude made a mockery of the proceeding, ending it in short order.

His accusers didn't waste precious time either, handing down a verdict without debate: "We find you, William Franklin, guilty as charged," said Tucker.

Billy was escorted back to his prison to cogitate while he waited for the Continental Congress to decide what to do with him, expecting any minute that his friends would rescue him or that his father would have a last-minute change of heart. Making good use of his time, he wrote a final farewell to Temple. Concluding, he said, 'God bless you, my dear boy; be dutiful and attentive to your grandfather to whom you owe great obligations. Love Mrs. Franklin, for she loves you and will do all she can for you if I should never return more. If we survive the present storm, we may all meet and enjoy the sweets of peace with the greater relish'.

Word came on the 25th that Governor Trumbull of Connecticut was chosen to provide housing for the ex-governor and to secure his parole. His horrifying nightmare had come true! Billy was beside himself. His situation looked grim and hopeless. Plagued by sleeplessness and anxiety over leaving Betsy to fend for herself, he took sick and ran a very high fever. In his delirium, he was on trial again. Sitting in judgment was his father, who pronounced him guilty of spousal neglect by not accepting one of the three locations of confinement offered him in his own province. Hallucinating another time, he watched helplessly as his wife withered away, reduced to nothing but skin and bone.   Aside from the bad dreams, for the first time in his life, Billy was thankful for a bout of illness.   It delayed his departure one more day.

And what of the elder Franklin while all this was going on? Had he experienced a turnabout or somehow planned to intercede? Let's backtrack and see: On Friday, the 21st, the day of his son's hearing, he was at home.   'His physical ailments were nearly behind him', he told General Washington in a letter.   That same day he received a draft of the Declaration of Independence from Tom Jefferson to review.   Sometime between the 22nd and the 25th, he felt well enough to travel and went to visit his friend, Edward Duffield, the clockmaker, at his country home in Moreland.   On the 26th, the day Billy was led from his province 'like a Bear through the Country', Benjamin wrote his second alibi to Dr. Rush.   In it, he said, 'I hope in a few days to be strong enough to come to town and attend my Duty in Congress'.   It appears that he was making himself scarce until the disgraceful impeachment was over.   No doubt he wanted desperately to intervene, but his hands were tied.   His motto forbade it: 'We

must all hang together, or assuredly we shall all hang separately'.
Nonetheless, in all probability his pain was caused by more than
boils, edema or gout.   What he suffered from was infinitely
deeper, would never fully heal and would bleed afresh with every
haunting memory.   Benjamin suffered from a broken heart, like
any father who has lost his son.

TO THE VICTOR GO THE SPOILS

Chapter XXVII

New England Coffeehouse – London
61 Threadneedle Street
October 1, 1782

Never getting his fill of the out-of-doors these days, Billy

walked from his rooming house at 28 Norton to 61 Threadneedle

Street at a rapid clip.   Nearing the New England Coffeehouse, he

recognized Joseph Galloway standing in the doorway, all smiles,

waiting to greet him.   They embraced like long-lost brothers, with

tears of joy and sadness alike intermingling.   They were like two

tall ships set adrift, bobbing aimlessly in the calm that follows the

storm.

After this brief, private reunion, they entered the public

place where a group of fellow compatriots swarmed around to

welcome the governor into the fold.   It was like old home week, and only after much backslapping and chitchat did Joseph manage

to steer his old chum to the privacy of a quiet corner table.   "I

want to hear everything," he said as soon as drinks were ordered.

"Where do I begin?"

"Start at the beginning of your confinement."

Billy shuddered as haunting memories of his inhumane

treatment in captivity flooded back.   Although four years had

passed since Betsy Graeme's ex-husband, Henry Hugh Ferguson,

arranged his exchange, recollections of his incarceration still

educed severe trauma.   Unfortunately, the Graeme/Ferguson

marriage ended when Henry joined the British army in November,

1777 and became the Commissary of Prisoners.

A strong mug of steamy-hot tea was plunked down in front

of him that Billy slurped as greedily as possible to help steady his

nerves.   He glanced across the room, catching the eye and

acknowledging with a nod the one who had secured his release and

arranged his exchange.

Getting a grip on himself, he began to fill Galloway in on

the fateful events of the intervening years.   "I stalled every way I

could, trusting that something would transpire to make the

Provincial Assembly rescind my sentence.   By the time we reached Lebanon, Connecticut I had given up, abandoned all hope of ever being rescued.   My only option was to give my written parole to Governor Trumbull.   It was either that or go to jail or the notorious Simsbury Mines.   Besides, by signing it, I was free to roam and ride within a six-mile radius of the city, which would allow me the leeway and leverage I needed to gather intelligence and to develop an effective, covert communications network."

"Like any prisoner of war worth his salt would do."

"My feelings exactly.   Initially, Trumbull sent me to Wallingford, but after a week I knew I could be of no use there, so I asked that my residence be changed to Middletown."

"And they granted it?"

"I have an honest face."   They laughed softly.

"Were you working with Lord Howe?"

"Yes.   He stayed on after the peace negotiations failed."

"By the way, did you know the peace talks were almost held at Proprietary House instead of on Staten Island?"

"No, I didn't."

"Guess whose suggestion it was.   Commissioner

Franklin's."

"H'm. That's interesting. In a roundabout way, maybe Papa was trying to get to see Betsy. Anyhow, getting back to my story, by using the underground, I succeeded in issuing countless pardons throughout Connecticut and New Jersey."

Galloway whistled through his teeth, showing approval for his compatriot's gutsy, do or die deeds.

"Ah, but then New Jersey's new governor, Livingston, confiscated several pardons bearing my name, and the jig was up. I was sentenced to solitary confinement at Litchfield jail."

"That must have been a living hell."

Billy's eyes filled as he dredged up the buried, degrading details of his unmerciful imprisonment. "It was like being buried alive. For 250 days I rotted in that squalid cell, the straw on the floor dank and matted, reeking with the stink of my own human waste and that of others before me. A tiny, four-paned window was my only light, my only ventilation, my only view of the outside world. I had no bed, no clean clothes, no pen, no paper, no books, no newspapers. I lost my teeth and honestly thought I was near death's door. But worst of all, news of my cruel treatment killed my precious Betsy.   Dr. Lawrence said she died of a broken heart."   Billy could not go on.

Joseph covered his trembling hand with his own.   "I saw her in early May of '77.   Then, when the British army evacuated Perth Amboy in late June and retreated to New York, I learned that she went along, bag and baggage."

"Thomas, bless him, got word to me, through Trumbull, that she was deathly ill."

"And they denied you a furlough?"

"Washington tried his best.   I must give him credit for that, but the Congress turned down my request the day she died. Friends buried her in St. Paul's Chapel."   His voice broke.   "One day soon, this man, 'who still laments her loss', will have a plaque erected there in her memory."

After a polite pause, Joseph asked, "What do you think brought about your release from solitary?"

"Certainly not compassion for me but guilt over the shameful way they were treating the son of Benjamin Franklin. The Congress didn't want my blood on its corporate conscience. How would it look if his only living son died at the hands of his captors?"

"Speaking of family, tell me about Temple.   I was in Philadelphia at the time, so I know he sailed to France in October, '76 with his grandfather as his paid, personal secretary."

"That's another sad story.   After he received my farewell note, he went to Perth Amboy to be with Betsy as I hoped he would.   The boy wanted desperately to visit me at Middletown, but Papa wouldn't hear of it.   Said it was too dangerous. Truthfully, I believe the disgrace of having a Tory grandson as well as a Tory son was the deciding factor."

"How old was Temple when he left?"

"Ripe for the draft.   Papa was protecting his interest. Temple represents his only hope for carrying on the Franklin name.   By the way, he took along his namesake, Benny Bache, also.   Papa never could stand being alone."

Joseph took out his handkerchief, blew his nose and looked away.

"I'm sorry, my friend.   How callous of me.   Your misfortune is no less than mine.   Tell me.   How did you and your family fare?"

"To make a long story short, when the rebels recaptured Philadelphia, I took Betsy behind British lines.   Grace stayed on at Trevose, hoping against hope that the old family homestead wouldn't be sequestered.   But, of course, no such luck. Supposedly, after my death, it will be returned to her lock, stock, and barrel.   Washington saw that she passed safely through the American lines on her way into Philadelphia.   Honest to God, Billy, that woman is braver than I ever dreamed.   Betsy and I miss her very much.   But enough of my troubles.   Continue."

"There isn't a great deal more to tell.   The last ten months of my jail term were spent at a private home in East Windsor. My captors were compassionate and my treatment lenient.   I was exchanged for the former governor of Delaware, John McKinley, and on November 1st of '78 arrived in the British stronghold of New York a free man, but a British subject, missing you by only a few weeks, I understand."

"Your reputation as mastermind of the Associated Loyalists in America has preceded you," Joseph said, raising his cup of green tea in a toast of appreciation.

"I rendered what service I could, but my efforts were

largely hamstrung by those in command.   When I wrote you to be

my mouthpiece here in London, I was desperate.   Our campaign

was a stepchild to General Clinton; I had to go over his head."

"I'm curious.   Just how did you operate?"

"Our objectives were twofold: diversion and harassment.

Our raids were swift and decisive.   Hit a target, take a few

prisoners, some spoils, and run.   The hostages were used as

pawns to free Loyalists held in rebel jails.   The men were paid

from the booty they collected."

"The clamor over your so-called retaliatory raids carried all

the way across the Atlantic."

"Hammurabi's eye for an eye," the governor replied, giving

a noncommittal answer.   "From what I'm hearing, you were no

slacker either."

Joseph grinned.   "I tried damn hard to spring you, old

friend."

"Really?   How?"

"I had organized my own cavalry unit.   One day I heard

that Governor Livingston was traveling to Burlington unguarded,

so I colluded with Major André, who was living in your father's house throughout the British occupation of Philadelphia…"

"Ha!" Billy laughed.   "I can only imagine how Papa reacted to that news!   I'm sorry, go on.   You colluded with Major André…"

"to capture the governor and exchange him for you."

"That was an ingenious idea, Mr. Galloway.   What happened?"

"Howe nixed it."

"That figures," Billy replied, looking glum.   Staring into his tea, he swirled the spent leaves round and round and let them settle, trying to rearrange his fortune in the bottom of his cup.

"How the hell did we ever lose this damn war anyhow?" Joseph questioned, sinking into melancholia himself.   "We outmatched them, outshined them and outnumbered them."

"It's simple," Billy replied, shaking his head.   "They had the best leadership plus the unwavering resolve to win that we lacked.   Papa insisted that these men were visionaries and not anarchists as I argued."

"I got to read their *Declaration of Independence*," Joseph added.   "As I remember, it said, 'When in the Course of human

Events, it becomes necessary for one People to dissolve the

Political Bands which have connected them with one another, and

to assume among the Powers of the Earth the separate and equal

Station to which the Laws of Nature and of Nature's God entitle

them…"

"I read it, too," Billy snapped, unable to quell his irritation.

"Now let's see how well they do after winning their independency

and severing the umbilical cord from the mother country."

PAYING THE PIPER

Chapter XXVIII

Southampton, England
July 24, 1785

Almost ten years had elapsed since Billy last saw his father.

Whether they would resume their former connection depended

heavily on the outcome of this four-day meeting.   Afraid of an

oversight, he checked and rechecked their room reservations at the

Star Tavern but decided against a third inquiry when the proprietor

gave him a dirty look as he approached.   Instead, he went outside

to take a walk in the bright sunlight to kill the remaining hour or so

until Captain Truxton's packet arrived from France.

As always, the smell and coolness of the sea beckoned him,

prompting the direction of his course.   The wharf was a beehive

of invigorating activity, a chorus of sounds and fascinating sights, schooners coming and going, captains shouting, green seamen and jolly tars whistling and singing as they tossed bales, rolled barrels and carted crates, filling and emptying the warehouses lining the piers as need be.

Engrossing as all this was, Billy could not get his mind off what lay ahead. He was glad he had made the overture last summer, relieved when his father agreed to correspond, but nervous about his hesitancy in renewing their former friendship. In fact, Benjamin used the opportunity to take a swipe at his son for taking sides against him.

He said in no uncertain terms that 'fidelity to one's father outweighed any political allegiance and that a stance of neutrality would have been understandable and bearable'.

The cut hurt him deeply, especially when it was evident that his father did not treat family loyalty as a two-way street. 'Your Nation,' Benjamin wrote Peace Commissioner Howe, '...by punishing those American Governors who have created and fomented the Discord ...might yet recover a great Share of our Regard'.

But Billy had served his time, endured his suffering and

wanted to forget the past.   Right or wrong, he had followed the dictates of his conscience and, after much soul searching, decided that, if given a second chance, he would undoubtedly take the same path again.

Benjamin did make one concession: As a reciprocal gesture, he permitted Temple to visit his father for six weeks in the fall.   Overjoyed, Billy took his 24-year-old son on the grand tour. Like he and his father had done a quarter of a century before, they traveled from the ruffled Lowlands to the craggy Highlands, hobnobbing along the way with no one but the crème de la crème of society.   Having the time of his life, Temple extended his holiday by dribs and drabs for another two months, not, however, without evoking the wrath of his 'neglected' grandfather.

Billy temporarily abandoned his watch and looked up at the sky, following the lead of everyone around him.   Something was creating quite a stir, and if it was Jean Pierre Blanchard and his hydrogen balloon, he didn't want to miss it either.   The adventurous aeronaut's maiden flight across the English Channel from Dover to Calais in January had made aerial history.   What was more, he launched the idea of delivering international mail by air. Billy immediately sent Temple a letter, thinking it would

please him to receive a post by such a novel conveyance.

There it was, a giant sphere thirty to forty feet in diameter

drifting along freely on the breeze. Its passengers, who were

carried in a tub like undercarriage, waved flags and fronds as they

passed overhead.

Carried away by the marvel of the spectacle, Billy missed

seeing the packet dock, for when he resumed his vigil, his nephew,

son and father were already ashore. His heart nearly stopped

when he saw that Benjamin was not navigating under his own

steam but was being carried in a sedan chair. As the distance

between them melted away, his chest tightened, and he felt like he

was being squeezed by a tourniquet.

Spotting his father, Temple broke stride and rushed ahead

with arms outstretched, leaving no doubt in anyone's mind that the

bond between them had survived the strain of separation.

Whether Billy could reestablish the same comradery with

Benjamin was a totally different story.

Coming abreast of the retinue, Billy welcomed his godson

warmly before turning to his father. "Hello, Papa," he said, offering his hand.   "It was good of you to come."   He was

careful not to let any resentment show.   Benjamin had shocked

him by pulling a fast one in the course of their recent

correspondence.   Riding high on the wings of victory, his father

demanded the payment of his overdue loans and presented him

with a viable plan for divesting himself of the bulk of his overseas

empire.   It should not have come as a surprise, however, because

Benjamin had given him ample notice, warning him in one of their

prewar verbal barrages that those who aided and abetted the enemy

had no right to share in the prosperity that would most assuredly be

forthcoming in postwar America.   Nevertheless, in spite of

mutual injuries and injustices, Billy kept alive the hope that his

father would forgive him and that he would get back in his good

graces.

"Hello, William," he replied with uncommon formality.

"Is the gout troubling you again, Papa?"

"When you're eighty, everything is troublesome."

"Seventy-nine, grandfather," Benny teased, winking at his

uncle.

"You know better than to contradict your elders, young

man," Benjamin said, soundly putting him in his place.   "I was

born January 17, 1706.   That means I'm in my eightieth year."

"I'm sorry, grandfather.   I was only poking fun."

With his mind apparently dwelling on the loose ends he

was here to tie up and sticking strictly to the business at hand,

Benjamin asked William if he had assisted Mr. Vaughan in

collecting the papers for the second volume of his political works

as he had asked him to do.

"Yes, Papa.   Your publisher will meet you here in a day or

so."

"Very well."

Small talk about the balloon, the Baches and the young

men's experiences while in France filled the evening hours.   It

wasn't until the following morning that Benjamin lowered the

boom and openly disclosed the real reason for his stopover: He

had come not to mend the breach between father and son but to

sever the relationship forever.   He was here on business, to collect

his son's outstanding debt for himself and to buy up as much of

Billy's American real estate as possible for Temple.   Billy was surprised to learn that, for some strange reason, his properties had not been confiscated during the war.   Was it because of his parentage?   He wondered.

"I am here to settle our affairs," Benjamin announced with dry candor.

Yes, Temple was Benjamin's new protégé, the one who had not betrayed him, the one who stood at his side at the signing of the Treaty of Paris and, more important, the one who would sire the next generation of Franklins, something Benjamin desperately wanted.   Interestingly, like his father and grandfather before him, his number one grandson had already fathered an illegitimate son in France, but sadly, the infant lived only three weeks.

Billy, the exile, the outcast, squirmed in his chair as he reviewed the preordained terms of the several contracts, somehow managing to maintain his outward appearance of calm and humility.   Inwardly, however, he was livid.   One glance told him that Benjamin was calling the shots.   This is highway robbery, he fumed to himself.   Temple buys my New York holdings for £1500, 40% below value, the exact amount Papa says I owe him. Papa buys my Rancocas Farm and my Burlington properties for

£2000, also at a discount.   Then he turns around and sells the

farm to Temple and takes the mortgage.   Poor Temple.   Now *he*

is beholding to Papa.

Billy studied the final document.   This was the

horselaugh.   He was to turn over half of his Vandalia shares to his

son now, bequeath the remaining half in his Will.   This was hard

to swallow, not because he begrudged Temple his due but because,

at age 55, he was not ready nor could he afford to dismantle and

dispose of his entire estate, living as he did on a £500 yearly

stipend paid him by the British government.

Too empty to fight, Billy scrawled his signatures on the

documents and dated them July 26, 1785.   "One other thing,"

Benjamin said, addressing his son as he passed the contracts

around the table to be witnessed.   "I asked you to give your law

books to Temple.   Did you bring them?"

"Everything I owned was burned in a warehouse fire in

New York," Billy replied passively, feeling as though he'd been

squeezed dry, like Benjamin's proverbial orange.   Looking pale

and gaunt, he struggled to his feet.   "If there is no further business

to conduct, Papa, I am going to the beach."   A stony silence was

his only reply.   Temple made a move to skip out too, but
Benjamin shook his head, keeping his grandson at his beck and
call.

"Mind if I tag along?" cousin Jonathan asked, catching up
to Billy.   Having arrived from the interior earlier that morning, he
was to accompany the family back to America.   "I hope you don't
hold it against me, witnessing those documents, I mean."

"Of course not," said Billy, slackening his pace.

"Can we still be friends?"

Billy filled up and could not speak more than to say,
"Thanks."

"I know you're hurting, but so is he."

Billy raised his eyebrows and quickened his gait.

"It's true.   I overheard him talking out loud one night.
He wrote it down, in a letter, I think.   Or a diary.   He said,
'There is no greater sorrow Than to be mindful of the happy time
In misery'.

Billy dropped to his knees in the sand and let it all out.

The Seashore – England

September 7, 1811

Billy came here to his summer home with his 13-year-old granddaughter, Ellen, to try to lift his spirits after the funeral. His second wife, Mary, who had given him twenty-three happy years was now gone. Also dead was his Papa, who he never saw or heard from again after the Southampton debacle. Benjamin did mention him twice, however, once in his Will: 'The part he acted against me in the late War, which is of public Notoriety, will account for my leaving him no more of an Estate (than) he endeavoured to deprive me of ' and once when writing to a friend, where he appeared to lay the blame for the perpetuation of the alienation on Billy: '(He) keeps aloof, residing in England'. Sally, too, was dead, but Billy was satisfied that he and his sister at least had been reunited. Richard brought her to England on an extended vacation, funding the trip through the sale of diamonds he extracted from the frame of a Louis XVI portrait, a gift to the Doctor from the King.

Billy limped along the beach at his own pace, taking great pleasure in watching Ellen up ahead searching for shells. Sedate and ladylike from her prestigious upbringing, she was the joy of his life.   Half Irish, her hair was dark and her eyes the blue of periwinkle.   She reminded Billy a lot of his father, talkative in private but taciturn in public.   Energetic and full of curiosity, she had an answer for everything.   Having reared her from infancy, Billy experienced for the first time the attachment that develops through parenting and knew he would miss her sorely when she returned to school.

Shortly after Benjamin's death in 1790, Temple sold the Rancocas Farm and moved to London, where he rented an apartment on Manchester Square, not far from his father and stepmother.   Taking a shine to Mary's young sister, Ellen D'Evelin, he fathered an illegitimate daughter in 1798.   Unwilling to settle down and too undisciplined to begin the tedious task of publishing his grandfather's memoirs, he ducked his responsibilities, turned his back on his family and pulled up stakes and moved to Paris.

Fed up with his son's laziness and neglect of duty, Billy rewrote his Will and cut Temple off, leaving his share to cousin Jonathan and children.

For thirteen years, not a word passed between father and

son.   Now eighty-one, lonely and grief-stricken, Billy yearned to

see his only offspring.   The crowd that once gathered in the

coffeehouse on Threadneedle Street had dwindled to a mere

handful.   Billy was an old man.   Soon, he, too, would die as his

dear friend, Joseph Galloway, had eight years before and Tho

Wharton thirty years before him.   Tho was 43 when he passed

away, dying of quinsy at Twickenham.   You may be wondering

why this staunch, hard-nosed patriot is remembered in the same

breath with Galloway.   Unlike the governor's friend, Charles

Thomson, until his untimely death, Tho remained steadfastly loyal,

surreptitiously footing the bill for Billy's keep throughout his years

of imprisonment.

    If little else, Billy inherited Benjamin's distaste for solitary

living.   Remember Polly?   No, Billy never thought twice about

wooing her on his return to London, even though she did end up

being an extremely well-to-do widow.   But just to make sure he

didn't get any ideas, Benjamin took her out of harm's way by

beckoning her across the sea to America to live under his roof,

which she did.

    Squinting against the glare of sun and surf, Billy saw that

Ellen had stopped to wait for her aged grandfather.   Getting his

gout-ridden feet to speed up was no easy matter.   He knew he

needed to come to some kind of a decision about the girl's father

but stubbornly decided not to give in.   He would stand pat and

make Temple come crawling back to them.

His perseverance paid off.   It wasn't long after Billy's 82nd

birthday that his wish came true.   Temple wrote to say he was

ready to tackle his grandfather's papers and that he was thinking of

repatriating.   Overjoyed by the overture and motivated by his

intense aversion to family quarrels, Billy began to prepare for the

return of his 52-year-old prodigal son.

His 83rd birthday came and went and still Temple had not

come.   But being the sucker that he was, Billy was not troubled,

because uncharacteristic of his profession but consistent with his

nature, he held that a man's word was as good as his bond.   On

this assumption, he went ahead and reinstated his son in his Will,

leaving him the remaining half of the Illinois shares and one-third

of whatever he could collect from the Croghan estate.   Oddly

enough, America was again at war with Britain, and due to a

sudden turn of events, Vandalia was once again under the domination of the union jack.   Until the day he died, Billy thought he was leaving Temple a sizeable fortune.   His granddaughter, Ellen, however, would inherit the bulk of his estate, with monetary bequests specified for his servants, cousin Jonathan's sons and close Loyalist friends.

In reality, the only wealth William Franklin attained was through marriage.   Mistakenly suspected of acting in collusion with his father during the Revolution, the British government allowed only £1,800 of his £48,000 Loyalist claim.   The only enduring affection he received came from the women who worshiped him.   His first love expressed her undying devotion in the epitaph on her gravestone:

'Elizabeth Graeme Ferguson Waits with resignation and humble hope for reunion with her friend in a more perfect state of existence'.   Whose face did she see when she penned this inscription, Henry Hugh Ferguson's or William Franklin's?

True to his word, Billy had a plaque placed in the sanctuary of St. Paul's Church in New York City to mark where his first wife, Elizabeth Downes' body lies beneath the altar.   It reads:

'Sense and Sensibility Politeness and Affability Godliness and Charity were with Sense refined and Person elegant, in her united(.)   From a grateful remembrance of her affectionate tenderness and constant performance of the duties of a Good Wife, This monument is erected, By him who knew her worth and still laments her loss.'

Billy died of a heart attack on November 16, 1813 and was buried by his faithful granddaughter, Ellen, who cared for him until the end. and then carried out his wish to be buried in the courtyard of St. Pancras Church next to his second wife, Mary, Ellen's aunt.

A decade later, Temple followed his father to the grave, dying in Paris at the age of 63, failing to sire a son to carry on the Franklin name and never experiencing the joy of a daughter's love. He did dutifully publish his grandfather's Memoirs and married his mistress of many years, Hannah Collyer.   His life can be characterized as 'a seed that fell by the wayside and withered away because it had no root'.

Benjamin's dream of a Franklin dynasty ended with his grandson's death.

AFTERWORD

After researching Ben and Billy in depth for many years, I have a supposition to propose. What if Benjamin had not taken his son to England to study law but had left him at home to enroll at Harvard, William and Mary or King's College. In all likelihood he would have married his fiancé, Elizabeth Graeme, possibly had a legitimate child (or children), not have become a royal governor or a Tory, but, instead, opened a law office in his hometown of Philadelphia. It seems to me that this estrangement could have been avoided. True, by going abroad, he was enlightened by the important people he met; however, graduating from the Middle Temple, instilled him with a sense of duty and a lasting commitment to England and the Crown. It may have been

Benjamin's aversion to being alone, needing family nearby, that was the driving force of his decision to uproot his son. b

On the other hand, what about William?   He thrived on the generosity of his hard-working, industrious father, becoming more dependent as he aged.

In exile, given a perfect opportunity to prove his mettle and break away from his tendency to rely on his father, wives' dowries or government, he squandered it.   Instead of partnering with Galloway to start a law firm in London, he spent his time trying to wheedle more compensation from the British government for the loyalists.   Perhaps he would have done well to remember Benjamin's maxim from *Poor Richard*.   'God helps those who help themselves'.

Made in the USA
Middletown, DE
23 July 2019